THE ATTACK!

A second later she had looked up, horrified to see Elk Woman riding like the wind toward the spur of low hills, Johnny kicking and yelling across the withers of her racing pony.

The next moment they had all been startled to see Tim leap on his saddle gelding and take out after the Indian woman. From his shouts and yells, they had assumed he was dashing off on an instant and brave attempt to catch the squaw before she could reach the sanctuary of the hills. But then, even as they were voicing their confused admiration for Tim's act, and before any thought of an organized pursuit of the squaw could be formed, the hills had belched out a cloud of screaming red warriors. Elk Woman and Johnny, followed by the hapless Tim, had disappeared into the belly of this cloud that then swept on unchecked, to surround the strung-out wagons....

—from "Medicine Road"

D1617060

MEDICINE ROAD

WILL HENRY

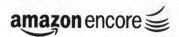

The characters and events portrayed in this book are fictitious.
Any similarity to real persons, living or dead, is coincidental
and not intended by the author.

Copyright © 2006 by Dorothy H. Allen
"Medicine Road" first appeared under the title "War Bonnet"
in Zane Grey's Western Magazine (2/52). Copyright © 1952
by the Hawley Publications, Inc. Copyright © renewed 1980
by Henry Wilson Allen.
Copyright © 2005 by Dorothy H. Allen for restored material.
All rights reserved.
Printed in the United States of America.

No part of this book may be reproduced, or stored in a retrieval
system, or transmitted in any form or by any means, electronic,
mechanical, photocopying, recording, or otherwise, without
express written permission of the publisher.

Published by AmazonEncore
P.O. Box 400818
Las Vegas, NV 89140

ISBN-13: 9781477831236
ISBN-10: 1477831231

This title was previously published by Dorchester Publishing; this version has been reproduced from the Dorchester book archive files.

~

TABLE OF CONTENTS

Orphans of the North

Chapter 1

There was no sound in the Hemlock Wood. The snow came to rest silently upon the forest's floor; the wind lay noiselessly among the spruce and balsam boughs. No movement disturbed the vast, uneasy quiet to hint that life still stirred the frozen pulse of the Arctic woodland—and yet it did.

So, too, did fear. The very silence smelled of fear. It was in the staleness of the air, the unnatural hush of the hemlocks, the slowing fall of the snow. Beneath its eerie spell the animals crouched waiting, fearing the stillness, wanting it to end, yet fearing even more the sound they knew must end it. Presently the waiting was done, the frightening silence broken. From the north, borne on the cold wings of an awakening wind, came the long, quavering, low-keyed and weirdly beautiful hunting song of the white Arctic wolves.

Thus was Awklet born into a world of savage uncertainty. The cow moose Bera was his mother. She was an old moose, gray with the snows of many winters. Awklet was to be her last calf, and that he might live old Bera was prepared to die. The wolf song was not new to her. She had heard it many times before. Always it came as it did now, when the animals were weak and thin from the wintertime's lack of forage, when they could not run or fight. They could only crouch in their hiding places and wait, hoping the wolf pack would pass them by.

Quickly old Bera worked with her newborn calf. Nosing the baby ever deeper into the alder tangle, her red-rimmed eyes kept searching nervously from right to left. The calf stumbled awkwardly on legs that were yet too new. Time and again he fell, but old Bera's great, humpy nose was always there to urge him up and onward. Presently the old cow moose found that for which she sought—dry ground, free of snow and heavily grown with tough, acrid forest grasses. She hesitated, sniffing and grunting eagerly, and was quickly satisfied. The dry ground would not hold their scent overly long, and the strong smell of the native grasses would confuse what little odor she and the calf might leave upon it.

The time grew short now. Hurriedly Bera forced the wobbly calf across the clearing and toward her chosen goal—an overhang of scraggly cedars whose branches were snarled in a thick, protective crown, and whose fallen trunks and limbs formed a perfect fortress-nest for her tiny young one. In the heart of this cover she made him lie down to await her return.

The calf uttered little soft noises and touched his velvety nose to that of his mother. He did not understand the reasons for the old cow's worried actions. With his weak baby's vision he could scarcely see the things about him. Even his mother was no more than a big shadow that made reassuring sounds and gave forth a comforting smell. But in the wild a parent's orders are obeyed instinctively. Directions are somehow comprehended and carried out at once, and without argument. So it was that tiny Awklet lay precisely as old Bera left him, although her reasons for having him do so were entirely beyond his hours-old intelligence.

Loki paused on the crest of a high snowbank and gazed down upon the silent Hemlock Wood. He was a tremendous wolf, deep of chest, thick of loin, heavy and powerful of flank. Great muscles rolled beneath his magnificent coat. Every movement he made was one of absolute power and certainty. He knew no hesitation, no doubt, no fear. And why should he? Loki was the king of the white Arctic wolves.

He gazed long at the forest, his face without expression, his body without movement. Behind him the crowded ranks of his followers were frozen images awaiting his signal. At length he turned to them. They drew back, growling and muttering among themselves. He gave no sign that he saw or heard their uneasiness. His stumpy little ears lay back close to his broad skull. The bands of muscle along his jaws quivered only slightly. His face was a scarred white mask from which only one eye glared at his nervous followers. Where the other eye should have been there was nothing save an empty slit. Even in the remoteness of the Arctic, the price of kingship is a heavy one.

Loki narrowed his one good eye. A low rumble shook his chest. Like released springs the muscles of the waiting wolves uncoiled. They went over the crest of the snowbank in a silent wave, cascading down its steep face like a waterfall of white fur. They melted into the forest below without a sound.

Old Bera listened intently. The hunting song of the wolves had fallen away and she heard nothing. Satisfied, she gave Awklet a last nuzzle, turned, and forced her way out of the cedar tangle. Stepping into the open ground of the clearing, she moved with decision and sureness. Her baby was well hidden. The wolves would not find *him*, and what matter her fate? The calf was safe, that was the main thing. It remained only for her to lead the wolves away from his hiding place. That was as far as the wild mind worked. The fact that the calf would surely starve without her never occurred to old Bera.

Through the snow-deep aisles of the forest the wolf pack coursed. Only the *hush-hush* of their feathery footfalls distinguished them from the ghosts they resembled as they followed Loki in search of game. In the rear of the pack, a little separated from the others, three big dog-wolves ran by themselves. They were One Ear, Bakut, and Scarface. Long dissatisfied with Loki's leadership, the three were growling and bickering angrily. Presently One Ear lagged even farther behind the pack's swift pace. His two companions dropped back with him. Soon the pack drew away and a turn in the trail hid them from its view. At once the three deserters struck out on their own, their course leading them at right angles to that of the pack.

They had not gone far before they blundered across the fresh tracks of a cow and calf moose. Following this sign, their keen nostrils were suddenly stung with the full body scent of their quarry. They cut away from the tracks and headed across a small, open meadow directly toward the new, stronger odor. Ahead of them was a thick stand of alder and birch. They slowed their pace, their noses telling them their prey lay just beyond the cover, their instincts warning them they must now proceed with the greatest care. Loki was not far off and the law of the wolf pack made no allowances for deserters like themselves.

Luck held with them. As they broke through the stunted trees, they stopped and dropped to their bellies in the snow. Across a second small clearing an old cow moose was putting the finishing touches to an amazingly clever calf nest. Had they not surprised her at it, they would never have known the calf was there. As it was, they would get two suppers for the effort of one.

There was no need for a signal. One Ear, Bakut, and Scarface knew their business. It wasn't as if this was the second or third, or even the tenth or twentieth cow moose they had stalked. Bakut would slash the great tendon in her right rear leg, Scarface that in her left. As she went down, One Ear would leap for her throat. It was that simple, and it would all be over very quickly.

Loki brought the pack to a halt in the big meadow that formed the center of the Hemlock Wood. Here, as they had since the oldest of them could remember, the wolves would separate into small bands and work the forest in an ever narrowing circle. By nightfall they would have closed the circle and completed their work of destruction.

Like the well-trained hunters they were, the various pack leaders took their followers and departed. Zor and Bigfoot were first, then Lukat, Split Lip, and old Sukon, the greatest hunter of them all save Loki himself. Watching them go, the king wolf's single eye narrowed suddenly. The meadow was empty now, the last wolf gone, yet he had not seen One Ear, Bakut, or Scarface with any of the departing packs. Loki growled, deep and ugly, in his throat. Unless his one eye was tricking him, the three must have left the main pack before it entered the meadow. Still growling angrily, he turned swiftly along the back trail, following the broad snow track the pack had made in reaching the meadow.

Old Bera speeded her ungainly gait as she came across the clearing away from the cedar tangle. She must not be seen leaving her calf. The wolves must find her before they found her baby. She must play the old wilderness mother's game of leading danger away from her helpless young. Suddenly she froze in mid-step. Was that a movement there in the snow ahead of her? Just at the edge of the clearing, where the forest began? She reached out her huge, humped nose, peering uncertainly toward the alder and birch clump.

The snow moved again, took sudden, frightening form. Wolves! Three of them. Crouched to their bellies in the snow, their furry haunches gathered under them, their almond-shaped, yellow eyes fastened upon her. Grunting hoarsely, she wheeled to face them.

They came at her in a silent rush, and, as they came, old Bera was ready for them. She braced herself, easing her great weight back upon her hindquarters so that her razor-sharp forehoofs would be free to lash out at her attackers. Nostrils spread, small, red eyes rolling wickedly, heavy lips laced with nervous froth, she presented no reassuring picture to Loki's three deserters.

One Ear hesitated understandably. Bakut and Scarface broke their charge, sliding to a stop at the same time. This was not going to be so easy as it had looked.

Presently One Ear slunk off to the right, circling around to get behind the old cow. Bakut and Scarface followed him. Bera turned with them, step for cautious step. There were no beginners here. All four animals were veterans of dozens of such encounters. None wasted so much as a single breath or motion as the endless, silent circling went on. But old Bera had only two eyes—and there were three wolves.

The circle was broken without warning. Suddenly Bakut charged straight in. As Bera reared to meet him, he sidestepped and dived in under her, slashing for her rear leg. She was forced to whirl and tuck the leg high to her side so that Bakut's fangs would strike only the tough muscles of her outer haunch, missing the inner, soft part of the leg for which he aimed. In doing this, she had to turn her eyes from One Ear and Scarface. They closed instantly, both leaping for her unprotected throat.

At the same instant, Bakut's teeth closed on her haunch. The pain of the wound caused her to rear suddenly higher, making both One Ear and Scarface miss their aims and bury their fangs in the bone and sinew of her shoulder. The hurt of the new wounds forced an explosive grunt from the old cow moose.

It was the first sound of the unequal struggle. It echoed like a pistol shot in the still air, startling Awklet to his feet within the cedar tangle. His action was purely nervous, could not be controlled.

His mother's deep grunt had been too loud, too close, too instinctively frightening. Then, before he could move again, he heard another, more terrifying sound—the guttural snarling of angry wolves. It was a sound as fascinating as it was frightening, and the young moose could not resist the strange excitement and curiosity it called up within him. Stretching his thin neck toward the source of the fearsome noise, he blinked his weak eyes in infant wonderment.

Loki traveled fast. Shortly he came to the spot where One Ear and his two companions had left the pack. Pausing only a moment to sample the freshness of their tracks, he swung off after them. He moved with the tireless gait peculiar to the hunting wolf, ears back, red tongue lolling, lone eye burning.

Before long the trail of the deserters joined that of a cow moose and her day-old calf. Loki lengthened his stride. The scent was very fresh now and he knew his followers could not be far ahead. They were not. Within the next minute he heard their snarling.

Swiftly the king wolf changed his course, racing toward the birch and alder thicket from beyond which the snarling came. As he ran, a new odor struck his nose—fresh blood. Then, suddenly, a fourth smell, strongest and deepest of them all, came to him.

Loki trembled as he bellied into the snow and crept through the thicket. He always trembled at that smell. He loved it. It was in his very sinews. He knew its harsh scent as well as he knew his own, and the excitement of it never failed to set every fiber of his great body on sudden, tingling edge. It was the smell of death.

As Awklet's straining eyes focused on the clearing, he saw his mother, gaunt old Bera, thrusting and slashing with her cloven forehoofs. First One Ear attacked, feinting and dodging, leaping and snarling. Then, when One Ear pulled away, Bakut and Scarface raced in, retreating swiftly when One Ear attacked again.

Suddenly Bakut slipped beneath old Bera as she turned to thrust One Ear away from her flank. With invisible speed his fangs slashed across the tendons of one rear leg. At the same instant, One Ear leaped in and severed the sinews of the other. The old moose staggered and went down as Scarface found her throat with merciful speed.

The young moose sank back into his nest, burying his head in its warm grasses. Wild confusion raced through him. He shook violently, his breath coming hard, his tiny heart pounding. Still, true to instinct and his mother's instructions, he did not move or make a sound. But blind obedience was not to save him now.

With the cow down, One Ear, Bakut, and Scarface turned to finish the hidden calf. But as they did, the tall grasses at the edge of the clearing behind them parted silently. Loki's lips lifted in a soundless snarl. The expression on the king wolf's face was not a good thing to see. Noiselessly Loki launched his charge.

Completely occupied with the hidden calf, his three followers did not hear his silent rush until it was too late. Scarface, trailing his two companions toward Awklet's nest, died first, his back broken by one grinding slash of Loki's huge jaws. His death snarl brought One Ear and Bakut to a sudden, sliding halt. Their stiffly braced forelegs were nearly touching Awklet before the two wolves came to a full stop. In wheeling to face their angry leader, one of the big wolves actually stepped on the terrified calf. It was too much for the nerve-wracked baby moose. With a bleat of terror he bounded to his feet, leaped blindly into the surrounding brush tangle. He had not blundered twenty feet before he was hopelessly caught in the snarled branches. There he hung, a trapped and helpless witness to a sight he was never to forget.

One Ear and Bakut now faced their king. The latter's position astride the dead Scarface told them what had brought Loki here. They knew they had broken the law of the pack and they knew their leader had come to punish them for it. They knew, also, as Loki stepped over the motionless body of Scarface and glided toward them, how he meant to punish them for it.

Awklet looked on, spellbound. Even in his instinctive dread of them, he could not take his eyes from the wolves. Nor could he, for all his frightened confusion, fail to note the contrast between Loki and his opponents. Where they were big, Loki was huge. Where the muscles of One Ear and Bakut rolled impressively when they moved, those of Loki bulged unbelievably. Where the grasses scarcely bent beneath the tread of the other wolves, they seemed not to bend at all under the footfalls of the king wolf. Yes, Awklet saw Loki, and he never forgot him. Of all his memories, that of the leader of the white Arctic wolves was to remain uppermost in the mind of the orphan moose calf.

Shoulder to shoulder now, One Ear and Bakut awaited Loki's attack. He was almost upon them, but they showed no fear. Whatever else they may have been, One Ear and Bakut were no cowards—and they were no fools. Despite their breaking of the pack's law against hunting alone and despite the long years of Loki's savage administration of that law, they had the king wolf outnumbered two to one. Such odds were insurmountable. Loki might get one of them. He would never get both of them.

At first it looked as though they were right. Barely two paces from them, Loki caught his foot in a protruding cedar root, stumbled, and fell, full-length, in front of them. They were upon him instantly, roaring and slashing crazily.

From his prison in the cedar tangle, Awklet stared in dumb amazement. The snarling of the wolves was terrifying, but the fascination of their fury was greater to the tiny calf than his fear of it. He continued to watch, and, as he did, the impossible happened.

With one great surge the king wolf regained his feet and shook free of One Ear and Bakut. Before the astonished wolves could recover, he dived past them. Then, turning with incredible speed, he was back upon them, all in one raging instant.

Bakut died as Scarface had, without a struggle. Loki, coming upon him from the rear, closed his huge jaws on the vertebrae of his neck. There was a single, crunching splinter of bone and that was all. In the next moment he whirled and leaped at One Ear. But the latter was ready for him and met him in mid-leap.

Shoulder to shoulder the two wolves crashed and reared upright, their forelegs tucked against their furry chests, their hind legs straining to gain an overthrow. Their fangs were clashing and grinding in movement too swift to follow as each sought the other's throat. For a moment the outcome seemed in high doubt, but Loki's fury was too great to be withstood. Slowly One Ear fell back before it, still striving to meet fang with fang, shoulder thrust with shoulder thrust. The end came abruptly.

Loki suddenly staggered back and fell heavily to the ground, as though he had lost his footing or had received some mortal wound and fallen from its injury. At once One Ear launched his body through the air, leaping forward for the kill. In the same moment the apparently helpless Loki struck upward from the ground like a great white snake. His jaws closed on the leaping One Ear's unguarded throat, ripped sideways and outward.

One Ear did not die so quickly as Bakut and Scarface. He lived long enough to see Loki come and stand over him, and to hear a last, deep growl rumble up out of the king wolf's chest.

As Loki turned to leave the clearing, the killing rage that had suffused his mind began to fade. Normal thought returned. He paused. There was something he was forgetting. The calf! By the trail that he had followed to the clearing, Loki had known that the old cow moose had a calf with her. It must still be somewhere close at hand.

He looked around the clearing very carefully. His lone eye hesitated, then lingered on the cedar tangle toward which the three wolves had been sneaking. The king wolf growled deeply in his throat. Wily old One Ear had not missed the calf. He had known where it was. Loki growled again. One Ear had been a good hunter. The pack would miss him.

In the cedar tangle Loki quickly noted the signs of Awklet's flight and rumbled his disappointment. He swung his great head this way and that, searching the air for odor signs telling of the way the calf had gone. There was none. There were no baby moose scents fresher than those in the nest itself, and they were clearly stale.

Loki looked anxiously about him, seeing the shadows growing swiftly deeper on all sides. The hour grew late. Darkness was closing in. He must get back for the gathering of the pack. With a third low growl, the king wolf turned to go.

At this precise moment Awklet sneezed. Loki stiffened and wheeled toward the sound. As though to make sure of his discovery, Awklet sneezed again—and found himself confronted with the awesome sight of an Arctic king wolf.

Loki towered over the helpless calf, his one baleful eye glowing in the semidarkness of the tangle. His black lips curled back over his gums, exposing the twin rows of his fangs. Death was very close to the orphaned moose calf in that moment. Then Awklet sneezed again.

A wolf, even a king wolf, is still a member of the dog family. As such, he has a certain sense of playfulness, savage though it may be, a sort of basic interest in the puzzling antics of other animals. The small moose's unnatural posture and born awkwardness aroused Loki's canine curiosity, delaying his wolf's instinct to kill automatically. The sight of the wobbly-legged moose calf sprawling rump heavenward and hopelessly tangled in the heavy brush made the old wolf sheathe his fangs and stand still for a moment, his great head cocked inquisitively at Awklet.

There was ample reason for the pause. And the undue mercy. A day-old moose calf, in the most favorable of circumstances, is close to Nature's least graceful handiwork. This one, with his grotesquely homely face, spread-eagle position, and ludicrous, calm-eyed expression surpassed his species in comic ugliness.

The king wolf wondered that the calf was not more afraid. He sat thoughtfully back on his haunches, regarding Awklet with the utmost gravity. The calf could not have been more than hours old, yet he showed none of the paralyzed terror Loki was accustomed to seeing in his victims. He simply hung there in his scraggly prison, staring back at the huge wolf with a blankly quizzical look. His furrowed brow, tremendous shaggy ears, and bright brown eyes concentrated on Loki as though the latter had come to help him, not destroy him.

The king wolf rumbled mutteringly in his throat, prolonging his head-cocked regard of the awkward youngster. He had killed more moose calves than this homely dwarf had minutes of life. Yet there he squatted on his haunches like a six-month cub, studying this particular calf as though it were his first encounter with one of his kind.

As Loki sat there studying Awklet, the mournful, weirdly beautiful howling of the gathering pack came across the snowy wastes of the Hemlock Wood. Loki threw up his head and howled in return. The hour grew late and the duties of leadership called. He gave Awklet one last thoughtful look, as though he might yet kill him, then turned and started to trot off without a backward glance. As he did, Awklet emitted a parting sneeze.

Loki stopped, turned around, peered back. Through the gathering dusk he could make out a small branch so placed beneath the moose calf's nose that its slightest movement tickled him, causing the sneezes.

Loki trotted back to the cedar tangle. His jaws parted, his huge head snaked out suddenly. There was a steel-trap clip of his two-inch fighting fangs and the bothersome branch fluttered earthward, severed not three inches from Awklet's soft nose. Then, without so much as another glance at the moose calf, he turned and disappeared into the night.

Thus did Awklet come to know Loki. And thus did Loki, through a chance whim, or through the one unconscious kindness of his life, set the seal of certain termination to the years of his reign in the Northland.

Chapter 2

Early calved as he was, Awklet was not the first born of the deer tribe in the Hemlock Wood. Far to the south of the dark thicket in which Loki had carelessly spared the moose calf's life, Neetcha, the caribou doe, huddled, trembling and waiting for the wolf pack to leave the forest. Close to her nervous flank pressed her young ones, two ten-day-old, premature fawns. The youngsters nuzzled her underside in inquisitive puzzlement and without reward. Demandingly the spotted babies shoved and pulled at the doe's udder. Nothing happened. No milk came. Imperatively they voiced their wants, their small bleats of protest echoing strangely loud in the stillness of the aspen grove that hid them.

Neetcha quieted them, her quick nose bunts and sharp snuffles warning them to be still, that grave danger was near. They obeyed without question.

Presently the danger drew nearer. Neetcha could not suppress the shudders that raced through her. Instantly the fawns caught something of the doe's nervousness. The smaller of the two pushed an in-quiring nose out from between his dam's forelegs, imitating her action in sniffing the dead wind. As he did, the breeze freshened for the first time in hours.

One fawn's dainty head recoiled. He blew out through his small black nostrils, every short hair on his spine lifted on end. His whole body was shaking with the fear of that terrible smell which lay so sud-denly in the wind. The other fawn caught the smell in the next breath. He, too, snorted in alarm and joined his brother in staring, spellbound, in the di-rection from which the dread scent came.

The doe grew tensely quiet, every nerve and mus-cle in her body stretched bow-taut. Unbidden, the fawns froze to her side. The time of waiting was done. Here came the makers of the smell!

Through the protective screen of the aspens, the fawns watched, transfixed, as the wolves loped into view. They could see their high-withered, swift-rolling gait, their slant yellow eyes burning in the twilight gloom, their red tongues lolling wetly, their nervous muzzles swinging back and forth in the stirring breeze. There were at least a dozen of them. They were easily counted as their ghostly shapes fled forward across the snow. One, larger than the rest, was in the lead. He had an abnormally big head with a gash of a mouth that seemed literally to split his face from ear base to ear base. The gray, lean look of age and endless experience was written in every expert flick of his stumpy ears, and quick wrinkling of his broad muzzle.

Then, even as the fawns watched, the old wolf slowed his gait and swung his huge head toward them. Shortly he stopped altogether. Of all the cruel hunters in Loki's pack, Sukon had the finest nose.

When he drew up like that, sudden and sharp, there was more in the evening wind than the smell of snow. His followers quieted their panting, closed in behind him, and waited as the delicate scent muscles in his blunt muzzle quivered and grew still. He inhaled with deep sniffs, facing toward the panic-stricken caribou in the grove. Then a vagrant shift in the wind moved through the aspens—toward Sukon.

The fitful breeze struck the aging pack leader fully in the nostrils, leaving him rigid with excitement. The hot, sweet scent of caribou fawn raced deliciously down his spine. From between his ears to his tail's root, the guard hairs on Sukon's back bristled. Without a sound, he leaped toward the aspen grove, his pack mates straining at his heels. In the trees, Neetcha and her twin fawns stood paralyzed. Then, in the last moment, they ran—the fawns away from the wolves, the doe directly toward them.

It was a brave act on Neetcha's part, but far too late. Where she sought to divert the pack and lead them away from her babies, she succeeded only in making their leader swerve enough to avoid being run over by her cloven hoofs. Sukon had smelled the fawns, and now he saw them. Let the pack handle the doe; he wanted younger, sweeter meat.

But the pack was not ready for Neetcha. She burst into its ranks too suddenly, scattering the surprised wolves right and left in the blind craziness of her last-minute race to save her young ones. Before they could come together again, she was gone. Three of them whirled to chase her, but the rest kept on after Sukon and the fawns. The three soon abandoned their effort and, fearing they would miss out on the more certain feast of fawn meat, returned to share in the fruits of Sukon's superior hunting judgment. They did not return in vain.

Even after the first overwhelming wave of fear had passed, Neetcha continued her wild flight. On through the deepening snowbanks she plunged, nor did she pause until she reached the innermost heart of the Hemlock Wood. Here she huddled in the deepest thickets, gasping until returning breath began to flow with cooling regularity through her lungs. Finally the shudders of exhaustion ceased to wrack her flanks, the tremble quieted in her limbs. Only then did she venture from her hiding place.

At first she could not eat. She was weak from her long race and sick with the memory of her fawns. But the air was turning swiftly colder, and she sensed that a harsh change in weather was coming. Instinct bade her fill her stomach in preparation for it.

An early spring blizzard was brewing, one of those fierce tempests that rage in the pause between winter and spring in the Northland. Neetcha feared such storms as did all the wild creatures. She made haste now, that the approaching one would not find her unready. Quickly she ate, first of the tender birch and alder shoots, then of the tough, nutritious bark of the larger limbs. Soon she was full, and turned to seek shelter from the coming storm.

Shortly she found it, a bone-dry cedar tangle, heavily lined with dead grasses. Here she made her bed. But as she prepared to lie down, her senses detected moose smell.

The smell was quite close. Investigation revealed that it was strongest in the very spot she had chosen for herself. And it was very fresh—so fresh that she looked about her, fully expecting to discover who was sharing her retreat. She saw nothing, and lay down puzzled. Sniffing again, she caught another smell, one that she knew and hated. But it was a dead scent and the wolf that had left it was no longer near. The moose smell, though, was very much alive and confusingly close.

The cold filled the air, growing more intense with each minute. Neetcha, settling wearily into her warm bed, started to doze. But sleep did not come, for suddenly a new fact of the moose smell began to turn in her drowsing consciousness. It was the smell of a calf, a very young calf.

A wave of mother feeling came up in Neetcha. Her milk udder, swollen with her dead fawns' untaken supper, ached and burned. Presently she fancied she heard a muffled bleating. Strange how real the sound was. It was almost *too* real. Neetcha rose awkwardly to her feet, stood, ears pricked and tense. Then she heard it again. Clearly and beyond any doubt this time—the helpless, frightened bleating of a very young baby. Swiftly she nosed out the soundmaker, a day-old moose calf hopelessly entangled in a mass of snarled small branches. The tracks of a gigantic wolf marked the snow all about him.

Neetcha, the caribou doe, had found Awklet, the orphaned moose calf. She needed no human intelligence to tell her what to do. In a moment she had the calf freed from his prison. Without question the moose baby followed the fawnless doe back to her dry-grass bed. Without thought the bereaved caribou accepted the cold, hungry calf. And without prompting, the infant suckled at his foster mother's warm breast, while Neetcha reveled in her relief and gratitude for the nursing.

Thus in the deepest tangle of the Hemlock Wood, with the fierce winds of an Arctic blizzard howling their approval, began the strange story of Awklet, the orphan moose.

Chapter 3

The storm lasted seven days and nights, then was gone as swiftly as it had come. With it went the wolves. Like shadows, shapeless and without sound, they drifted northward. Fifteen, twenty, thirty—fully fifty of them. Eyes burning like live coals in the gray half light. Restless heads swinging constantly, nervous jaws chopping quick flecks of yellowed froth. Homeward bound. North and north and ever north. Hour after tireless hour. Mile after trackless mile. Northward, ever northward and homeward went the killer pack.

In its forefront went Loki himself, aloof and unapproachable as befitted his hard-won rank. Behind him moved his scarred lieutenants, the elite of the adult males in their full prime, the seasoned hunters and fighters like Zor, Lukat, Split Lip, Bigfoot, and the crafty Sukon, who stood just below Loki in the pack command. Behind them came the rank and file—the females, the old males past their prime, the yearling cubs not yet in theirs.

Looking back through the swirling snows, Loki found grim reason for satisfaction in his kingship. The hunting had been and still was good. Even now, in the thin scrub of the barren ground beyond the forest, scattered pockets of game were to be found. Yesterday it had been a tough old caribou stag in company with four young does. The day before that, two yearling moose were caught outside the shelter of the last timber. So it had gone, excellent the entire way, the finest winter hunt in many years.

In times past, the caribou herds had wandered the entire Arctic. Since the earliest of Loki's memories, the herds had supplied the wolf pack with its main food. From the treeless wastes of Loki's own perpet-ually frozen homeland, across the vast sweep of the barren-ground tundras to the stunted timber at the northern approaches of the Hemlock Wood, the caribou had come and gone and grazed as they pleased. But a succession of severe winters had kept them from the tundra mosses and forced them southward into the sparsely wooded lands north of the Hemlock Woods. This move, in turn, had forced the wolves to follow them. Weak from starvation, the once great herds had scattered before the inroads of the white killers, seeking the last sanctuary avail-able to them—the heart of the Hemlock Wood. Thus, even in the years of Loki's life, the caribou had been reduced from proud, free, fearless rangers of the open tundra to shy, skulking, frightened crea-tures of the forest darknesses.

Nothing could have pleased Loki more. For in the confinement of the deep woods the caribou lost the courage and resolution to defend themselves, which had always marked them in their tundra days. They fell into the dangerous habit of "yarding up" like the forest-dwelling deer tribes. That is, they gathered together in a packed disorganized mass in some protective stand of birch and alder. There, easy feed was within immediate reach and the old, hard days of tundra foraging could be quickly and happily forgotten. The very fact had provided the climax to this present year's wonderful hunting.

After leaving Awklet, Loki had found the main caribou herd—what remained of the once great tundra herds—in its winter yard in the Hemlock Wood, and had led the pack in a tremendous killing of the helpless creatures. It had been a feast to remember and to think about for the next year's hunt. Very clearly, the herding-together instinct and the fierce will to fight of bygone years no longer existed among the stupid remnant of the tundra herds. The caribou still fought back when attacked, and their heavy antlers and razor-sharp hoofs were still deadly, but they no longer clung together to make a circle of hoofs and horns on which the wolves would impale themselves. Instead, they broke away and ran in small groups and forsook one another and made the killing an easy, very pleasant thing. It became very evident to the king wolf that the former defensive power of the great herds was forever gone.

Loki licked his lips and chopped his jaws with the pleasure of that prospect. Already in his savage brain thoughts were forming up for next year's hunt. With the blood of this year's killing still warm in his mouth, he was tasting that of the next. Even now, while far to the south Neetcha, the caribou doe, was contentedly dreaming of her wobbly-kneed adopted calf's life, Loki was coldly thinking about his death.

* * *

Neetcha had been absent from the yard when Loki and his pack entered the Hemlock Wood. To this accidental fact she may well have owed her life, for the pack's toll had been particularly heavy among both the early calving does and their sisters yet heavy with unborn young. The rest of the herd had stampeded and scattered through the nearby forest, instead of forming a fighting circle and attempting to defend themselves as was their almost forgotten custom. The frightened survivors of the king wolf's raid were just beginning to filter back into the yard when Neetcha approached from the south with her new son.

Among the does destroyed or still missing was old Aldera, the herd queen. As in most animal tribes of herding instinct, the real leader of the caribou had not been a male, but a female. The usual picture envisioned of any of the woodland deer herds—be they elk, moose, caribou or dainty black- or white-tail—is that of some lordly antlered bull or stag moving proudly in the lead. It is a popular picture but not a true one. Actually the real leader is nearly always a cow or doe. And usually, as in the case of old Aldera, this leader is one of advanced years, gaunt and gray and cautious with the wisdom of many winters.

Aldera had been the mother of Neetcha's mother and the mate of Neetcha's grandfather in the days of the retreat from the Barren Grounds. But whether or not she was Neetcha's grand dam did not matter. What did matter was that the old doe had consistently grazed with the younger and had, since the days of the latter's fawnhood, unconsciously instructed her in the ways and warinesses of herd leadership. Now, with their old queen missing, the

remaining caribou would naturally look to Neetcha
as their new queen.

Of this the young doe knew nothing as she plodded northward through the deep snow of the departed blizzard. The steady *swish-swish* of her broad,
splayed hoofs trod and kicked clear an ample path
for the ungainly moose baby that followed her.
From time to time she would swing her bony head
rearward for a quick glance at the awkward calf. It
was a glance that seemed to say she cared not at all
whether the struggling youngster were there or not.
And at each such glance Awklet would bleat plain-
tively, demanding like some tired child that the pace
be slowed or a halt called altogether.

Neetcha paid no heed to these pleas but forged
steadily ahead through the deepening snows. Puff-
ing complainingly, the moose orphan lunged and
stumbled in her wake. Occasionally he would fall to
his knees or, striking a pocket of soft snow, plunge
completely out of sight. At these times he would
bawl piteously, but Neetcha did not wait or give any
sign that she heard her adopted son's wails of de-
spair. Straight ahead and unheeding, she continued,
as though for all of her the calf might be left behind
to lie in the snow forever. And somehow, on each of
these occasions, Awklet found the strength and will
to struggle onward and to come again, eventually, to
his rightful place at her flank.

Although he could not know it, Awklet was getting his first and greatest lesson in leadership. There
could be no place for weaklings in the wilderness
future that faced him. Yet for all her Spartan forcing
of the pace and for all her apparent disregard for her
adopted heir's welfare, there was in the eye of
Neetcha, when she looked at Awklet, an entirely dif-

ferent story. It was a look of motherly pride and fierce devotion that went well beyond a normal parent's love. The circumstances surrounding her meeting with the moose calf were so poignant as to guarantee a deeper bond between them than any to be forged by blood alone. A new leader, possibly one who might someday head the caribou themselves, was being trained. His first hard lesson must be that the wilderness gods, no less than any others, helped those who helped themselves.

Neetcha at once assumed her leadership of the herd. Her first act was to lead a cautious search for the white wolves. If the latter were still in the forest, she must know it. If they had gone, all was well. They would not return until the following late winter. Once they quitted the Hemlock Wood, they never turned back; they headed steadily into the polar darknesses from which they came. But as the new caribou herd queen, Neetcha had to know if they had started their return journey or were yet in the woodland and still on the hunt. Toward this purpose she led her search.

With her went Bektan, Bela, and Blue Nose, all trusted elder stags. For two days they drifted through the Hemlock Wood, circling every meadow, probing deeply into every thicket and windfall. With nightfall of the second day they returned to the herd yard satisfied that the wolves were finally gone.

Gazing about her at the grim reminders of Loki's visit, Neetcha knew she had no time for rest. Yonder, by the base of that slender balsam from which she would never move, lay Olanchi, the friend of her fawnhood. There by the ledge rock beyond the balsam, still and huddled, lay

Santu, the sister of her mother. Among the alders behind the rock sprawled the motionless, frozen-legged form of Lepak, Neetcha's beloved brother, while all about lay scattered the other pitiful victims of the king wolf's recent passing.

There was but one thing to do now—find a new yard for the remainder of the herd and find it, not tomorrow, but tonight. As the frosty moon rose an hour later, it shone on the long straggling line of the caribou herd, winding south through the silent forest aisles. At the head of the shuffling, nervous-eyed column moved Neetcha, studying with wary glances the trail ahead in anxious search for the new hiding place and bedding ground. By her flank, very much excited by the whole adventure, ambled the spraddle-legged Awklet. He was getting his second lesson in proper herd leadership, and enjoying it immensely. All was exactly right with his innocent world. He had not a worry in the whole wide woodland.

Meanwhile, far to the north, across the frozen sweep of the tundra, roamed the huge, white-furred, one-eyed Loki. Running now at the head of the pack, the king wolf had lost some of his recent good feeling. Well as the hunt had gone and smoothly as the home journey was progressing, Loki was growing troubled. Something far back in a hidden crevice of his savage brain kept bothering him. His uncanny sense of memory had served him too well throughout the years of his kingship to be ignored. And it was warning him now that he had somewhere and recently committed a serious error.

His lone eye narrowed, his broad skull furrowing with the effort of animal concentration. Presently

he began to growl, low and deep. His pack mates
running near him drew quickly away, knowing
from the quality of the growl that their king was
angry. From past experience they had learned that
it was not good to run close to Loki when he was in
such a mood.

Then, suddenly, the growling ceased. The king
wolf suddenly knew what he had done wrong back
there in the Hemlock Wood. He should not have allowed that trapped moose calf to live. That had been
an act of weakness, a characteristic foreign to the
wolf nature. And the guilt of it was sufficient to send
Loki's memory back across all those frozen miles.

He slid his furry haunches in the powdery snow.
So abrupt was his halt that the first of the following
pack actually piled into him from the rear. His deep
snarl lashed out at once, warning them back. They
fell away from him instantly, sensing the quality of
his excitement.

Again his chest rumbled, the hoarse growl going
this time, and with less anger, to old Sukon, his favorite. At once the aging wolf understood that he
was to lead the pack homeward from that spot. His
replying growl to Loki was quick, and there was no
complaining from the others. It was the law of the
pack. The leader was to be blindly obeyed. Any wolf
that thought otherwise would have to fight Loki to
the death.

For a matter of seconds the great wolf stood alone
in the trail, watching the last of his pack mates follow old Sukon obediently northward. Then Loki
turned his broad head southward. His stumpy ears
flicked erect and for another moment he paused, as
though taken with some last questioning thought of
his decision. Then, swiftly, he was gone, leaving the

emptiness of the halting place to the lonely sweep of the Arctic wind. Only the deep impressions of his giant pad prints remained to mark the direction of his return to the Hemlock Wood, and even those soon disappeared beneath the shifting snows.

When the king wolf reentered the southern woodland, he loped directly toward the cedar tangle where he had left the entrapped moose calf. He found it precisely as it had been, save for one small detail. The calf was gone.

The story of his going, although nearly five days old, read very clearly to Loki. The double line of cloven-hoofed tracks, one set large, the other tiny, stitched its way neatly out of the windfall and across the snows of the meadow beyond it. The king wolf's delicate nose told him even more. The big tracks were those of a caribou doe, and the smaller tracks belonged to the moose calf orphaned by One Ear, Bakut, and Scarface. And that particular moose calf was the one for which Loki was looking. Swiftly and silently the huge white wolf took the trail of Awklet and his foster mother.

It was full dusk when Loki came to the outskirts of the abandoned caribou yard. Belly down, he sneaked forward through the heavy snow, his keen ears pricked for the first sounds of his quarry. Presently he heard them— the coughing, stomping, and grunting of caribou moving restlessly about. Warily as a monster cat he halted on the crest of a snowbank overhanging the yard.

Below him a dozen old stags wandered in lonely misery. Headed by Bartok, a grizzled elder jealous that the herd leadership had gone to such a young doe as Neetcha, the twelve old stags had stubbornly refused to follow the new queen. But in the whole snow-packed confines of the yard nothing else moved. The main herd—and with it the doe and the moose calf—was gone. Loki lifted his lips in a soundless snarl of disappointment and turned back to his quest.

The moon was good, the trail of the departed herd broad and clear. Following its deep-rutted snow track was cub's play for an old warrior like Loki. Once away from the yard, he settled into the tireless, mile-eating lope of the wolf that knows where he is going and is in grim haste to get there.

Meanwhile, Neetcha had been in luck. What had started out discouragingly with Bartok's refusal to follow the herd had wound up nicely. The young doe had succeeded in finding a fine new yard only a few miles from the old one. Now, from the vantage point of a ledge of rock in the center of that new yard, she studied it carefully and grunted, soft and deep, with satisfaction.

It was an excellent hiding place and the herd was well placed within it. The does with early fawns were bedded in its center, just beneath Neetcha's look-out. Beyond them were the does due to fawn shortly, and beyond them in turn the old stags, yearling stags, and the aging, barren does without fawns. Within this outer ring of seasoned veterans, the young mothers and their newborn infants rested peacefully. For most of them it was the first time they had known what it meant to bed down and drowse and feel safe doing so. Yes, Neetcha had good reason for satisfaction. And the herd had equal reason to reflect her feeling. It had found a real leader at last.

To the watchful young doe on the look-out rock,

this new faith was rewardingly evident. It could be felt. It arose from the herd in a continuous murmur of subdued night gruntings. It made itself known in the lack of moving about and place shifting among the ordinarily nervous animals. And indeed this confidence did not appear misplaced. It would be next to impossible for any intruder to enter the new yard.

Downwind from her, on the far side of the herd, a single narrowed eye was conveying the same thought to Loki, the Arctic king wolf. It had required all his vast woodcraft to creep this close to the sleeping caribou. Now he was still faced with the problem of crossing 100 paces of open, snow-packed yard to come at his quarry. And every step of that 100 paces was blocked by a bedded-down member of the herd. Through the magic of his wonderful nose, the king wolf knew that Neetcha was the doe he had trailed out of the cedar tangle. In the still of the night and with the light, fresh wind blowing toward him, he was able to single out her scent from that of all the others. And he knew, of course, that the moose calf would be close by her.

Yet, providing he was skillful enough to work his way within striking distance of her and the calf, how would he get away after the deed was done? The herd would be instantly on its feet and he would be caught in the middle of 100 panic-stricken caribou. Even for a king wolf, these were weighty questions. And the odds against his getting away unscathed were impossible.

Loki uttered another of his soundless snarls, his decision made. It was typical of his breed that the difficulty of escape failed to stop him. Attack was the only problem. Following the old wolf-pack logic that the truest trail is the straight one, he flattened himself to the snow, wormed his way into the sleeping herd and directly toward the look-out rock. His intention was to cover what ground he could before discovery, then to race for the rock and the doe, trusting that the moose calf would be there beside her.

It was a daring move and it almost succeeded. The king wolf was within six paces of the rock when a thin snow crust broke beneath his great weight and brought a wild-eyed little figure out from the shadow at the very base of the rock. For the second time in his short life, Awklet stood face to face with Loki and lived to tell of it. And tell of it he did. His bleat of terror rang out in the night quiet like a trumpet blast. Instantly the entire yard was alive with the noise and movement of the herd coming to its feet.

For once Loki could not act fast enough. He had made his approach on the assumption that the calf would be with the doe on top of the rock. The blunder of nearly stepping on him and causing the terrified calf to let out such a high-pitched squall inflamed the king wolf's savage temper. In the confusion of his rage, Loki hesitated.

It was all the time Awklet required. With a great clumsy sideways leap, the moose calf bounded out of striking range. Had he been a moment later, Loki would have cut his throat from ear to shaggy ear. As it was, the king wolf would now do well to get the caribou doe.

Snarling, he gathered his great haunches for the leap that would end the life of the new herd queen. Neetcha, up on the ledge, had at last begun to drowse just before Loki had started toward her through the sleeping herd. Her startled eyes opened to the picture of a huge Arctic wolf hurtling through the air toward her. Awkwardly she lunged up and forward, her one instinctive thought to get to her adopted calf. In consequence, Loki's murderous leap was met in mid-air by the driving weight of a full-grown caribou doe. The momentum of Neetcha's 300 pounds of bone and sinew carried both her and Loki over the edge of the rock.

They fell apart as they struck the hardened snow ten feet below. When Loki came to his feet, shaking the snow and ice from his eye, he saw nothing before him but charging hoofs and horns. For once, the caribou were unafraid. They knew he was alone and they knew they could kill him. Sensing this, Loki leaped to the attack, knowing he must escape at once.

Neetcha scrambled to her feet in time to see the maddened herd pour in on him, and in time to see his fearless return of the charge. Then, before she could move to join her fellows, Loki had brought off his 100-to-one chance. He was free and clear of the herd and fleeing for the safety of the black forest beyond it. The herd, although it was fully aroused and in a fighting mood, made no effort to pursue him. Its new courage, taken from Neetcha's brave example, was not yet that strong. The excited caribou only stood sniffing the giant wolf's tracks and snorting into the darkness. Joining them, Neetcha gazed long and thoughtfully at those tracks, while at her flank the curious Awklet also studied them. In that stretching line of huge pad prints lay lesson three in the calf's wilderness education: an Arctic wolf, like any other living thing, could be defeated.

Loki fled northward, full of rage and set on finding the pack and returning at once to the Hemlock Wood. To Loki, skilled in the dangerous art of leadership, it was all too clear that the woodland caribou had found a fighting queen in Neetcha. One who might rally and guide them to the point where next year's hunt could be quite a different matter than the easy slaughter the pack had just enjoyed. His wolf's instincts, and indeed his very pride, demanded an early end to both the caribou queen and the upstart moose calf.

Loki reached his Arctic homeland and rejoined the pack ten days later. But he no longer wanted to start back to the Hemlock Wood. An early spring wind, blowing suddenly warm and constant, had commenced to set the ice going out in the great rivers. There was no foreseeing at the moment how far such an unseasonable thaw might go. Loki could not gamble on having the pack trapped south of its frozen habitat. His infallible instincts warned him not to try the trip, and as usual his uncanny intuition was rewarded. The thaw continued and within two weeks the ice was going out of the rivers in full flood. What had looked like a false touch of spring had turned into the genuine thing. An expedition south would have been disastrous.

Six weeks later the growing spring was fat with a bumper crop of the small Arctic game upon which the pack fed during the whelping season, and all its members were busy hunting and foraging for the cubs now being born. All was still well with the king wolf's rule. An early spring meant an early winter. With the first freezing of solid ice across the wide rivers, Loki would go south ahead of the main pack with a chosen few of his best hunters. They would find the caribou herd and cut the queen doe and her hump-nosed moose calf out of it, and that would be the end of that. The herd would drift apart again and the hunting in Hemlock Wood would fall back to being as fat and easy as ever. With that thought, the big wolf was content.

He lay down and slept soundly, his only concern being that he would awaken in good time to join his old friends, Split Lip and Sukon, in digging out a warren of buttery young snowshoe hares Sukon had discovered only that morning. His dreams were very pleasant.

Chapter 4

It was a beautiful soft summer in the Northland, and the same bountiful nature that fattened the wolf pack in the shadow of the pole caused the caribou to prosper and put on tallow in their forest land to the south. For the first time in many years small bands of them ventured up into the stunted timber north of the Hemlock Wood and even beyond that out onto the sweeping reaches of the old barren-ground tundra pastures. Happiness was in the herd, and a fresh sense of confidence and security.

It was a time, in that far northern land, of long daylight and little darkness. The young of the herd could see to play at their head-butting and hoof-fencing games until after ten o'clock at night. And even then the brief dimming of the sun's warm light lasted no later than four o'clock in the following morning. Very nearly around the clock, the young of the caribou gamboled in the golden light. Very nearly around the clock their elders browsed or rested or watched them with utter content.

As for Awklet, the orphaned moose calf, it was an unbroken time of pure enjoyment and adventure. Perhaps it was because the herd's luck had changed for the better with his coming among the caribou. Perhaps it was simply his association with the new queen that had led them so well. Or perhaps it was only because there was so much succulent tundra moss and leafy forest browse to eat that especially fine summer. But for whatever reason, the entire caribou herd took the comical-looking moose calf to its gentle-natured heart.

Wherever he went, and whichever members of the herd he might seek out, he found constant welcoming snorts and friendly sniffings to greet him. His particular favorites, however, were the crusty old stags. It almost seemed as though he felt sorry for them, or at least was sensitive enough to sense their loneliness. It is a law of Nature, and a cruel one, that the aged and the infirm are shown no attention and given no help whatever. But Awklet acted as though the law did not exist for him, and the grateful graybeards of the herd clearly regarded the young moose as something very special.

As to the fawns of his age, there was a little trouble. They were much smaller than he and nowhere nearly as powerful. Even in play it was difficult for him to keep from hurting them. As a result Awklet came gradually to draw apart from them, tending to graze and herd with the older animals—always, of course, within sight and smell and easy reach of his beloved foster mother, Neetcha.

This companionship between the caribou doe and the moose calf had been from the first a thing of the most touching devotion. But in the course of that first sweet summer they grew inseparable. To see them together in those sunlit, long, and cloudless afternoons was to see a rare picture of Nature's deepest and most vital instinct—mother love. And nowhere does that mother love burn so intensely as in the breast of a female wild thing deprived of her own natural young and adopting, in consequence, some other child of the wilderness.

The absurdity of the strange mating made its tenderness only the more compelling. The woodland caribou doe is one of the least lovely of all creatures. Its head is long and coarse, somewhat resembling that of a common barnyard cow. It carries this great awkward blob of a head so low it nearly touches the ground. At the same time its shaggy shoulders are as high and sharp and bony as an old hallway hat rack. Its tremendous clumsy hoofs, cloven nearly to the hock, splay out and *clack* across the frozen ground of winter or the sucking mud of summer like great misshapen snowshoes. It is a big and muscular animal standing four feet at the withers. A coarse, horse-like mane of hair covers those withers, and its tail looks as though a frayed-out stub of a used paintbrush had been pinned on the opposite end of the animal's paunchy body. It has a shuffling, slouchy gait and, whether moving or standing motionlessly, is surely one of the homeliest animals in the world.

Yet an early-born bull moose calf such as Awklet, observed in mid-term of his first year's summer, will by way of sheer contrast make a caribou doe look handsome. Nothing in nature's entire comic opera cast, from the dress-suited penguin of the South Pole to the Humpty-Dumpty puffin of the northern Atlantic Coast, can compare in purely ludicrous appearance to a first-summer bull moose calf. With his head as big and shapeless as a nail keg, and with his slender trim-legged hindquarters looking as though they had been cut off some other animal half his size and grafted upon his own bulging barrel of a body just at the hip line, Awklet was easily the superior in lack of animal beauty to his ungainly foster mother. His nose was as bulbous and broken in profile as that of an ancient desert camel's; his great lips, whiskered and bristled, hung slackly as a tired old plow horse's, and his shoulders were topped by a huge chunk of meaty gristle like the neck crest of a Spanish fighting bull.

Yet to Awklet his foster mother was the most beautiful thing in the Hemlock Wood, and to Neetcha he was the grandest sight to be had south of the Arctic Circle. For Awklet, that first summer was to remain the happiest time of his life. And truly it was a memorable summer. All of the northern deer tribe prospered throughout it, and none so amazingly as Awklet. Nature had made him a large calf to begin with. His mother, gaunt old Bera, had been unusually big for a cow of that area. His father, a chance migrant from far Alaska's Kenai Peninsula, where grow the largest and most powerful moose in the world, had been a tremendous bull standing nearly seven feet at the shoulder and weighing almost 1,600 pounds. Awklet had inherited truly from his giant sire, and as summer waned into early autumn the sheer bulk and power of the young moose became startling.

At eight months he was very nearly as large as are most moose at maturity. He weighed close to half a ton and was already within a few inches of six feet at the hump of his ungainly withers. His rear and forequarters were as thick and rounded as those of a draft horse, yet his lower legs were as clean and trim as a racer's. His face, despite the great barrel-like head and lumpy nose of his kind, wore an expression of intelligent gentleness. His eyes, small and deep-set and dark as midnight, held a look of calm assurance and pride in growing strength, difficult to define but unmistakable when observed.

With this raw material, Neetcha had worked the summer through, teaching him all she knew of caution and cleverness in the ways of wilderness survival, while certain of the old stags instructed him in the fighting use of his head and hoofs. As the fall days grew short of sunlight and the nights sharp with cold, Neetcha felt she had done everything in her power to ready Awklet for his second winter in the Hemlock Wood and his next meeting with the Arctic wolves.

Even so, she was not able to rest. The instincts of the born leader would not let her forget the wolves. There must be something else she could do to put the herd beyond the reach of Loki's killers. The caribou were fat and soft with the ease of the summer living, not yet ready to fight the wolves. The moose calf needed time to grow. He was not yet, by many months, in his prime or prepared to face the white-furred invaders. Suddenly an instinct of self-preservation struck Neetcha, the caribou doe. Where it could not yet fight, the herd could still run away!

When the wolves came, they would find only the small creatures awaiting them—the wandering hare, the slumbering squirrel, the snow-hidden ptarmigan, the deep-burrowed deer mouse. Unable to live on such scant prey, the murderous pack would be forced to return and starve out the winter in their own bleak polar homeland. Still, where could the caribou go? How could they live? What would they find to eat in some strange new land? These were questions beyond Neetcha's reach, but she knew one thing and one thing alone. Anything was better than to stay and wait for the wolves again.

Awklet, listening to the coughing and grunting of the elder caribou objecting to the young queen's decision to leave the Hemlock Wood, shook his big head in puzzlement. He would not have known, any better than those quarrelsome old stags, what should be done. But Neetcha knew. She knew instinctively, and she followed her instincts.

With the first snow flurries of an unusually early winter, a wondrous migration began. Before the snow had a chance to pile deeply enough to hold the telltale tracks, the caribou started drifting south. In bands they went, in dozens and scores, and singly or in twos and threes. By night and by day they traveled, never stopping, never resting, and bearing always and continually southward.

Within a week there were no caribou in all the vast land from the barren-ground tundra to the far southern border of the Hemlock Wood. The hare, the squirrel, the deer mouse, and the ptarmigan came out of their cover and listened and looked and wondered. In all their lives they could not remember such an empty, silent forest.

True to his hunting habits Loki was in the Hemlock Wood with the first solid river ice. But wolf after wolf of his small advance pack returned with the same news: nowhere within a long day's sight, sound, or smell were there any caribou. The herd had vanished. With it, of course, had vanished the young queen doe and her weanling moose calf.

Loki's one eye blazed green with rage. He growled and snarled in a towering fit of black anger, the froth and foam slobbering from his great jaws. Sukon, Split Lip, and the others had never seen him like this. He was behaving like a yearling cub that has just been soundly thrashed by a full-grown male in front of his favorite young she-wolf. All of them, tough and battle-scarred as they were, backed away and lay down well out of his reach, waiting for his madness to pass.

Before long the king wolf grew quiet. This was no accident, this empty forest. Those caribou had been led in their escape by that new queen he had tried to kill last spring. The young doe's action would mean great and immediate trouble for him. The main pack was due to arrive in a day or two and would expect and require heavy feeding upon its arrival. Instead, it would find only a shred of winter-thin snowshoe hare or bony Arctic ptarmigan to reward its members for their long, hard journey and their trust in his leadership. And worse. There was nothing Loki could tell them except to turn around and go back home. They could not, as a full pack with fifty-odd bellies to fill, continue on after the caribou. As it was, even turning back at the Hemlock Wood, they would be weak and starving before they reached home. This was Loki's first failure, and he knew that the wolf people were not of a nature to allow their leaders to fail more than once.

Leaving Sukon to wait for the pack and lead it back north, hunting as they went, Loki decided to go on with the others in search of the caribou. Loki and his pack would be gone as long as need be. They would find the doe and the calf and the rest of the herd if it took them all winter. When they did, there would be no more blunders on Loki's part. This time they would kill the herd queen and her ugly orphan calf.

At first the caribou had found their southerly flight an easy success. After the first hurried week, they slowed down and began to feed. The farther south they went, the richer became the new pasturages. Even though Neetcha still kept them traveling a certain number of miles daily, they were steadily gaining fat. All were in fine spirits, with Neetcha's place as leader growing more firmly established with each night's resting grounds. Even old Bartok, his rebel nature quite aware of the young doe's success, kept his peace and browsed with the herd.

Yet with all this easy living, Neetcha was not content. Something was wrong here; her leader's instincts sensed it. Vague feelings of unrest and danger arose within her and would not be quieted. But there was so much rich pasture on every hand, with no sign of a natural enemy of any kind to disturb the herd's present tranquility, that anxiety seemed foolish. And yet there was something wrong. Here was the herd, two months' safe journey from its threatened homeland, with all its members brighter of eye and glossier of coat than ever before. Here were all Neetcha's faithful followers alive and happy at a time when they would normally have been dying under the fangs of the white Arctic wolves. Here were peace and safety and better browse than any ever found in the Hemlock Wood. Why, then, had not the caribou tried wintering in the south before? If it was all this fine and simple, why had the herd not done it before? Or had it? And if it had, had it found the answer to the doubts now assailing Neetcha? Had it discovered some degree of evil possibly greater than Loki and the white wolves?

Meantime, the herd came into a wonderland of lakes and waterways and open meadows. To be sure there was ice on some of the water and snow on much of the meadow, but nothing of any real account—nothing, surely, to keep an enterprising caribou from digging out a fat supper of the wonderful summer-dried prairie hay and southern moss which lay everywhere just beneath the snow.

The herd, now ten weeks south, felt it had found the Promised Land at last, and nothing could move its contented members out of it. Neetcha, although warned by her inner senses to keep traveling, could offer no good reason for not halting. Within two days the caribou, with perhaps as many as 500 in the big herd now, were spread over a ten-mile area, browsing and resting after their long migration.

On the third day Neetcha had the answer to her forebodings. In seeking to lose Loki she had found something worse than all the wolves in the Arctic world—man! In the far north country of the Hemlock Wood there were, of course, men. An occasional half-breed trapper or Indian hunter would pass through in a season, but whole years had sometimes gone by without the sight of a single man. For this reason the caribou had acquired no fear of these rare travelers. Now Neetcha had led the herd into a land where Indian tribes lived the year around. Unknown to her, sharp-eyed red scouts had been trailing the migration for days, only waiting for it to halt in just such open country as now surrounded it. It had been a long time since caribou had been seen so far south and the Indian rifles welcomed them eagerly.

All that day the shooting went on. The caribou, ringed on all sides by the unfamiliar, terrifying flash and roar of gunfire, fell like settlement cattle. Darkness brought the only relief and under its cover Neetcha fled northward. Others of the herd, singly and in scattered small bands, followed her. There was no question of leadership now. Each animal, Neetcha no less than the slowest-witted fawn, was guided only by instinct.

When, ten days north of the Indian ambush, the weary stragglers found one another and gathered again into the herd group, there was less than half the number that had started south. Neetcha knew that they must go on and did her best to lead them homeward. But their trust in her was no longer the same. The line of march strung out a mile long. Weaklings dropped out or wandered away. A growing number of the older animals hung back and began to herd with old Bartok, who had all along distrusted Neetcha's leadership. The young doe sensed this disintegration but did not know what to do about it. Confused, and for the first time in doubt of her own judgment, she hesitated. Bartok made no move to take the lead in her place, and the caribou came to a halt. Exhausted, discouraged, leaderless, they gave up and lay down where they were. And they were in a very bad spot.

Since fleeing the Indian rifles, they had traveled by night and rested during the day so that no pursuer could approach without being seen. Now, although night was coming on, they clearly had no intention of continuing the march. And while Neetcha grunted and moved nervously among them, still striving in every animal way she knew to force them to their feet and back onto the trail, a silent white watcher narrowed his lone eye and lifted his lips in a soundless snarl of pleasure.

Loki and his small, picked pack had found the herd the day after the Indians discovered it, and they had trailed it every day since. But with the caribou resting and watchful during the sunlight hours and moving only at night, there had been no chance for anything save a broad daylight stalk. And even Loki had known better than to try that brazen course with a herd that still numbered nearly 300.

Worse luck yet, in the presence of man, Loki's fellow wolves had begun to grow restive. Soon their fear of the two-legged red hunters was greater than their fear of their one-eyed leader. One by one they had dropped away and turned back north, leaving the king wolf at last alone to continue his long and fruitless hunt. Their desertion had worried Loki a great deal at the time. Now, suddenly, all was changed. The fortunes of the stalk had shifted his way again.

Obviously the caribou were not going to move this night. Dusk was already thickening and they were crowding loosely together and bedding down with scattered carelessness. This was the end of the trail. Loki sank lower still in his sparse cover of birch saplings. He could afford to wait a while longer now. The hour of the young doe he hated was at hand. And next would come her miserable moose calf that he so heartily despised.

An hour passed swiftly. The unsuspecting herd slept soundly. Like a great shadow Loki drifted from the birch trees, out and across the unguarded bedding ground. Exhausted by ten hopeless days on the trail, the caribou never stirred as he slipped among them. Neetcha, worn and weary beyond animal endurance, slept even more deeply than the others. It was good that she did, for it made the end seem only like a long dream—a dream that went on forever, without fear, without sorrow, without awakening. Loki destroyed her as easily and quietly as he might have destroyed an Arctic hare. She uttered no sound, made no struggle, died in peace and dignity and without pain.

Awklet did not feel his foster mother's muscles relax and go limp, although when the end came, he was lying flank to flank with her—as he had since tiny calfhood. He, like the others, was too trail-weary, too far gone in heavy slumber to hear or heed such a slight movement. Loki did not wait to savor his luck. The doe was dead, the hulking young moose still asleep at her lifeless side. The great wolf's haunches gathered beneath him, then uncoiled like steel springs.

But Neetcha and his other tutors among the caribou had taught the big calf well. Among the lessons he remembered was a certain trick shown him by one of the old stags, a way of sleeping with the neck so curved and tucked between the forelegs that no stalking wolf could strike at the soft under part of the throat. Awklet had admired this trick and adopted it for his own. Thus it was that Loki's fangs missed the great vein of the throat, struck instead the gristle-tough muscle of the upper neck. The shock of the unexpected error nearly dislocated the king wolf's slashing jaws.

Awklet was up instantly, blood streaming from the gaping wound in his neck. Loki, seeing he had blundered again, and not choosing to face the maddened young bull moose in addition to a stampeded herd of caribou, sprang hurriedly for cover in a nearby thicket of ground pine. Awklet immediately charged the thicket, raging and stomping through it like a demented thing. He had seen in the moment of Loki's retreat the silent form of Neetcha and the telltale blood upon the snow at her side. Again and again, blind with rage and heartbreak, the yearling bull ripped and thrashed through the cover into which his enemy had disappeared. It was too late. He found nothing but wolf tracks. The murderer was gone.

Chapter 5

Once away from the caribou herd, Loki slowed down and began looking for a place to sleep. He was very tired from his long following of the southern migration, but showed the wolf's typical cunning in selecting his bedding spot. It was on high ground along the very edge of a rocky cañon overlooking a swift-tumbling river. There was a good moon, and no trees blocked his view of the surrounding country. Satisfied, he lay down and curled up with a great, weary grunt.

Downwind from him, a hundred paces away on the riverbank, a wicked-looking little pair of bloodshot eyes watched his every move. Many minutes after he had lain down, a huge shadow detached itself from the stream edge willows, gliding from them toward the king wolf's bedding ground. The shadow was so big and grotesquely hump-backed as to appear unreal. Only the deep-set, tiny eyes, burning like pinpoint coals in the darkness, labeled it a living thing.

Loki fell asleep at once. In the first fleeting moments after unconsciousness overcame him, he dreamed briefly of the night's adventure. He had done exceedingly well. With the young queen doe accounted for, the caribou herd would break apart again. He would, of course, have been better pleased to have gotten the big bull moose calf in the same stroke. But then, the latter could safely wait until next winter. Big as he was, he was only a yearling. Far too young as yet to be reckoned a serious threat to the continued easy hunting of the stupid caribou with which he grazed. All was well in Loki's savage world, and he could slumber the night away on that pleasant fact.

The king wolf sighed in his sleep and was content. He had forgotten about another young giant who had not been too youthful to be a threat in another time and distant place far back along the trail. Another young giant had also been only a little over a year old when he won his great victory. The price of that victory had been the kingship of the white Arctic wolves, and the name of the young upstart who had claimed it—Loki! The king wolf sighed again, going deeper still into his weary rest.

The great shadow paused, standing motionlessly a dozen paces from the sleeping king wolf. It seemed to gather itself, hovering huge and bat like for a moment. Then it plunged forward, breaking for the first time into the full glare of the Arctic moon. It was Awklet.

But too many years of light sleeping had trained Loki for such a surprise attack. The ground-shaking rush of the young bull's charge awakened him and sent him leaping and rolling to one side. Yet, fast as he was, Awklet was faster. A razor-sharp forehoof lashed out with the speed of a striking snake. The double-edged slash of the huge, splayed hoof caught the king wolf on his blind side, ripping across his bad eye, smashing him to the ground. He lay, stunned and motionless, and Awklet wheeled savagely to charge again.

From some last resource of his great store of courage, Loki forced one last movement. Senseless, crippled, blind with the blood coursing over his good eye, he staggered to his feet. In the way of his breed he drew one more breath, took one more step. That step carried him over the cañon's lip, sent him plunging into the icy waters below.

Checking his charge with braced forehoofs, Awklet was barely able to keep from following his enemy into the torrent. Recovering his balance, he searched with his small red eyes for a sign of his adversary's body in the foaming rapids. But, although he remained for many minutes, silent and watchful, upon the cañon's rim, his vigil went unrewarded. Loki, king of the white Arctic wolves, had disappeared. It seemed that never again would he lead a killer pack into the winter hush of the Hemlock Wood. But fortune sometimes favors the wicked as well as the bold.

The stream by which Loki had slept poured through its narrow, rocky gorge for perhaps a quarter of a mile. Above and below the abbreviated chasm the river was frozen from shore to shore. But within the gorge itself the water ran as rapidly as a millrace and was free of ice. To this fact Loki owed his life.

Striking the water, his body sank like a stone. He was carried along the gravelly bottom for several hundred feet, then spewed to the surface. He bobbled downstream like a furry cork for the remainder of the distance to the solid ice at the open water's end. Here the current spat him safely out onto that ice, as though he made a bad taste in the stream's mouth and it could not rid itself of him soon enough.

The shock of his short ride through the icy waters revived Loki, cleansing his head wound as neatly as a skilled surgeon and leaving him, although sick and weak, clear-headed and able to travel. He regained his feet, tottering and stumbling shoreward. At the edge of the ice he found an open stretch of dry, rocky ground leading northward. As he staggered along, his strength returned and, with his strength, his anger.

That yearling moose calf was a demon. It was incredible that a lowly forest browser should trail and attack a wolf—and a king wolf at that! But he had. In all his long reign, Loki had never been nearer death. And for the rest of his life he would carry a mark to remind him of it.

Loki's deep growl rumbled. Yes, he and the young bull had marked each other. Stamped forever across the left side of Loki's face was the brand of the cloven hoof reading: this wolf is mine! And upon the crest of Awklet's neck was the sign of the fang, scarred there for life, and warning by its cruel signature—beware, let be, touch not, this moose belongs to Loki!

After seeing that his enemy did not come to surface within sight, Awklet followed along the edge of the ice downstream to make sure he had not done so below. There he found the stark evidence of Loki's survival and escape. Awklet did not linger over the familiar marks of the great pad prints. No moose, no animal at all, could trail a wolf once the wolf knew he was being trailed. Awklet had beaten Loki this time, but the battle was not over. If he could read nothing else in the blood-stained footprints leading off into the polar darkness, Awklet could read that his war with Loki was only beginning. With a soft, deep grunt the ungainly young bull turned away to the south.

When Awklet did not return from his disappearance along the attacking wolf's trail, the caribou assumed he had met the same fate as his foster mother. The thought only heightened their fright and confusion. They milled around the dead queen, sniffing warily at her still body, stamping and snorting their hatred of the lingering wolf smell that clung to it.

Seeing their uncertainty, old Bartok quickly took over the leadership of the herd. Bunting the nervous fawns, herding the sulky does, threatening the younger stags, he soon had them all rounded up and moving away to the north. There was none to challenge him now and Bartok stood and bugled in senile fury as the docile herd obeyed his bluffing. But suddenly, from the darkened forest beyond the moving caribou, a voice far younger and more menacing than the old stag's took up the challenge.

The herd stopped moving, and a deep hush fell over it as Awklet stepped from the tree shadows and stood revealed in the gray light of the coming dawn. He was indeed a sight to produce dead silence. His head, neck, and shoulders were caked with clotted blood. The great wound on his neck, forced open in his attack on Loki, was bleeding afresh, staining his humped withers with its bright crimson. His right foreleg, from hoof to knee, was drenched in the same color. His heaving flanks were smeared with the dried lather of perspiration, his pendulous lips flecked with angry froth.

The young moose bellowed again, pawing the snow in great surging showers, and the herd drew hurriedly back, sensing that Neetcha's gangly calf had overnight become a fearsome bull. Again he bellowed, thrashing his huge head among the crowding pines, showering ice and snow broadside. Then he started slowly toward Bartok.

But the gaunt old stag wanted none of him. He was half the enraged youngster's size, ten times his age. Very wisely, and with no delay, Bartok lost himself in the comfortable middle of the herd, in this way admitting he had no further interest whatever in contesting the moose bull's claim to the leadership. Disdainfully Awklet allowed him to go. Then, after a suitable number of admiring younger does and dour old grand dams had sniffed at the wolf's blood on his foreleg, he calmly ambled away and bedded down. Following his confident example, the herd gratefully resumed its interrupted rest.

But although he lay quietly enough, there was no sleep for Awklet. That moment there on the cañon's edge had been brief, its action lightning fast. Yet for an instant he had been within hoof's reach of the wolf—and the moon had been very bright and good. His foster mother's slayer had been no chance wanderer, no stray hunter, no outcast, no lonely killer for food. He had been the same one-eyed white giant Awklet remembered from the first hour of his life. This was the king wolf of the Arctic killer pack. There could be no two wolves like that one. Awake or asleep, Awklet would never forget him.

Shortly after daybreak, the return of the herd to

the Hemlock Wood continued uneventfully. There was no question of leadership. The caribou for the first time had a leader in which they could have utter faith, one who actually pursued and attacked wolves! At last the herd had courage at its head. And not courage alone, but wisdom. For Awklet had learned the fourth hard lesson of wilderness survival: no enemy can be defeated by running away. In leaving the Hemlock Wood, Neetcha had been wrong, but in being wrong she had taught Awklet to be right.

With sunup, the herd was moving north. None of the caribou showed any further curiosity over the body of their dead queen. Antlers swaying, splayed hoofs clacking on the frozen ground, they filed past her. Within minutes, the last of them was gone and Awklet remained alone in the snow-swept meadow.

He walked slowly forward, stood for a long time looking down on the huddled form of the only mother he had ever really known. At last he stretched forth his great ugly muzzle and placed it alongside the dead doe's soft-haired ear. For a moment only he nuzzled her, using the gentle, lingering nose bunts she had taught him in babyhood. Then he turned away.

He did not look back again, nor did he slow his pace. Awklet had said his last good bye to Neetcha.

Chapter 6

It was a long, severe winter but at last the ice went out of the rivers and the brief, lush spring of the Northland came again. It was time, Awklet's instincts told him, for a herd leader to be at work.

Throughout the short months of the sub-Arctic summer, he restlessly led his followers over every trail of the vast domain that had been the grazing grounds of their ancestors. This meant exploring places the oldest members of the herd had never seen. But Awklet forced the herd to move constantly, and by autumn's close he had achieved the purpose toward which the impulses of leadership drove him. The caribou now knew every main track and side trail of the sub-Arctic tundras to the north, as well as all those of the Hemlock Wood to the south. No longer would they need to run in blind ignorance and panic when the white wolves came. This time they would know the land for which they must fight, and they would be prepared should they have to take life-saving flight.

In either event, the land itself held certain grim advantages for both the invaders and the defenders. To the north, beyond the tundra, stretched the unbroken sheet of polar ice that was Loki's frozen lair. To the east ran the low jumble of the Boulder Hills. To the west stood the high, ragged teeth of the Icy Mountain. Through these hills and mountains led the two historic trails by which the wolf pack traveled southward each winter. Where they entered the Hemlock Wood, each trail narrowed into a deep and difficult pass—Retreat Pass to the east, Blizzard Pass to the west.

But countering these inviting entrances to the Hemlock Wood was the great natural shield of the Rotten Lakes Swamp. This phenomenon of Nature stretched entirely across the northern border of the woodland between the two mountain passes. It was not actually a collection of lakes at all but one continuous marshland fed from beneath the ground by boiling-hot springs. From somewhere deep in the smoldering core of the earth, these springs flowed summer and winter alike. The potency of their heat was so great that not even the sub-Arctic icecap could subdue it. The result was a constantly crumbling honeycomb of rotten moss ice and spongy tundra snow to which no wild creature would trust itself.

Awklet had plodded patiently along the southern edge of the great thermal swamp, looking for a way to cross over it northward. When he found none, he turned back to the Hemlock Wood. Nature had told him in her mysterious way that no animal could travel across those smoking morasses of rotten ice. Loki would not be coming that way. No mortal wolf, not Loki or any other, would come into the Hemlock Wood across Rotten Lakes Swamp. In fortunate consequence, Awklet could leave to Nature the guarding of four-fifths of the border between the Hemlock Wood and Loki's land to the north.

With his explorations accomplished, Awklet lost his restlessness and settled down to await the coming winter. He was content and the herd was ready. They had followed him wherever his instincts had taken him, and they had done it quickly and without question. Clearly they were happy with their new leader and just as clearly they would obey him when the time came to do so. Indeed, both the powerful young leader and the big-eared, gentle-eyed followers had real cause for content with one another and with the woodland they loved so well.

The forefathers of the present herd had chosen well when they ended their barren-ground retreat in the Hemlock Wood. It was surely a region that resolute fighters might hope to defend. The caribou had only to keep herd sentinels on watch over the two trails, Boulder Hill and Icy Mountain, by which the white wolves always came south. That was an easy task and one that came quite naturally to a deer tribe whose safety had depended for generations upon just such herd sentinels. Once warned in good time of the approach of the Arctic raiders, the fighting circle could be formed successfully, as in the old days of the tundra ancestors.

The only small danger was that Loki might know of some third way into the Hemlock Wood, but that was scarcely any danger at all. The white wolves had always used those same two ancient roads. It seemed unlikely that there were any other trails into this peaceful land. And so the contentment of the caribou herd grew greater and their sense of security more false.

Summer grew late, autumn disappeared like quicksilver, winter shut in swiftly. The first two months brought nothing but light snows. The big cold did not come. The short gray days passed endlessly with no sign of the wolf pack. Awklet became extremely concerned.

The winter deepened into December. The new year turned. January and February fled by. Still the animals of the Hemlock Wood awaited the deep cold that always brought the white wolves down from their Arctic homeland. But the cold did not come. Nor did the wolves.

It was the strangest winter in the memory of the eldest caribou, yet its mystery had a simple answer. Once in a very long while, the great cold would not come with its usual fierceness to the land of the midnight sun. As a result, the wolves would not be frozen out of their far northern hunting ranges, would not be driven south to seek food. This was such an unusual time, such a rare and open winter.

Spring came. The forest browse grew rich and heavy on every hand and the living was good for Awklet and his caribou followers. Another golden Arctic summer swiftly faded. Autumn lingered briefly. Soon the snows of early winter whitened the Hemlock Wood. The animals sniffed the cold north wind and wondered about the wolves.

Surely they must come now. Surely this winter would bring them. But where were they? What had happened to them? What were they waiting for?

The caribou grew dangerously tense. They would not stay in one place, and Awklet had constantly to lead them to new bedding grounds. Fortunately his own calm confidence was contagious. And for this there was great physical evidence. The appearance

of the massive young bull moose in the full strength
of his fourth winter would have inspired courage in
a pine mouse. Fully 1,300 pounds in weight, he
stood five inches over six feet at the shoulder. His
coat, a dull shaggy red-brown in earlier calfhood,
was now sleek and deep and very dark, almost black
in color, with the belly and lower legs a bright,
creamy, fawn-yellow, after the striking pattern of his
Alaska-bred sire. His antlers, while not yet of the
magnificent rack and spread that later years would
bring, were still sharp-tined, clearly dangerous
weapons. For all his tremendous size, his movements were lithe and quick as those of a lynx, his
every attitude suggestive of alert, fearless, highly
dangerous fighting power.

The ugly scar that Loki had left upon him, and
that ran like a streak of angry red lightning across
his great hump-muscled neck from crest to jaw base,
served only to increase his look of savage fitness.
Small wonder that the caribou, looking at him, grew
quiet and, for the time at least, unafraid.

The third month passed and still the wolves did
not come. The cracking cold of deep winter was
upon the woodland now, the normal time for the
appearance of the Arctic killers, long past. The waiting became intolerable.

At last, early on a frosty morning in the fourth
month, a lone caribou sentinel far out on the barren-
ground tundra sighted the main pack of white
wolves traveling south. By the use of good snow
craft and the fine caribou art of moving unseen in
vast fields of white, the crusty old stag was able to
outrace the pack and come ahead of it to the borders
of the forest, thus bringing the warning to Awklet.

The latter at once departed for a well-hidden look-out post above Blizzard Pass, from which he could observe the approaching pack. Loki was in the lead and the pack was at full strength, guaranteeing that the wolves did not intend splitting up to attack from more than one direction. They were entering the woodland openly, boldly, and confidently. They were not even moving fast, just coming on at a steady jog trot.

Awklet's fierce little eyes snapped with excitement. Returning to the herd, he swiftly led it deeper into the forest, guiding it carefully along the broad open trail that ran from the base of Blizzard Pass to the heart of the Hemlock Wood. Now he could make his own defenses, secure in the knowledge of the exact direction from which the wolves would attack.

For his battleground he selected the very meadow where, three years before, Loki had made the mistake of sparing a wobbly-kneed moose calf's life. Driving the last year's fawns and young does into the center of the clearing, he herded the older does and the stags of all ages into a solid ring of protection around them. That done, he took his own position on the northern edge of the circle. He was ready. On the basis of what he knew of Loki's movements, it was an excellent disposition of forces. From the standpoint of what he *did not know*, it was a possible deathtrap.

Loki had spent the preceding summer scouring the Arctic for new recruits and had succeeded beyond his hopes. To the east of his own domain was a polar waste of rock-girt ice floes ruled over by a mangy outcast called Boron. This crafty old scavenger had a following of perhaps thirty wolves, the outlaws and unspeakables of every decent wolf pack in the Northland. Loki, accidentally crossing trails with Boron, saw in him the perfect ally for his vengeful return to the Hemlock Wood. The skulking renegade did not dare refuse to join his scabby pack to the king wolf's powerful force.

So Boron, a wolf entirely unknown to the caribou, was traveling far to the east of Loki at the moment of the latter's entry into the Hemlock Wood. With Boron coursed his outlaw pack. Only minutes after Awklet had led the herd away from Loki and Blizzard Pass, Boron and his wolf scum poured, unseen, from the mouth of Retreat Pass and into the forest behind the caribou circle. While Awklet watched only to the north for the approach of Loki, Boron closed silently in from the south.

Loki struck first, from the north. He and his yammering followers attacked without warning, out of the four o'clock blackness, slashing into Awklet's side of the antler-lowered circle. But Awklet raged at the front of his circled herd, bellowing and charging the surprised wolves with such successful fury that the caribou took fire and fought like demons. Coughing and grunting hoarsely, slashing and hooking with hoof and horn, the tough old does and stags drove back the wolf pack's first howling wave.

Loki wisely called off the assault and ordered the wolves to retreat a short way into the surrounding forest. From this cover, an occasional wolf charged the herd to keep it from resting, but the main pack did not return to the attack.

Awklet sensed that something had gone wrong with the king wolf's plans, but he could not guess what. Neither could Loki. Loki had expected Boron to strike the herd from the rear while he came at it from the front, thus stampeding the caribou and finishing the killing quickly. But Boron had failed to strike, or even to appear. Now the herd, alarmed and aroused to nerve-strung courage by Awklet's utter fearlessness, was going to be very hard to handle. Still, Loki would wait a while for Boron. He could afford a little time, and the treacherous old rascal would not dare to fail to show up.

The king wolf watched Awklet and narrowed his lone eye uneasily. This great hulk of a moose bull was giving bad signs of knowing which end of the breeze carried the odor, and that was not a good thing. Perhaps, after all, he had better not wait for Boron. He looked about him for old Sukon. The old wolf heard his summoning snarl and slunk quickly toward him.

Boron, meanwhile, was in trouble. His way into the Hemlock Wood was not so easy as he had expected. A small band of old stags under two tough, experienced leaders, Horsa and Kajak, had been bedded near Retreat Pass. This straying group had heard Awklet's gathering bellows when the young moose began calling in the caribou after sighting Loki approaching by Blizzard Pass. The small band had started to fall back toward the main herd just before Boron entered the forest.

The renegade wolf and his pack were moving with the wind; hence they did not scent the caribou so close ahead of them. But the latter, being downwind of the wolves, scented them at once. Instead of fleeing in panic, Horsa and Kajak halted their two dozen seasoned fighters in a screening stand of ground pine and waited for the white raiders. They let the surprised wolves run right into them, then charged point-blank into the pack's midst.

They trampled over and injured at least ten of Boron's followers. Half of them were so badly hurt they were out of the fight for good. The caribou did not slow their rush, continuing straight on into the heavy timber toward Awklet and the main herd. Boron and the remainder of the wolves, taken completely off guard, made no attempt at pursuit. Instead, they swung far to the south and circled through the forest to come at the herd from the west.

Had Loki waited for them, the sun would have been long up and shining before they could ever have joined him. But the king wolf was not waiting. Old Sukon had been eager for an immediate, all-out attack on Awklet's antlered circle. So while Boron skulked through the woods to the west, the attack was being carried out.

Loki's huge pack leaped forward, snarling. Awklet and the caribou fought back desperately until Horsa and Kajak, with their excited band, raced in from the south, fresh from their encounter with Boron's wolf pack in the forest. Momentarily confused and for the first time shaken in his confidence, Awklet began to retreat. Encouraged, Loki's pack redoubled its slashing attack, thinking that the old panic had begun to break up the herd. It had not. Nor had Awklet's confusion been more than momentary. As he saw the caribou hold firmly in their determination to defend themselves, his own resolution returned twofold. Slowly and skillfully the big herd, following its moose leader, continued its retreat, the old does and stags keeping the outer circle closed up and unbroken. As the daylight hours wore along, still with no hint of Boron's whereabouts, Loki again slowed the attack. He was now content to follow the herd, meanwhile trying to determine where its young moose leader was headed.

At dusk that night, he found out. At first his lone

eye lit up wickedly. Awklet had led the herd squarely into one of the two entrances to Half Moon Valley, and the old wolf thought that the herd was now trapped. This valley was a steep-sided place flanked on one side by Sleeping Bear Lake and on the other by the impassable granite cliffs of the Boulder Hills. The two outlets were Bear Tail Pass to the south and, to the north, Ice Rock Cañon, through which Awklet and the herd were presently crowding. It looked as though the wolves had only to seal Bear Tail Pass at the other end and drive the caribou in through Ice Rock Cañon, bottling them up in Half Moon Valley. Once this was done, the pack could either cut them down or starve them out, with no chance for escape either way.

But Loki was no inexperienced yearling cub. Suddenly the gleam of eagerness died out of his lone eye. He knew he did not dare divide the pack and send one part to seal up Bear Tail Pass. Instead, he must keep the pack together, surrounding and holding the caribou right where they were. They could not get away and the longer they hesitated, the more surely they were lost. In the Arctic, it was the wolf that always won the waiting game.

Loki was rounding up his pack with Sukon when from the forest to the west came a sound that made the old king's savage heart leap—the eerie, long-drawn howling of a trailing wolf pack. It was Boron. The rascally scavenger had at last caught up. Now everything was different. Now Boron and his mangy ones could go south and watch Bear Tail Pass while Loki and his full pack drove the herd on into Half Moon Valley.

When Boron and his pack limped up out of the darkness, Loki at once fell to snarling and growling at him. Boron was tired and his wolves were bruised and footsore, but they were killers by trade, and this was just the sort of hunting made to order for murderous outlaws. After a short exchange of growls and snarls with Loki and Sukon, Boron led his pack quickly off into the southern darkness.

The king wolf watched them go. When the robber pack had disappeared, he flattened his stumpy little ears, narrowed his cold yellow eye, and curled his lip at old Sukon in a soundless snarl of cruel pleasure. Now, surely, the end of the orphan bull moose was very near.

Chapter 7

Shortly before dawn a mysterious movement began in the caribou herd. Loki and Sukon, crouched and waiting on the outer edge of the herd circle, could not believe their eyes. The moose was leading the caribou into Half Moon Valley, and without being driven to it! But surely there was something wrong here. Could it be as simple as it looked?

Cautiously Loki led the pack into Ice Rock Cañon, following closely in the tracks of the last bunch of old stags guarding the withdrawal. There was no need for hurry now. Boron would be coming up from Bear Tail Pass, trapping the herd between his pack and Loki's. After that, the only way the caribou could move would be into Blind Cañon and they would never do that. The young moose was too smart. He would know that there was no escape from Blind Cañon. Its tiny valley opened off the main meadow of Half Moon. Its sheer walls were naked ice and rock. No living animal could climb out of it and there was no feed for the caribou on its barren, boulder-strewn floor. To enter it would be only to destroy any slim chance the herd might yet have of fighting its way out of the present trap. Half Moon Valley was bad enough, but Blind Cañon was far worse.

Suddenly now, just as Boron and his outlaw rag-tag pack broke into sight along the southern edge of Half Moon meadow, Awklet gave a mighty bellow and led the herd in a lumbering gallop straight across the meadow and into the narrow, high-walled entrance of Blind Cañon. Both Loki and Boron at once gave chase, but again they had been outwitted. The caribou gained the cañon's mouth and crowded through it before the racing wolves could cut them off. As the two packs slid to a snow-showering halt, Awklet and a dozen old stags turned to face them, crowded shoulder to shoulder in the choked throat of the deep crevasse.

Although the main herd was for the moment safe from attack, both wolf packs immediately set up a growling, snarling yammer of excitement. The caribou were finally and forever trapped this time. To the last frightened fawn and stumbling old doe, they were crowded into Blind Cañon. Their moose leader had blundered. The king wolf had led his brothers well and demonstrated his superior hunting craft. This time there had been no mistake. Loki had more than made up for the disastrous hunt he had led them on last winter. Now all that remained was to drive the caribou on up the cañon and out into the bare rock of its little valley. There a tremendous kill could be made once the herd had been starved into weakness. But the pack would make certain that plenty of seed stock was left to breed an ample supply of meat for the following year, and all the years thereafter.

As soon as daylight broke, full and clear, the pack would start the last drive. It would be a great hunt. When it was over, the caribou herd would be broken apart, its moose leader destroyed. With the great young bull dead, the caribou would never again gather to fight as they had the past, bloody day. It was an exceedingly pleasant prospect. The three huge dog-wolves—Loki, Sukon, and Boron—snarled and bickered over it delightedly. To the east, the first faint streak of coming day broke behind them.

Meanwhile Awklet stood alone in the blackness that hovers so deeply just before daylight, his tired brain struggling to stave off sleep. He had not shut his eyes or stopped moving for twenty-four hours. His whole aching body cried out for rest. But there would be no rest, and he knew he must stay awake or die. He must somehow, for a last time, fight back the wolves.

Summoning his great strength, Awklet lurched forward toward the panting, slowly pacing ring of wolves that again began to bedevil him and the old stags at the cañon's mouth. The old stags charged bravely after him, their assault bringing the wolf pack up off its crouching bellies. For five minutes Awklet and his stags kept up their short charges and retreats. Then, after three of the stags had been cut down by the wolves and another two so severely wounded they could barely stagger, Awklet and the surviving stags once more fell back into the cañon's throat.

They had paid a hard price, but they had succeeded in gaining the precious time the herd needed. When the fighting stopped, Loki could see by the growing daylight that once again the herd had disappeared. Loki could not see through the narrow opening of the cañon's walls into the inner valley, but he had no need to. While the young bull and those tough old stags had fought so well, the other caribou had probably panicked and fled into the little valley of no return. All Loki had to do now was cut down the moose and finish off the rear-guard stags. After that, the way to the inner valley and the big kill would be wide open.

As the king wolf allowed himself one last con-quering howl, the big moose started to move. Loki narrowed his one good eye suspiciously. As he watched, Awklet looked across at him and bellowed defiantly. Then, surprisingly, the moose turned, forced his way through the old stags and fled up the cañon.

Instantly Loki snarled the signal to attack. The waiting wolves leaped forward. Snapping with rage, their king led his combined packs down upon the nine old stags.

Awklet, stumbling with exhaustion, caught up with the herd in mid-valley. As he did, the howling and yelping of Loki's attacking wolves rose to a sud-den climax in the cañon behind him. Forging to the head of the slowing herd, Awklet led it out and across the rocky ground toward the sheer north wall and his last goal—the brawling, rushing course of Lost River. Gallantly the tiring caribou lumbered af-ter him, struggling to keep up with his giant strides. None of them questioned why the young moose was leading them in this direction.

The strange, deep stream of Lost River drained the tiny glacial lake at the widened end of Blind Cañon. From the lake the stream ran a short dis-tance across the mile-wide inner valley, then disap-peared abruptly and mysteriously into the perpendicular face of the northern cliffs. Thence it raced in a silent, black flood underground beneath a high spur of the Boulder Hills to issue forth again in the outer spaces of Half Moon Valley. It ran open and unfrozen all year, for the little lake that was its source was fed by the same great subterranean hot springs that underlay the Rotten Lakes Swamp.

Long before, Neetcha had brought Awklet into Blind Cañon. To a wobbly-kneed calf, the purpose of the visit was far from clear. The gentle caribou doe led him to the eerie place where the roaring waters of Lost River smashed into the rock of the north wall and disappeared. Here she paused on a granite ledge high above the stream, urging him to join her and look down. As he did so, she had deliberately shouldered him over the edge, sending him sprawling into the racing waters. His single piteous bleat of terror had been lost in the roar of the churning flood.

Short minutes later, wet and bewildered but unharmed, he had been shot forth from the Half Moon Valley side of the cliff, to come to a floundering stop in a quiet, broad pool from which he easily struggled to shore. The next moment he had been joined by Neetcha herself, who came bobbing out of the apparently solid rock as magically as had he.

Awklet alone knew that the friendly, warm current of Lost River would carry any animal from the apparently hopeless trap of Blind Cañon back out to the freedom of Half Moon Valley—and do it in less than three minutes! It was something that he had never forgotten, and he was remembering it now as he urged the tiring caribou toward the spray-splashed rock from which his foster mother had pushed him those long years before.

Horsa and Kajak and the other old stags in the cañon's throat fought to the last. But no such small band could stand before Loki's fury. Shortly the last of the brave oldsters went down, and the wolf pack poured over them into the inner valley. Instantly they saw Awklet and the main caribou herd making for the north wall and Lost River. Loki threw back his huge head, howling deeply and hoarsely. Like mad things, the white wolves streamed off after their quarry, their wide red mouths hanging open, their slobbering jaws chopping furiously. By some dark instinct bred in their killer kind, they knew that they had to catch those desperately racing caribou before they reached the river.

But Horsa's stubborn stags had done their work well. They had given Awklet a few minutes of precious time. Time for him to lead the herd to the rock overlooking Lost River. Time to urge the timid and the frightened into the fearful stream. Time for the swirling flood to bear its antlered, strong-swimming burden beneath the mountain and away to freedom.

When the first of the pack reached the rock, the last caribou had disappeared. Loki was amazed and furious. And a little frightened. High boulders had hidden the herd from the pack's view in the last minutes of its race across the little valley. Now there was not so much as a crippled fawn in sight. And no least sign of what had become of better than 300 woodland caribou. But the king wolf's uneasiness disappeared before his renewed anger. There were high boulders across the swift river, beyond where it disappeared into the north wall. Somehow the herd must have forded the stream higher up and gotten into those far-shore boulders. It seemed impossible that the entire band could have done this and vanished so completely in the little time it was out of the wolf pack's sight, but there was no other explanation.

Snarling wickedly, Loki turned on Boron. The caribou must be across the stream somewhere. Any living thing falling downstream in the current of the river would have been smashed to a pulp against the face of the cliff into which the water plunged. The river came within inches of the top of the great cave through which it flowed under the mountain. The caribou could not have gone that way and lived. They must be upstream. Loki swung his followers on up Lost River, seeking the secret way across it. Boron and his rabble waited at the rock for his return.

Certainly Half Moon Valley had never seen a stranger sight. Certainly the crest of Lost River had never borne a stranger freight. Without warning, from the bare rock of the stream's outer issuance spewed forth a torrent of waterborne caribou. Within seconds the big landing pool was alive with the antlered, bobbing heads of the entire Hemlock Wood herd. Not a single animal had been lost in the swift-churning ride through the mountain.

By the time Awklet reached the rocky beach, the herd had swum clear of the stream and reformed on its southern bank. At this point the caribou could easily have fled back to the beloved fastnesses of their forest home, but Awklet's bravery did not end with merely escaping from Blind Cañon. And, refreshed by their miraculous journey through Lost River's underground caverns, the herd did not falter nor fail to follow him.

Leaving the yearling fawns and their mothers under a strong guard of the older stags and barren does, the balance of the herd swung obediently off after Awklet. Doughty old Bartok took charge of the band staying behind to watch over the does and their fawns. In spite of his past actions, Bartok was the best and angriest fighter among them, now that Horsa and Kajak were gone. And for all his surly ways, he could be trusted when the wind fell still among the aspens and the hunting song of the Arctic wolves was in the winter air.

Awklet led his followers at a lumbering gallop back toward the narrow rock passage of Blind Cañon. Sensing instinctively their leader's intention, the slowest-witted, least resolute of the embattled caribou began to grow fiercely excited.

Chapter 8

As Loki searched pantingly for the secret crossing place of the caribou herd over Lost River's swirling torrent, a sudden snarl from Split Lip brought him up short. Swinging his huge head, the king wolf looked back toward the entrance of Blind Cañon. Something was happening over there by the cañon, something unexplainable, something possibly very dangerous.

The king wolf's pack was on high ground with the whole width of the inner valley spread below it in the glaring snow light of full sunup. Far over by the cañon's outlet to big Half Moon Valley, the wolves could see a dark mass of living forms surging into the little inner valley's mile-wide arena. The missing caribou! The very animals they had been seeking just now along the banks of Lost River. The herd that had disappeared without a trace had now reappeared in the same mysterious manner. This time, however, there was one sinister difference. This time it was the wolf pack that was sealed in the valley from which there was no escape known to them or their leader.

A deep and terrible anger struck the great wolf. His single snarl was so heavy it shook the very snow beneath his huge pads. With that snarl and without another signal or thought for the pack behind him, Loki turned and started alone for the cañon entrance. Over there, waiting for him, was the young moose he had come to kill. Loki did not think of himself. He did not think of the pack. He thought only of Awklet.

Meanwhile, over by the cañon's rock-grit throat, where a mid-valley range of ragged boulders hid the wolf pack from his anxious view, the exhausted young moose thought of Loki. He knew that somewhere out in the stillness of that little valley the king wolf was waiting to kill him. Awklet was not afraid, but he was very, very tired. He had waited a long time and with an anger of his own for this final meeting with the giant wolf. Yet now that the time was near, he feared that his great weariness might cause him to fail the herd and thereby to fail the memory of the soft-eyed foster mother from which he had inherited his leadership.

Across the valley Loki's followers now made their own last decision. As their snarling leader started toward the caribou herd, his faithful pack, to the last red-tongued wolf, fell in behind him. They had lived with their king and now, if it were time to do so, they would die with him.

Typically Loki thought nothing of this fierce show of loyalty. It was simply the way of the wolf pack. Without looking back, he led the way down and off the higher ground and into the great boulders of the valley's broken floor. As he went, his savage heart burned with the desire for revenge. The pack might be trapped and facing a fight to the death. So be it. Loki was willing to sell his own life for a price—the life of a giant young bull moose standing five inches over six feet tall at the shoulder and weighing a full 1,300 pounds.

Awklet waited a little longer, then led the herd a cautious few steps out into the valley. Here he paused again, every sense straining for a sign of the wolves. He still could not see or hear anything of them. After another careful time of waiting and listening, he took a small band of seasoned old stags and started off to look for his enemies, leaving the main herd on guard at the cañon's entrance. He went with confidence and without fear.

There was realistic cause for the young moose's calm lack of fright. From time immemorial the caribou had fought the wolves by gathering in a tight circle, with the females and the fawns inside and the males outside facing the attackers. Thus the wolf had always been the offensive fighter, the caribou the defensive fighter. Now the young moose had unknowingly changed the old order. The wolves were in the position of an attacked herd, while the caribou were taking the place of the attacking wolves. The outcome of the threatened battle, therefore, was not at all reassuring for the wolves.

No wolf is a match for a ring of adult, aroused caribou in a stand-off fight. The wolf always operates as a raider. He attacks, slashes inward, leaps outward and away. Loki had always killed what he wanted and withdrawn before his surviving prey could recover enough to start dealing him punishment with razored hoof and crushing horn. When, upon rare and notable occasion, he was trapped as

Awklet's herd now had Loki trapped, the wolf king
was an entirely different animal. A cornered wolf
will fight, as will any cornered wild thing. But he
will not fight with the same fury and self-confidence
displayed in the bloody attack. Somehow Awklet
must have sensed this. His triumphant situation
must have produced the courage and brave assurance with which he led the old stags out into the valley in search of Loki.

But that had been back by the cañon's throat. Now
he was out in the open center of the valley and suddenly the courage and calmness went out of him like
water wrung from a shrunken sponge. Through a
narrow opening between the great ten-foot boulders
that for the fortunate moment hid him and his followers, the young moose caught a fleeting glimpse
of the slavering king wolf and his full pack bearing
soundlessly down upon the very boulders behind
which he cowered.

The sight shocked Awklet into a state of near
panic. All of his inherited terror of the wolf smell
and the close sight of the white killers flooded up in
him. In an instant, the roles of hunter and hunted
were reversed, and the reversal very nearly stampeded the youthful bull who had borne himself so
bravely up to that last nightmare moment. He had
started out merely to *look* for Loki—to locate the
hiding place of his murderous pack, so that he might
then return to warn the herd and lead them in the
flight that would follow. Of course, his great mistake
had been in presuming that such an enemy would
be hiding. Now the frightened young bull moose
stood needlessly trapped, carelessly cut off from the
main caribou herd.

It was the type of blunder no animal could make

more than once with Loki's kind. Yet, having made it, all Awklet could do was crouch behind the gray boulders with his equally paralyzed stags. Crouch there and watch the king wolf lead his pack like a ghost band of frost-furred furies straight past Awklet's rocky shelter and toward the leaderless herd at the cañon exit from Blind Valley. The only chance of survival for the fearful moose and his trembling caribou companions was to remain unseen as Loki swept past their hiding place. If they could do that, they might then make their way back to the main herd while the wolves were preoccupied with their attack upon it.

Like carved statues the frightened old stags and their giant young leader stood among the protective cover of the mottled boulders. Not a muscle twitched. Not a breath stirred. And, fifty paces beyond, the wolf pack poured by in a panting white flood.

At this instant Loki needed the wondrously keen nose of his faithful Sukon to catch the all but nonexistent odor of the hidden enemy in the whistling Arctic winds. But old Sukon was dead, fallen but the hour before in the savage fight to break past Horsa and Kajak in the cañon's outer throat. The winds of Arctic chance whistled in vain. Yet the nose is not the hunting wolf's only weapon. Nor even his best one. The eye is even more deadly keen. And Loki had an eye. Just one eye, it was true. But such an eye as no other wolf ever had. Through the years of its cruel using, that lone orb had developed within itself an incredible power of sight. If a deer mouse moved at twenty paces, Loki saw it. If a ptarmigan or a snowshoe hare ruffled a feather or twitched a white whisker at thirty paces, it was also seen. If a shifting caribou antler dislodged a puff of powdered snow no bigger than a chickadee from a rock ledge of the boulder behind which its nerve-ridden owner was hiding, Loki saw that, too. Suddenly the great king wolf twisted in mid-stride, his hoarse voice breaking into a yammering snarl of discovery. Behind him the wolf pack veered its course and raced amid a mad chorus of whimpering yelps and whining growls straight toward Awklet's boulder pile.

Back by Lost River's edge, Boron watched the king wolf's pack stream toward the caribou herd. He made no move that would cause his own disreputable pack to follow Loki's courageous lead. For Boron knew something that the king wolf did not. The caribou herd's mysterious vanishing and return was not so baffling to the crafty scavenger as it had been to Loki, nor was his character so valiant as the latter's. Boron was as devious and shifty and cunning as the king wolf was bold and brave and straightforward. And he had seen something Loki had missed.

Having raced across the valley on higher ground than Loki's pack, Boron had seen the last of the herd plunge into Lost River and disappear under the apparently solid rock. Seeing them again, still dripping wet from their journey, he sensed that in some way the mysterious river had carried them to safety outside Blind Valley. With a scavenger's dishonesty, he had kept to himself his knowledge of the herd's plunge off Leaping Rock. Something about it had puzzled his wily mind enough to warn him to silence. It had been troubling him constantly while Loki had been up the river looking for a caribou crossing place that did not exist. And now, as he hesitated to follow the king wolf across the valley into the danger of a fight with the aroused herd, his skulker's knife-sharp instincts suddenly told him what he and his cringing companions must do. Let Loki die alone in his fight with the caribou. All the better for Boron and his robber pack. With Loki dead there would be only one king wolf in the Northland—Boron!

The gaunt wolf growled and bickered with his followers a moment. They, too, had seen the caribou disappear and now they were thinking, as their leader had already divined, that the mysterious warm river must lead out through the rock. Quickly there was an agreement. Abandon Loki, of course. Save their own skins and, more, have all the future hunting in the Hemlock Wood to themselves.

Boron growled once more, then crouched and sprang from Leaping Rock into the river. Eagerly the others followed his example and, in their swift turn, were sucked out of sight beneath the high rock of the north wall. The trip through the great rock was pleasant, even beautiful. Boron's ragged cowards enjoyed it hugely. The river's cavern was high and arching and full of good fresh air. Great stalactites and stalagmites of weird, unearthly hue and faint phosphorescent luminosity decorated the entire way. The water was tepid and relaxing in temperature, its current swift and smooth with no bothersome undertows or whirlpools. It was indeed a high-spirited band of deserters that bobbed out of the Half Moon Valley exit of Lost River some few moments later. It was indeed a happily panting pack of Arctic wolf scum that swam shoreward through the quiet waters of the exit pool. And it was indeed a lovely shallow landing beach they found waiting for them at the pool's edge, so peaceful and serene and entirely deserted.

Boron's treading paws struck bottom. He scrambled momentarily for footing, found it, started wading out. Suddenly his slit-eyed glance focused unbelievingly on the dark forest rimming the gravel edge of the pool. Suddenly the guard hairs on his back, from skull to tail root, stood straight on end. Caribou stags! At least fifty of them! Gathered there and waiting in the black shadows of the timber, gathered and waiting for him and his two dozen mangy deserters.

The stags did not wait long. Boron had only time to snarl a warning to his nearest fellows before old Bartok was lunging across the narrow beach and into the shallow landing waters. Perhaps a third of the wolves, those still in deep swimming water, managed to reach the far shore and escape. The others, including Boron, had no chance at all. Floundering helplessly in the beach shallows, they were driven under and drowned by the sheer weight and vengeful power of half a hundred angered old caribou stags.

Chapter 9

Awklet and his isolated stags were waiting for Loki when the Arctic wolf pack rounded the boulders and bore down upon them. Rump to rump they stood in their tight circle, antlers lowered, nostrils wide with fear, eyes rolling in desperation. The young bull moose, although terribly afraid, did not give way to panic. He set his great muscular hindquarters beneath him and swung the spreading rack of his sharp-tined antlers almost to the snow as the wolves came in. To his right and left, the caribou were as frightened as their leader but seemed to take sudden heart from his defiant example. They were prepared to die as gallantly as had Horsa and Kajak and the others of their bravely departed fellows before them.

For half a minute the wolves poured in at them, leaping, slashing, snarling. They downed two of the old stags and crippled a third, but the circle closed up and fought on. They were blooded now, and a blooded animal begins to fight on instinct, losing his natural fear in the heat of the battle. With his life at stake and no escape possible, even so gentle a creature as the caribou, once badly injured, becomes extremely dangerous.

A full-grown stag is twice the size of a common American deer. Big specimens will often exceed forty-eight inches at the shoulder and weigh upward to 400 pounds. The antlers of the woodland caribou are tremendous, having a short heavy beam with a spreading rack that commonly carries more than thirty tines or sharpened tips. Their skill in using these huge tree-like weapons against predatory enemies is all the more amazing in contrast to their otherwise clumsy and inoffensive appearance.

Thus it was that Awklet and his gentle friends went well armed into the battle with the white Arctic wolves. And for a little while they gave them blow for blow in the fierce struggle. But only for a very little while. A few valiant old stags could not long stand against the fury of a full wolf pack, no matter how high their courage or how great their fighting skill. Especially when that wolf pack was led by Loki.

The king wolf, backed by Split Lip and Zor, now drove in three times in rapid succession, attempting to cut Awklet away from his fellows and thus hasten the breaking of the caribou circle. On the third rush, the big bull caught Zor with a lightning slash of his forehoof, splitting the eager wolf's skull like a ripe melon. In the same whirling instant he got one rack of his young antlers under the charging Loki and hurled him twenty feet away.

The king wolf landed with a jarring crash against a nearby boulder. He was more surprised than hurt, but the blow sobered him long enough for his first blind rage of killing lust to subside. At once, his wily brain began to function with its old-time cruel cunning. While the rest of the pack, momentarily slowed by the almost simultaneous death of Zor and downing of its giant leader, continued to circle the caribou, Loki hung back to watch the way the battle was going. Every instinct of his hunter's mind and all the training of his long career in deer killing came into play as he focused his lone eye on the little knot of caribou and the ring of wolves that surrounded it.

Beyond question the pack could finish off the big moose youngster and these few old stags. But to do so would take time and cost more of Loki's followers their lives. This did not make either for good hunting or good leadership. It was true he had to finish off the moose, but he had also to get his pack out of the trap it was in. And he had to do that without losing any more of his valued pack leaders or old friends. Here was a grave problem and the crafty old leader of the Arctic wolves hung back quietly.

At the same time, Awklet sensed that he could not stay where he was, and survive. The wolves would kill the caribou one by one and then finish him. But his keen intelligence told him not to try a straight-away race to rejoin the main herd. Strung out on the run, the caribou would be easy prey for the pack. They could not run away; they could not stand and fight. There seemed no answer—no choice save to stay and fight to the end where he was.

Then, suddenly, a desperate alternative suggested itself to his anxiously moving eye. They were not impossibly far from the main herd. Perhaps he and the stags might *fight* in that direction, where they did not dare run. It was a slim hope, one suggested by his instinctive leader's desire to be at the head of his herd. The moment it occurred to the young moose, he took action upon it.

Lowering his huge head, he gave a deep bellow of encouragement to the stags. Then he started hooking and slashing his way toward that side of the wolf circle that shut him off from the main herd at Blind Cañon. The old stags, perhaps realizing his purpose, perhaps just blindly following their herd leader, fell in behind him, protecting his rear and presenting nothing but hard horns and knife-sharp hoofs for the wolves to come in against. The latter, apparently not conscious of the slow drift of the fight toward the distant herd, kept up their standard circling tactics. They darted constantly in and out in their attempts to cut down single caribou, but it was clear they were making no concerted effort to stop the movement of the running battle.

Aroused by this success, Awklet fought onward like a thing possessed. The wolves, nonplussed by this sudden new fury in the young bull, fell back and gave way to him. Then, in the very moment when it seemed that the few stags could not fail in their bold fight to rejoin the herd, Loki returned to the fray.

Awklet heard the king wolf's deep and summoning snarls and the next instant saw the whole pack break off the attack to crowd, panting and growling, around its huge leader. Shortly the whole horde of the white raiders, save for six big dog-wolves, broke into a chorus of excited howling and at once swept away across the valley toward the main herd at the exit of Blind Cañon. Loki, too, had a last desperate plan, it appeared. And like Awklet he clearly meant to live or die by it.

It was significant that one of the six big wolves that remained behind to deal with the young moose and his caribou stags was a tremendous, deep-furred brute with one eye. Plainly Loki put a very high value on the life of that hulking monster of a bull moose. Furiously he led his five followers back at the young moose and his ten old stags. In five minutes of deadly in-and-out wolf fighting, too swift for the poor caribou to react to, four more stags were hauled down and left kicking in the snow. But victory in Nature's harsh struggle is never lightly taken. Two wolves also lay crippled and bleeding in the same snow.

Loki and his three remaining fighters, and Awklet and his six, faced each other panting heavily. All of the contestants were blooded now. Yet even here there was a singular difference in the blooding. The wolves carried only minor wounds while three of Awklet's stags were gravely injured, perhaps only steps away from going down for the last time. Excited by the prospect, Loki now launched his second attack. When it was over, his followers were less by one, and one whose loss burned like a tearing fang, even in Loki's cruel breast. Big Foot, fond companion of his cubhood days, faithful fighter at his side through the growing years, lay motionlessly beneath the still pounding hoofs of the enraged Awklet.

Still Big Foot had died very hard. He had taken two of the injured caribou with him. Two other badly wounded stags had somehow survived, but, even as the fighting paused with Big Foot's passing, one of them pitched forward in the snow and lay without moving. The other stood with eyes glazed, head down, tongue protruding slackly, dying on his feet as he refused to fall in surrender.

Three wolves now. Three caribou. And a giant young moose. The wolves all still in fighting condition. The caribou and the moose bleeding from dozens of ripping wounds in foreleg, hock, haunch, belly, and shoulder. Awklet gathered his weary hindquarters under him, awaiting the next charge. There remained but one last hope in his numbing mind. It kept him on his feet, still trying to fight, when every demand of his great tired body pleaded with him to lie down in the snow and let the wolves have their way. Perhaps his three brave fellows would stay upright long enough and fight skillfully enough to take Loki's two remaining wolves with them when they at last went down, thus leaving the king wolf and Awklet finally alone and face to face.

Suddenly from across the valley came the startling outcry of fifty hunting wolves closing for the kill. The battle with the main herd at the cañon exit was being savagely carried forward by the pack. Loki could now afford to take his time with the orphaned moose calf whose tiny life he had so carelessly spared in the beginning, and whose great frame he was now determined to bring down. With a ripple of his crouching shoulder muscles, the king of the white Arctic wolves turned with cold wrath to the final business of destroying Awklet, the adopted moose leader of the Hemlock Wood caribou.

Loki himself went for the moose, his two companions driving into the three caribou and splitting them away from Awklet. But Loki's lunge was only a feint, designed to pull the big bull off balance. And it worked viciously well. Before Awklet could recover and wheel back to join his fellows, all three caribou were down. Loki himself swerved away from Awklet at the last moment to take one of them, his followers each hamstringing one of the remaining two stags.

Thus Awklet found himself at last alone against the king wolf. But scarcely as he had hoped, with only Loki facing him. It is said that all brave things know final fear. That when death is really lurking in the next breath, there are no brave beings, animal or human. There could be no doubt of the young bull moose's courage, or of the quality of his fighting spirit. Equally there could be no doubt that, as the third old stag gasped and ceased to move in the reddened snow, Awklet knew the creeping cold of pure terror.

It was nearing mid-morning of the short Arctic day. A sharp wind had risen, driving a low-scudding pall of snow clouds before it. The light was bad, growing rapidly worse. The youthful bull was wounded, weary, out of breath. And he was terribly, tremblingly, frighteningly alone. Alone with three white Arctic wolves.

Across from him a guttural, nameless sound rumbled deeply in Loki's chest. Awklet, remembering that sound from the dim past, shuddered uncontrollably. He had heard that ominous mutter once before, as he lay, a day-old baby, in the cedar tangle where old Bera had hidden him in her useless effort to outwit these same wolves. He could even recall the picture of Loki, standing over the lifeless form of One Ear as the king wolf made that same sound that now shook his cavernous chest. Awklet knew that sound. He had always known it. It was the death snarl of the white Arctic wolf.

In the darkening shadows of the coming blizzard, the three wolves crouched for what seemed an eternity, their glowing yellow eyes staring unblinkingly at the fear-bound moose. Then, in a bewildering, snow-showering rush, they came for him, Loki straining in the lead.

The king wolf's gaunt form rose up under the fruitless lashing-out of Awklet's forehoofs. Upward and inward the great wolf leaped, driving for the soft and unprotected pulse of his victim's throat. In a wild surge to avoid the murderous slash, the young moose tripped across the body of one of the dead caribou, stumbled wearily, and crashed heavily down into the waiting eternity of the Arctic snows.

Chapter 10

Where it should have meant death, Awklet's stumbling fall meant life. At least for another brief moment. Loki, unable to check his momentum, leaped clear over him and landed in a deep bank of soft snow. Before the king wolf could extricate himself, Awklet was back on his feet.

Loki's reign would have ended in the next half breath had it not been for his two fellow wolves. He was still struggling to free himself from the snowbank when Awklet charged. But the other wolves, momentarily disconcerted by their leader's miss of what had looked like an easy kill, now recovered and closed in behind the big moose as he rushed the helpless Loki.

Both struck viciously for the great tendons of his hind legs, striving to cripple him and bring him down. Both missed, slicing their fangs instead into his upper haunches. The searing pain of the double wound swung Awklet around, and saved Loki's life. But it cost the king wolf heavily, nonetheless.

The quicker of his two followers leaped for Awklet's throat as the young moose came around. Instinctively Awklet lowered his head. The wolf, missing his mark, landed full upon the crest of Awklet's massive neck. Before he could scramble off his precarious perch, the big bull dropped to his knees, throwing his enemy forward and into the trap of his palmated antlers. Rearing upright again, Awklet lunged at the nearest boulder, pinning the wolf between it and his bony forehead. With a crushing thrust, he brought his 1,300 pounds of bone and muscle to bear against the ungiving surface of the rock. The shapeless mass that an instant later was shaken free of his antlers to fall into the snow could not be called a wolf. It was a nameless bundle of blood and fur.

But the second wolf had been given time to leap once more for Awklet's rear leg. The repeated attempt at hamstringing the raging bull ended as had the first—with the death of a wolf. As the brute's jaws closed on the leg, they missed the tendon by inches, burying themselves in the tough bone and sinew of the hock above it. For a fraction of a second the wolf could not free his fangs from their grim hold. Rearing on his hind legs, Awklet came backward and downward, literally sitting down on his attacker.

It was not a dramatic or a brilliant feat, but Awklet was not trying to be dramatic or brilliant. He was fighting for his life, and an awkward death counted just as decisively as a skillful one. The second wolf died in the crunching moment it took for the bull's immense hindquarters to come fully down upon him. But Loki, at the same moment, freed himself from the snowbank where Awklet's life-saving stumble had caused him to land. Even so, the king wolf did not come at once to the attack, as he would certainly have done with any other moose of his long experience.

The old wolf's hesitation was inspired by cunning, not fear. Here was really dangerous work, and work that even a king wolf had better undertake with every bit of craft gained in a long lifetime of killing the hoofed and horned tundra grazers and forest browsers of the Northland deer family. Loki knew this. His every instinct told him to be supremely careful now. It was a tribute to his utter confidence, however, that the giant wolf did not once consider the possibility of defeat coming to him. That any single animal in the Arctic world could vanquish him in individual combat was beyond the brute comprehension of the king wolf.

He began to circle Awklet intently and with cat-footed caution. Yet, even in the act of doing so, he was already concerned, not with the killing of Awklet, but with taking command of the rest of the wolf pack the moment the brave but doomed young moose was down. The angry caribou herd at the cañon exit would have to be split apart so that the wolf pack could escape through it to the outer safety of Half Moon Valley.

But where a confident old wolf thought ahead, a desperate young bull moose was thinking back. A towering young bull with blood on his body and vengeance burning in his small black eyes. A long-memoried young moose with the indelible picture of his gentle foster mother's cruel murder imprinted on his angry heart. He and his mortal enemy were face to face at last. Wolf against moose. Fang and paw against hoof and horn. Victory and life against defeat and death. Awklet against Loki!

The king wolf struck first. And missed! That is, if he meant to try for the throat, as it appeared he did, he missed. His ripping fangs merely opened an ugly gash in Awklet's right foreleg. The wound bled freely but did not seem serious. The young moose ignored it.

Loki's second rush had the same result. It looked as though he drove in, seeking to come at Awklet's throat, and failed. In missing the throat, as before, he succeeded only in inflicting another free-bleeding leg wound, this one below the right knee.

Twice more, in seemingly similar frustrated fashion, he repeated the tactic. The third and fourth wounds thus inflicted on his desperately dodging prey appeared in turn to be minor ones, although they bled well enough even so.

Now, belatedly, it was Awklet who took the offensive. He struck at the king wolf once, twice, three times, each hoof blow so fast it was actually a part of one continuous action. Yet each of the blows missed widely. Loki seemed to evaporate, to disappear completely. When the heavy cloven hoofs whistled into a spot where he had been, he was no longer there. He moved like magic and Awklet presently had the feeling he was fighting a ghost.

No animal of a moose's vast bulk could hope to match a wolf in the speed with which a blow was struck or evaded. Four more times, in as many lightning rushes, Loki now darted in to counter Awklet's attack. Each time his fangs found their mark with unerring accuracy, while he leaped back and away, unscathed. And each time the young moose's hoof blows and antler slashes missed by wider margins.

Actually the pattern of the king wolf's attack was chillingly simple. A veteran of a hundred such wilderness murders, he was not trying for the throat at all. That was sheer and pure wolf cunning. Instead, he was deliberately and methodically inflicting a series of minor wounds, the sum of which would be a great and rapid loss of blood. With blood went strength. That, again, was elementary killer's arithmetic. And shortly the understanding of that fact began to beat its way into Awklet's tired brain.

If his wolf enemy could put enough of those ripping tears in his weakening body, without getting himself seriously hurt in the process, the end was only minutes, perhaps seconds away. He could feel his great strength ebbing as he stood swaying helplessly in front of his will-o'-the-wisp adversary. He was very frightened, and very near final defeat, for there was apparently no way in which he could stop Loki's deadly blood-letting attack. Yet he would not give up.

From some far corner of his indomitable courage, in that last minute, the young moose summoned up strength for one more attempt at survival. If he could lure the king wolf close to his antlers for just one off-guard second, for just one fleeting instant of last-minute carelessness. . . . But old Loki knew a thing or two about killing a wounded moose. He certainly knew far better than to be drawn in close to the antlers of a bull of this one's temper. Nor was there any need for such risk. Not the way things were going. Each new rip he put into his dark hide was spurting more freely than the last. Half a dozen deep gashes were already flowing; another three or four would finish the job. After that, he had only to stand back and give the brave young fool room to fall. Shaking his huge head, growling softly and deeply, Loki started in once more.

Awklet felt his strength going now. He knew that the next minute held his life. Either he killed Loki within that minute, or he would never kill him. His own life was bleeding away as he stood there, waiting for the king wolf to come in. But if his great strength was failing, the workings of that fine animal brain that Neetcha had trained so patiently were not. Awklet, the orphan, was not dead yet.

The advancing Loki saw a weakening tremor shake the body of the young bull. He knew the moose was trying desperately to brace himself, to keep from going down. But another racking shudder ran through his huge body, and another. Loki stepped back, waiting. He was long familiar with these tremblings. They always came when the body was through fighting and the heart and brain would not admit it. The end was nearer than he had thought. The moose would need no more bloodletting. Any moment now would bring that sliding pitch forward to the knees so typical of the deer tribe in dying. From the knees, after a slight pause, the great, awkward body would roll sideways, rump over into the snow, and lie still. There might be a convulsive kick of a hind leg, and that would be all.

Even as the thought took Loki, Awklet made a final, staggering effort to stand, then pitched and slid slowly to his knees. His head was still feebly upheld, his small eyes, already half closed, still watching Loki. The big wolf moved two steps forward, his tongue nervously flicking the froth from his jaws. This was death; he knew it all too well. Tensely he waited for the rest—for the powerful hindquarters to collapse, for the upreared rump to slump sideways into the snow.

But the hindquarters did not collapse. Awklet re-

mained with rump in air, forelegs doubled beneath
him, glazed eyes staring stupidly at Loki. The king
wolf twisted his lips in a soundless snarl. Well, this
was a tough one! Dead and did not know it. Down
in the front, paralyzed behind, bleeding to death,
cut to ribbons, and still holding his stubborn head
up! All right. There was one quick way to end it now.
A simple, clean slash across the throat and jugular
vein would be all that was needed.

Relaxing, Loki moved in. Awklet's dulling eyes
followed him, helpless, uncomprehending. The wolf
paused, his broad muzzle less than a foot from the
dying moose's throat. In the one unguarded moment, in the tiny, fractional hesitation, Loki made
his last mistake. 1,300 pounds of doomed moose exploded in his face. Nearly three-quarters of a ton of
antlered dynamite blew up in the snow alongside
him. Awklet struck and he struck to kill. His thick
neck twisted back and down, catching and pinning
Loki beneath the crushing impact of his antlers.
With a supreme effort the king wolf wrenched himself free, his shoulder and half his scalp laid bare to
the bone by the ripping thrust of Awklet's blow.

He staggered away, fell, struggled to get up. Behind him, Awklet reared to his feet, wheeled, and
came for him. Loki tried to gather himself, to get his
legs under him, to rise and meet the hazy, hump-
shouldered form looming above him. But there was
a great weakness in him now, a vast roaring and
ringing in his head, a numbness as of strange cold in
all his limbs. The trees, the snow, the rocks grew
dim. All he saw was a great black, palm-antlered
mass rising high above him, then coming down and
down and down.

The moose. It had to be the moose. The one he had

been about to kill. Something had happened. He
was down and the moose was not. He strove desperately to get up. To force his jaws to open. To strike
upward. But he was too dazed. Where was that
moose? Which way was that cañon? Where was the
caribou herd? His wolf pack? Where was he?

No matter. It would clear up in a minute. . . .
There, it was better already. Very clear now. He
could see every battle scar on that old wolf sitting
over there in the snow watching him. But something
was still wrong. Something about that wolf. Had he
not met him somewhere before? Did he not know
him? That huge head? That broad, keen-nosed muzzle? It could not be. Move a bit closer to him. Make
sure. It was, it was! Sukon! Sukon, old brother! But
wait? How could it be Sukon? What was he doing
here? Sukon had been killed. . . . Loki knew where
he was then.

He knew where he was, and why Sukon was waiting for him over there across the snow. North of that
snow, stretching far and away into the endless twilight of his beloved Northland, lay that last, long trail
from which no wolf returned. Faithful even unto
death, his old friend had come to take him home.

There remains but little to tell. It is caribou legend
how Awklet reappeared before the herd at Blind
Cañon. Weak from his fearful loss of blood, he staggered out of the noonday blackness of the beginning blizzard at the very moment the herd was
breaking away under the wolf pack's frenzied attack. Old Split Lip, the last of Loki's lieutenants, saw
the moose's towering bulk loom out of the storm
and knew from that the king was dead. Stunned,
the wolves fell back as the herd, inspired by Awk-

let's return, raged into them. It was all over in thirty minutes.

A third of the pack was destroyed in that grim half hour. Another third was badly hurt. The survivors fled back into the jumbled boulders of Blind Valley from whence, long after Awklet and the herd gave up hunting them and were gone, they skulked out into Half Moon Valley and followed Boron's straggling cowards northward. They never regained their former pack strength, never ran again beneath another king like Loki. Peace came at last to the Hemlock Wood and to the ancient borders of the barren-ground tundra.

Perhaps Awklet was no hero, no perfect one. Probably he lived and feared and fled and fought as he did because he had to. And certainly he brought nothing to the caribou they did not already have. He only reminded them of a very small thing they had forgotten. Freedom and the will to fight for it.

Medicine Road

Chapter 1

The long roach of timber on Fat Cow Island in mid-stream of the Black Fork bristled against the red stain of the twilight, harsh as the hairs on an angry dog's back. The foreboding hills across the river crouched, still and quiet as so many monster, gray cats. Above the subdued mutter of the stream's sharp current, the hushed voices of the teamsters sounded hollow and foreign. The *chonk* of an axe in a piece of firewood carried half a mile in the heavy silence.

An hour went by, and then another. At nine o'clock, with the black prairie night folding in around them, close and stuffy as the inside of an old saddlebag, Andy Hobbs told the crew to go ahead and turn in. He and Morgan Bates, quiet smoking, quieter talking, sat the night away, waiting for Jesse Callahan.

From the night two weeks back, when Jim Bridger's red-haired, right-hand man had ridden into the wagon corral outside Fort Laramie, Choteau

& Company's whitebearded wagon master and his swart boss muleskinner hadn't known a good night's sleep. And with perhaps better than a fair-to-middling reason. When a mountain man of Jesse Callahan's reputation walked his barefoot pony up to your fire and told you that Brigham Young had set a hostile chief of Black Coyote's caliber onto your wagon ruts, you had a mighty good excuse for staying awake nights. At least you did, if you knew anything about what a high plains hostile would do to get his hands on ten pounds of low-grade gunpowder, let alone on twenty-four full kegs of prime Du Pont. Like, say, those two dozen fat, black canisters you had consigned to Fort Bridger in number four wagon, there.

Now, stretching into your third week out of Laramie, you hadn't seen so much as an unshod pony track to tell you that you were being trailed by the most white hating chief on the Medicine Road— the high plains Indian name for the Oregon Trail. And you were beginning to wonder if Jesse Callahan hadn't been feeding you a mess of trapper's lies about old Brigham and Black Coyote being in cahoots not only to knock over your supply train but to burn out Fort Bridger as well.

Then, at 2:00 A.M., the mountain man rode in. And five minutes after he did, you had all the answer to that last wonder you were likely to need. Happen you were half smart, you did, anyway.

While the wagon master stirred up the fire, Jesse chewed a slippery fistful of cold sowbelly, gulped three dippers of cool branch water. With the edge off of his all-day thirst and hunger, the red-haired mountain man wiped the grease from his mouth, made his talk quick and strong.

"Well, they're tailing us, all right. A big bunch, near onto a hundred, I'd guess. They've gone into camp back there a few miles. Lucky we beat them around Jackpine Slash. I was late getting back because I wanted to belly in on them, thinking maybe I could find out why they were laying back instead of being up front, setting a trap. Well, I didn't find that out, but I spotted something else a sight more unsettling."

"Such as?" the dark-faced boss muleskinner prompted.

"Such as a white man squatting to their smoke, cozy as a blood brother. I wasn't so close I could see who it was, but he was for sure white and for sure nobody well knowed in these parts."

"Now!" Morgan Bates was incredulous. "You ain't saying there's a white man other than old Brigham Young mixed up in this deal?"

"I'm saying just that." The mountain man scowled. "And I'll tell you something else I ain't mentioned before. When Bridger told me about Brigham Young hiring Black Coyote to knock off this powder train, and asked me to mosey back to Laramie to guide you on into Fort Bridger, he said Washakie, the old Shoshone chief who told him about the Mormon plot in the first place, had warned him there was a strange new white man working between Brigham and the Injuns. Bridger laughed at that and so did I. Injuns will always claim there's a white man to blame for leading other Injuns into trouble." The narrow-eyed mountain man paused. Shortly his hard gaze frosted over. "Well, boys, me, I ain't laughing no more. There is a white man steering those red sons."

"Find anything else?" Andy Hobbs frowned the

question, like Morgan Bates, not knowing how to figure the full importance of Jesse's discovery.

"Nothing else. But I'll tell you something, boys. Old Watonga, he's got all his head men along with him. I seen Yellow Leg, Dog Head, Toad, Blood Face, that lousy little Skull which is Black Coyote's shadow, and a couple of older chiefs I didn't recognize." Jesse removed his squat cherry-wood pipe, spat disgustedly into the fire. "I mean to say that right now I'm smelling more Injuns than we've yet seen. And, by God, I don't cotton none to the stench of them."

For a long minute, then, the bickering snap of the dry cottonwood twigs and the sibilant hissing of the older coals in the fire bed made the only disturbance in the night quiet. Finally Morgan Bates found a frame for his thoughts.

"I reckon none of us wants to see no more hostiles," he muttered uneasily. "What you aiming to do, Callahan?"

"Push on," replied the mountain man, "and push on fast. When I'm smelling them, I don't like to squat around with the stink in my nostrils. The wagons ought to roll at five."

"Stopping at Paiute Crossing, tomorry?" Andy Hobbs knew they would, wanted to get a little more out of the taciturn wagon scout.

"Yeah. I'll leave ahead of you, about three. She's moon dark the early part of the way, and I'll jog slow. Want to make sure them sons don't get around and flank us, again. I had them figured to leave us be once we got here to Wild Hoss Bend, but with them toting that white man along, I don't know. Something's up, likely. It's got me fretted, too. Happen the crazy scuts might yet take another cut at us."

"Well, you go ahead and have your look, Jesse."
The wagon master chucked his head confidently. "But
they ain't going to bother us no more. You'll see."

"I hope so," was all the mountain man said.

"You ain't just a-wolfing," was Morgan Bates's
fervent amendment.

Jesse rode slowly but even so his Sioux mare,
Heyoka, had him far up the Cut-Off by first light.
The scant morning gray let him refresh his remembering of this part of the Fort Road, quickly showing him it hadn't changed so much as a buffalo chip
since the last time he'd covered it. It was an open,
desolate country, lonely as a dog wolf crying the sun
down back of the Wasatches. What grass there was
had become so dry it powdered under a horse's
hoofs like he was walking in a sun-baked puffball
bed. The hills on the far side of the Black Fork built
themselves rapidly into a regular range, fish white
in color and bare of cover as a mangy hound's head.
And withal, high enough to hide all the Arapahoes
in the Northwest behind the lowest one of them.

Hell. Watonga could be over there a mile away,
with half the Arapaho nation, and not show himself
any more than a tumble bug rolling a rabbit berry.

As soon as the sun got up enough to allow a man
some far looking, Jesse began spotting distant
hands of quick-drifting dust puffs. Antelope, by
damn, and him so sick of stringy old mule meat and
sowbelly he could scarcely bear it. Still a man
wouldn't dast shoot one of the cussed goats if it
came up and begged him for the favor. In a country
like this, where the loudest morning noise was a
hawk's shadow chasing a white-foot mouse through
the buffalo grass, a shot would carry almost to De-

seret and back. One pop out of his Hawken just then would like as not have a man up to his armpits in Arapaho hostiles before the powder smell blew off his buckskins.

By ten o'clock, the smooth-walking Heyoka had covered sixteen miles, bringing the mountain man within long sight of that night's wagon camp at Paiute Crossing.

The burned-out frontier post at this spot had always been an interesting place to Jesse, and what he spied when he got up on it this time did nothing to dull that interest. At the site of the gutted log walls, the south-bank hills threw a spur of their range over onto the north side of the Fork. This wing of hills sheltered a good grove of big pines, protecting them from prairie fire wipe out and letting them survive to furnish firewood, sun shade, and storm shelter to the Cut-Off traffic. The crumbling walls of the old post made a handy breastwork to get back of in case of an Indian attack, and the cool Black Fork ran close by, with its bottoms meadows thick with excellent forage grasses. It was the favored campsite on the old Fort Bridger Road—of both white and red traveler.

In this case what intrigued the narrow-eyed Jesse was that it was being favored by *both* colors! Even at the distance, the mountain man could see that the white outfit was an emigrant train, and a poor one. Their shoddy wagons were corralled around the ancient log walls about as sloppy as any outfit could be, their cook fires and camp rig scattered around outside the protecting timbers.

The red camp was something else. Or it would be once the Indians, now methodically rearing their lodges, got it set up. And for a spell of years thereafter, certain surviving members of that shabby white caravan were going to be blessing the fact that Jim Bridger's close-mouthed protégé and hastily appointed supply-train chaperon rode into their lives when he did—which was in good time to see those lodges going up. And to read from the number of lodgepoles employed in the teepee frames and the distinctive markings of the buffalo-hide coverings, their exact tribal identity was Northern Wind River Arapahoes.

Jesse watched the Indians for a string of long minutes, saw they were intent on setting their village straight, knew from that, and the absence of picketed war ponies close in, that they were planning no immediate trouble for the whites.

Putting Heyoka to a stiff lope, he sent the smoke-gray mare up the Fork bottoms, keeping her down behind the shelving banks that buttressed the stream at this point. When he got upstream, past the old log walls, he turned the mare into the heavy timber of the grove, came silently down behind the straggling white camp.

Midway through the grove, an old channel of the Fork, cut there by some forgotten year's high water, protruded from the main channel like a probing finger feeling back into the woods. After a wet spring like the past one, this side channel held a trap of backwater well through summer. Called Paiute Slough, this sometime wilderness pool made a perfect spot for secluded bathing, particularly welcome to pioneer white womenfolk who had likely been on the trail many a dusty day's drive from Fort Laramie without any such god-made grove to hide their ablutions. With Heyoka stepping neat and dainty as a cat, Jesse came up to the slough without being seen—but not without seeing. And what he was seeing was six white women bathing in Paiute Slough. Six *Wasicun* squaws just as naked as the day the Lord had delivered them.

Heyoka's ears went forward and she got her nostrils flared for a good loud snort. And that was all she got. Jesse clamped his paw so tightly on her snout, she nearly swallowed her teeth before the snort got halfway down her Roman nose. Muzzle-wrapping her with a quick turn of the hackamore, the trapper slid his buckskinned leg over her crouching rump and stepped noiselessly to the ground. Only after that did he grant himself the pleasure of a silent whistle of plumb-center satisfaction.

A man sort of got women out of his head living the life Jesse Callahan had been living these past lonely years. Seeing these white womenfolk got his thoughts moving again to his restless and uncertain future. Jesse was of an age for a man to start figuring on a female and young ones. These women made him remember that, just as quickly as they had set him to thinking of the other thing. But God certainly knew a man like him had crawled through enough teepee flaps and known enough Arapaho women to last him till kingdom come. And now maybe Old Man Above was trying to tell him that what Jesse Callahan wanted more than all the gold in California was a real woman of his own color. A white-skinned one, by damn, and light-haired. And one with real blue eyes. That was his idea of a woman, by cripes! One with yellow hair and blue eyes.

Right now, though, he wasn't seeing any that fitted the bill. Besides, the whole bunch of them were having such a proper time of it, yelling and splashing each other with so much honest ginger, it couldn't help, after those first minutes of getting his hunger of normal curiosity quieted down, but take a man's mind back to what he was doing there. And what he was doing there wasn't supposed to be brush-spying on a bunch of middle-aged emigrant women taking themselves a decent bath!

Jesse backed away from the slough brush, careful to put his feet so as not to startle the bathers with any twig poppings. Then, swinging up on Heyoka, he began walking her on around the slough. He had gone perhaps forty yards, coming to the inland end of the water, when he saw her.

Maybe if God had set it up otherwise, a lot of things might not have happened. A red-wheeled Pittsburgh full of gunpowder might have wound up in Fort Bridger where it belonged. Jesse Callahan might have gone on wandering around the Rockies until he was as old and knee-sprung as Andy Hobbs. And Watonga might have headed for home with a full hide of hair and an unsmoked reputation. But God had it in mind otherwise. She was sitting on a sandbar at the far edge of the slough, maybe fifty feet from the staring mountain man. She had been out of the water long enough for the morning sun to get into her hair and fluff it out. And, man, that was some hair to get into! Yellow as July corn silk, it flooded down over her shoulders clean to her rump and, damn it, the way she was sitting, it covered a lot a man would admire to see. Even more than he would the hair.

She had her long legs drawn up under her, her body sort of angled forward to the slant of the sun, and that way about all a man could make out of her was that she was naked! Jesse, blood pumping in his head until his temples were near bursting with the hammer of it, was wishing she would move a mite.

Obligingly she did. Stretching slowly, she brought her arms up to brush the gold wave back where it belonged. She had been crouching on an old piece of buffalo robe and now she lay back onto it with an ease and smoothness reminding Jesse of nothing so much as a big, slim cat sprawling out to sun soak. Arching her back, she flung her arms and legs out to let the mountain man see she was a real blonde, the soft down curling under her arms and nesting below her belly curve, fluffing a thick wavy-gold in the sunglow.

Apparently she had lain back only to stretch, for after a minute that had Jesse's stomach wrapped three ways around his backbone, she rolled to her knees, and stood up. Then you saw her. By cripes, you really saw her! She was tall, five-ten, anyway, Jesse guessed, and a pure cross between a cat and a young willow for slender-moving grace. But that slender part of it went only as far as it should. Like the waist, the slim wrists and ankles, the tapering hands, small feet, symmetrical calves and clean, straight knees. Otherwise, what she was supposed to have, was where she was supposed to have it.

Her breasts were hand-size, for a man with real hands, and pointing out to the sides just a trace, the way Jesse liked to see them. And they had that sweeping upcurve along the bottom line of them that put the nipples to standing with their erected points nosing upward. Her arms and shoulders and thighs had that full roundness so rare in slender women, her hips, that sudden, soft, jut-out over the upper bones, together with the sculped hollows and cuppings of the big buttocks that, to Jesse's thinking, made a woman.

That the enchanted mountain man could have sat

still for much more of this unplanned peep-tomming will have to remain in the realm of the highly improbable. Fortunately the young woman took this moment to turn with her retrieved dress over her arm, looking for the first time across the slough.

In riding up on the emigrant woman, Heyoka had carried Jesse out of the covering brush. For the full term of his high-blood preview, the red-haired trapper had sat there in plain view, fat and stupid as a tickbird on a buffalo's bottom. The girl didn't waste any effort screaming; she just went diving behind the nearest brush clump, immediately popping her head back over the top of it. There, she poised herself, wide-eyed, motionless, waiting for the stranger to speak.

A man couldn't help liking that, too, her not yapping like a stepped-on puppy just because a strange man had seen her naked. Most women would have still been ki-yiying about it. There was another thing he liked, too. Something he hadn't noticed about her until she'd gotten that slinky, wildcat's body of hers covered up: her face, by damn!

Breaking out his best set of teeth, Jesse flashed her a spreading grin. " 'Morning, ma'am. Trust I didn't startle you. I didn't aim to ride up on you thisaway." As he talked, he watched her face, liking it better every second.

He'd always cottoned to high cheek-boned women, with thin nostrils and short, straight noses. If those noses turned up a midge on the end, like this one, he didn't mind that, either. At the same time, he liked a good jaw on a girl. And a full, wide mouth. And above all, a juicy lower lip that pouted out a mite like hers was doing, right now.

"You frightened me, all right, mister." The voice had just enough satin in it to go right with the face and figure. "What do you want?"

Jesse ignored her question to put his own. "What's your name, ma'am?"

"Lacey. Lacey O'Mara."

"O'Mara . . ."—he let his tongue curl around the name like a kid slurping blackstrap off a bent pewter spoon—"Lacey O'Mara! Sure, the whole thing's the luck of the Irish, ma'am. Mine's Callahan. Jesse Patrick Callahan."

For the first time the girl's face relaxed. Jesse thought he had thrown her a real dazzler with that smile of his but he abruptly discarded his whole previous scale of smile values. He had never seen a real smile before. He practically had to squint his eyes shut to bear the way the sun bounced off her white teeth.

"That's fine, Mister Jesse Patrick Callahan, but I'm not Irish and you're not in luck. That O'Mara didn't come with me. I picked it up along the way. It's *Missus* O'Mara to you, mister!"

Jesse clucked to Heyoka. The little mare stepped into the slough, started splashing through the shallows toward the hiding girl.

"It's all right, ma'am!" the mountain man called, noticing the alarm that straightened the smile-curve of her mouth. "I'm just coming over to see the color of your eyes."

When he had reined Heyoka out the far side, the girl found her voice. "You bring that mangy little horse one step closer and I'll scream bloody murder!"

"This is close enough," breathed Jesse, studying her frowning face. "Glory to God, they're pure blue!"

"What are? What are you talking about?"

"Your eyes, ma'am. They're bluer than a South Dakota sky, and that's somewhat. I allow they had to be, too, ma'am. Seems I just knowed that all along."

"Look, I don't know what you mean, mister, and I don't care. You go away right now or I'm going to start yelling. It's silly to stand here like this, and, besides, these leaves are scratching me."

"I envy them, ma'am," said Jesse rashly.

"All right, I warned you. Here goes the yell."

"Wait a minute, Missus O'Mara." She caught the earnestness in the plea, checked her shout. "I'll ride along, but I just want to say this." His eyes bored into hers, making her drop her gaze, blush hotly, feel, all at once, the hard-framed man of him. "I always said that, if I ever found the woman I wanted, and she had blue eyes, hell couldn't get that water high enough to keep me away from her. Well, ma'am, I've found her and her eyes are just as blue as a man could dream."

She didn't answer, keeping her lashes downswept. When she did raise her head, he was still sitting there.

"Good bye, Lacey." The blue-eyed, prairie-burned look of him ran down her spine, chilling her whole body with its excitement. "I'll see you, again."

He was gone after that, jogging his ugly gray pony toward the old fort walls, leaving her in mouth-parted silence.

Lacey O'Mara gasped. The nerve of him! The sheer gall! Sitting and watching her walk around naked, then quietly telling her he was going to have her, hell or high water—mainly, to judge from his laconic remarks, because her eyes were blue! Hah!

Well, the world was full of strange people and he was a relief, anyway. Not many had his clean, fierce look and easy, straight way of talking.

She watched the tall ramrod of his figure going toward the timber, sitting the little horse like an Indian, long legs dangling straight down. There was plenty in those wide shoulders, hanging red hair, narrow sun-blackened face, and piercing eyes to excite far less hungry women than Lacey O'Mara. He was just another man, though, for all his hard good looks and outlandish buckskin fringes. If you were a woman as old as Lacey, you had to remember that. You couldn't let yourself get to thinking about any man when you were thirty years old and had two kids of your own. Two kids and a bad lot like Tim O'Mara for your husband.

Nonetheless, she was still looking at Jesse when he checked the mare short of disappearing in the timber. Wheeling Heyoka, he called softly back: "Ma'am, you get them other women and come on into camp! It's the Injuns, ma'am, but don't scare them up about it. Just hustle them on in."

She nodded, waving a bare arm in reply. He waved back, turning the horse out of sight behind the screening cottonwoods.

Chapter 2

When Jesse rode into the emigrant camp, he found the men folk gathered around the ashes of the morning cook fire. They were a seedy, whipped-hound bunch if a man ever saw one. The kind of an outfit, Jesse allowed, that God spent his off nights sitting up looking after.

He came to them without giving any greeting or getting any. Swinging off Heyoka, he dropped the hackamore rope to the ground, went in long, bent-kneed strides toward them.

"Howdy." His lean, square-shouldered figure in its grease-blackened buckskins and loose belt of blazing Sioux beadwork worked in sharp contrast to the slovenly homespuns, flat hats, and crude cowhide boots of his listeners. "I'm Jesse Callahan as works for Jim Bridges up to the fort."

"Howdy," a couple of the men mumbled replies, not bothering to get up with them. The rest sat and stared, saying nothing.

"Who's in charge?" Jesse demanded, his eyes not

liking what he saw of these scarecrows, his knowledge of the Medicine Road telling him their story before they had a chance to.

"Tim is, I guess," one of the men vouchsafed. "Leastways, he says he is."

"Tim who?" Jesse asked, directing his question to the man who had answered him.

"O'Mara," the other grunted.

"Well, which one of you is O'Mara?"

"He ain't around," said the spokesman.

"And where might he be, mister?" Jesse was beginning to get nettled with the plumb dumb attitude of the emigrants.

"Down yonder by the fork. Relieving hisself, I reckon. I think I seed him head in behind them bushes a few minutes ago. 'Course, I wouldn't know."

"You don't appear to know much." Jesse nodded, turning his back on them. "O'Mara! Where are you? Sing out."

The mountain man threw his call toward the brush the other man had indicated, got his answer in a surly growl from behind the screening foliage.

"Over here taking care of myself, damn you! What's it to you?"

Jesse thought that over. It stumped him enough so that he hunkered down with the others to await the pleasures of Mr. O'Mara's peristalsis. Meanwhile, he fired questions at the hollow-cheeked men, got enough answers to add up to what he had already figured.

The group was emigrant land seekers from east Kansas Territory, around Shawnee. They had banded together and headed West with eight ox wagons. They had been California bound, had gotten as far as Fort Bridger with fair trail luck and no Indian scrapes.

Jesse had nodded, understanding that last part of it. No self-respecting Sioux or Cheyenne, much less any high-caste Arapaho, would bother a scrubby bunch like these.

At Fort Bridger the outfit had found themselves dangerously low on funds, had listened to the friendly advice of Jim Bridger, and turned back for the settlements. The old mountain man had pointed out to them the lateness of the season, the poor condition of their wagon stock, and the good chance of their running into a fatal snow trap in the distant Sierras. Jesse could understand that, too, and it made real sense.

When the emigrants had voted to turn back, Tim O'Mara, their hired guide, had refused to head back with them, saying he had business that wouldn't keep waiting for him in Salt Lake. They had paid him off and he had taken out for the Mormon capital alone, abandoning his woman and young ones who, for some reason, refused to go with him.

The emigrants had pulled into Paiute Crossing the night before Jesse found them. But it was only this very morning, just after the Arapaho village had arrived, that Tim O'Mara had suddenly and unaccountably shown up again, saying only that his affairs in Salt Lake were in hand and that he was offering to guide them back to Shawnee without wages.

At this point in the discussion, Tim O'Mara came slouching out of his leafy privy. One eye-tail look at him and Jesse knew he had his hands full. Tim was a big man, far bigger than Jesse. He was that kind of a bear of a man the Irish frequently breed. Hefty,

ham-handed, a meat slab of a face, roughly handsome a few years back, now coarsening up fast.
Small-eyed, hot-tempered, not smart. A bad man
sober, a pure bastard drunk.

"Howdy." Jesse nodded. "I'm Jesse Callahan."

"Yeah, I heard your big mouth going. What do
you want?"

"Looks like you could use some help. Leastways,
your folks can. Maybeso, I can give it to you."

"We ain't got any money." The statement wasn't
an apology, it was a challenge, and Jesse knew the
big emigrant was watching him, sizing him up,
fighting wise.

"I said *give* it to you," the mountain man replied,
careful to see that his words came out without fla-
vor, one way or the other.

"You mean *guide* for us? Hell, I guess we know
the way by this time. Backwards, anyway. We just
come over it."

"I didn't say *what* I meant," announced Jesse
slowly, "but I'm aiming to if. . . ."

"Why don't you climb your hoss, mister?" The big
man's interruption was harsh. "We've had all the
trouble we need and we ain't lost no squawman in
buckskins and Injun shoes. Go on, get moving!"

With the words, O'Mara moved toward the
mountain man, the glint in his pig eyes saying, clear
as glass, that he'd be mainly pleased if Jesse didn't
aim to accommodate his order. The red-haired trapper stood up easy and cautious. He'd seen his share
of Tim O'Maras, handled them as they came along.
You didn't talk to a slob like that. Leastways, not
with your mouth.

Tim stopped two steps away, feet braced, tiny eyes
pinning Jesse's non-committal glance. "You getting

on that hoss by yourself, little man, or is Tim
O'Mara boosting you up?"

The other men were finding their feet, moving
away from the fire.

"Help yourself," said Jesse quietly, and made his
move.

None of the bystanders saw how that Hawken's
butt got switched around in the mountain man's
hands, much less Tim O'Mara seeing it. But they all
heard the grunt that exploded out of the hulking
Irishman as the rifle stock drove itself halfway to the
trigger guard in the hard fat of his belly. Tim doubled forward, covering his stomach, stumbling
toward Jesse. The mountain man side-stepped as he
came, letting him fall past him, the rifle swinging in
another blurred arc as he did. The crack of the barrel
steel on Tim's thick skull sounded like a double-bit
axe bouncing off an elm burl.

"Prop him against that wheel," Jesse directed,
"and slosh him with that can of coffee water."

A belt on the head with a rifle barrel will slow a
bear down. When he came around, Tim stayed
where he was, sagged against the wagon wheel, listening sullenly to Jesse's talk. While the latter was
having his say, the womenfolk, returning from the
slough, drifted up to stand, gray and silent, behind
their men.

"The first thing," the mountain man began, "is
that Injun camp, yonder. They're meaning you some
trouble, or I don't know red skin when I see it. Soon
as I'm done talking to you, I'll mosey over there and
palaver with them. See can I get a line on their aims
and ambitions as regards you folks. Meanwhile, I
want you should listen close to what I've got to say. I
got a twelve-wagon freight outfit due in here this af-

ternoon. With them spanned out around you, you'll be safe for right now. But I got to roll them wagons on up to Fort Bridger. We can't lay over here, at all. Now, if you're smart, you'll tag on up to Gabe's fort with us, then hook up with a strong outfit heading east. Next to that, you can wait right here until one comes through, eastbound. But on no account should you head east alone. I've just had some trouble with a strong bunch of Arapahoes back yonder where you're bound for. They're regular trail raiders and spoiling for any kind of bait right now. We whipped their tails offen them, the way that Injuns look at such things, and I allow the next white outfit they see will get charged for the lesson. I advise you not to let it be yours."

"Mister," the man named Tom Yarbrough, the one who had spoken to Jesse before, answered him, "I believe you. We should ought to do what you say. But hang it all, we cain't. We ain't got the food, nor the extry draft cattle, no more. If we head on back right away, we might just last it out to Shawnee. We ain't got no choice, mister. We got to go on back."

Tim, his wits unscrambling gradually, was watching the talk now. Not looking at Jesse, he grunted an obscene agreement with Tom Yarbrough's objections. Encouraged, the other men began speaking up testily. Jesse, seeing he was licked for the minute and hoping he could get the emigrants to listen to Andy Hobbs when the powder train got in, broke up the meeting.

"All right, we'll leave it the way it is till my wagons get in. Then we can put the whole thing up to the company wagon master. He's been with the Choteaus for thirty years, and working this Oregon Trail for fifteen of that time. I allow you'd listen to him where likely you wouldn't to me."

Several of the men nodded. Jesse looked at Tim
O'Mara, waiting for him to speak.

"What do you say, Tim?" he asked finally. "You
willing to talk it over again, tonight? When Hobbs
and the company outfit gets here?"

The burly emigrant got up, bracing his back along
the wheel to let himself make it. When he stood, he
swayed a little before his legs steadied. A thin trickle
of blood was seeping from his nostrils, a blue lump
the size of a horse-collar gall growing behind his left
ear. His eyes, beginning at the ground, ran slowly
up Jesse's leggings and across his hunting shirt,
came to rest squinting fully on the mountain man's
dark face. His tongue ran over his upper lip, clearing it of the blood. He drew in through his nose,
gathering the phlegm and mucous in his mouth. His
words, along with the blood and spittle, were spat
viciously into the ground at Jesse's feet.

"You can kiss my butt, squawman. I'm through
talking."

When he walked away, the flushed women parted
to let him through, the white-faced men going awkwardly back to their staring into the sifting cook-fire
ashes. A pin, dropped in the ankle-deep dust of the
campground, could have been heard in Kansas City.

For an hour Jesse sat in the noon shade of the outer-
most emigrant wagon, watching the activity in the
Indian camp across the meadow. It never ceased to
amaze him the way these red nomads would move
in on a chunk of sagebrush and make a city of it in
sixty minutes. This bunch was no exception. Every
lodge had its assigned place in the pitching plan,
carried its own cover skins, poles, floor robes, and
sleeping-furs. Even as Jesse watched, the teepees

sprang up like dirty brown mushrooms, growing in a *dopa*, or square, of four groups of lodges centered around an open, middle square. This central square was the dance and council grounds, the middle space always reserved for the communal palavers and various ceremonial stomps forever taking place in any high plains village. The mountain man waited until the last lodge skin was in place and the older Indian boys had started scattering the pony herd out along the riverbanks to graze, then he took a look at the pan of his rifle, eased the Sioux skinning knife in its sheath, and stepped up on the dozing Heyoka.

Riding toward the camp, he was struck by two things—the abnormal quiet of the red village, and its respectable size. The first, a man would know from his vivid memories of the usual pandemonium of squealing children, strident-voiced squaws, and yapping camp curs that provided the audible atmosphere of the average plains village, particularly one that had just been set up. Among these tall, smoke-stained lodges, even the dogs seemed to move in unnatural and skulking silence. The second, any mountain man could gather by counting his fingers five times. There were fifty lodges of the red sons, and putting the prairie rule of thumb to that number (five Indians to the lodge) you came out with around 250 Arapahoes.

The minute Jesse had noted, from his first sight of this village, that it was a Wind River band, he had thought of the warrior pack of the same tribe that had attempted to waylay old Gabe's supply train in Jackpine Slash. This village was just of a size to be Watonga's, for the same rule of thumb that gave you five Indians of all cuts to a lodge, gave you two warriors. Hence, two warriors times fifty lodges came out Black Coyote. Maybe.

Nearing the village, a third thing began working in the back of his head. So far he had seen half-grown boys, squaws, small children, oldsters. Dart as it would through the camp streets and around the center square, his roving glance failed to bounce off a single, full-feather buck. From what a man could see, granting he was seeing wide and guessful, there wasn't a trail-grade warrior in the camp. One thing about that hunch. He could nail it down once he got into the camp.

That was a good guess, as far as it went. Trouble was, it didn't go far enough. 100 yards out from the lodges, three Indian horsemen broke from the nearest cluster of teepees. Riding abreast, the Arapahoes bore down on Jesse, blocking his approach to the village. The mountain man reined in Heyoka, sat waiting, slack-shouldered and watchful.

The riders were old men, each of them clearly an elder chief and warrior of past reputation. Their spokesman, a withered giant wearing a red-flannel undershirt, U.S. Infantry pants, and a single scarlet heron plume slanting through his gray braids, pulled up his pony, facing Jesse.

"*Hau*, the white brother comes in peace?"

"*Hau*," Jesse responded, gravely touching the fingertips of his left hand to his forehead. "*Woyuonihan!*"

It was the Sioux word and gesture of respect for the elder warrior of undoubted reputation. The old man was pleased but not, in this case, to be flattered off his original query. "The *Wasicun* comes in peace?" he repeated, his rheumy eyes lingering on the beautifully engraved rifle resting across Heyoka's withers.

Jesse upended the gun, firing it into the air. *"Wolkota wa yaka cola."* He intoned the phrase in the rumbling growl of the Minniconjou Sioux.

The three oldsters nodded seriously. *Waste,* good, this *Wasicun* talked with a red tongue. The words Jesse had used were those engraved on the sacred ceremonial pipe of peace of the Sioux nation. Their text and translation were known to every plains tribe west of the Mini Sosi. By their use the mountain man had pledged his real honor that he came without war in his heart.

"Hohahe," the old man responded, using Sioux in courtesy, "welcome to our teepees. I am Old Horse. Here are Beaver Face and Bull-In-The-Pants."

Jesse threw a snap glance and a nod at the other two, swallowing the smile that wanted to follow the greeting. Man, you try and tie a redskin when it came to slapping the right tag on a package of goods! That Beaver Face had a set of filed buckteeth fit to make stove wood out of any six-foot saw log. As for Bull-In-The-Pants, the old devil's loose-lipped countenance showed such a clear trail of pockmarked lechery that a man had to know, right off, that he was as well named as his companion.

"Ha ho, thank you." Jesse made the courtesy sign again. "I am Tokeya Sha, the Minniconjou. The Fox lodge brother of Ikuhansuka, Long Chin, and Mato Luta, Scarlet Bear."

He threw the names at them, hawk-eying their graven faces for a wrinkle shift of recognition. Those were big names on the war shield of the north plains, and, if the old coots were Black Coyote's boys, they'd likely know them.

But the old men sat still. They didn't share the flick of an eyelid muscle among them.

"Who is chief of your village? Whose village is behind you there? Whose name do you serve?" Jesse barked the questions peremptorily, like a Sioux chief talking to mound dwellers.

Old Horse was no mound dweller, and barked right back at him. "Heavy Otter. That's young Heavy Otter, not the old man. And you will not talk to me in a voice like that again."

"*Wonunicun*, it was a mistake. Tell me, father"—Jesse caught the old man's eye, pegging it down—"are you sure this Heavy Otter does not have a black skin? Big sharp ears? A bushy tail? You know, father. Much like those of a very dark-colored coyote?"

If the old man took the barb on that hook, he didn't break water over it. "My voice was clear. I said Heavy Otter. There is only one young Heavy Otter. Him, I serve. And no other."

"What does he look like, this Heavy Otter? I knew a Heavy Otter among your people when I was a boy." Jesse had never heard the name, was rebaiting his line for another cast.

"Short. Big belly. Weak chin. Bad color. Pale, almost like a *Wasicun*." Old Horse eyed the mountain man, daring him to call the lie.

Jesse moved his shoulders deprecatingly. "Let us go, my brothers"—nodding toward the too-quiet village—"I would meet this Heavy Otter. He sounds like him I knew."

"No!" There weren't any two ways about the tone in which Old Horse snapped that "no". It didn't mean anything but "nix". The Arapahoes were turning their ponies with it.

"How do you mean that, father?" Jesse tried for a delayer, caught one.

The old man halted. "He's gone. Heavy Otter is gone. *Nohetto.*"

"No!" The mountain man's own denial was as flat as Old Horse's had been. "That's not all!"

"Now what do *you* mean, nephew?" The first ripple of interest spread across the blank pond of the old chief's face.

"The warriors are gone, too. All gone. Every one of them."

The two gaunt oldsters backing Old Horse shifted their trade muskets to let them look at Jesse. Old Horse warned them with a scowl, turned to regard the white man. His leathered lips lifted, exposing the yellowed fangs beneath. Jesse imagined it was intended for a grin.

"Oh sure. You are right, nephew. Why should I deceive you who has lived among us? They're all gone. With Heavy Otter. Hunting buffalo. Trying to find some fat cows. Down there, some place. . . ." He pointed east, down the Black Fork. "That's why we are here. Just us old ones and the women and children, as you see. Waiting for the braves to find those young cows. That's how it is. Do you see it now?"

"Of course, uncle." Jesse knew the talk was over, carefully mimicked the old man's indifference. "That's how it is. I see it now. Well, thank you."

With the words, he was turning Heyoka for the emigrant camp, checked her suddenly, as though he had only now been taken with a major idea.

"Say. Listen to this. My manners are like an untaught dog's. Will my father not come to the *Wasicun* fires tonight? Do me that honor, will you? There will be some roast mule, just the tenderloins and the back fat, and a few presents. A little sugar, maybe, uncle. Some tobacco, too, perhaps. Who can tell? My goddams come from the east at sundown, heavy-loaded. Choteau goddams, uncle. Big Company goddams. Carrying many things to the blanket chief at the fort. You savvy Big Throat? You see?"

"Ha ho," grunted Old Horse delightedly. "We will come. All of us."

"Oh, no!" Jesse was quick. "Just those of reputation. Just you real warriors. Just you chiefs. Tokeya Sha feeds no squaws."

Flattered, Old Horse bobbed his head. *"Waste,* just the chiefs, then. We will come. When the night hawk whistles."

Jesse saluted them as they rode away, turned Heyoka for the emigrant camp, his dark face scowling. Damn their night hawk whistles. He didn't like the looks of those old birds, nor of that big, empty camp they had come out of. The whole damned river bottom was getting so thick with Indian smell it stank clean to a man's moccasin tops. *Aii-eee,* brother. If Heavy Otter's other name wasn't Watonga, Jesse Callahan would chaw the core out of Andy Hobbs's beaver hat!

Chapter 3

Back at the emigrant camp, Jesse found Tom Yarbrough and three of the other men, Seth Mason, Brown, and Hanks, waiting for him. There was no sign of Tim O'Mara and the others, or of any of the women.

"Folks are resting back in the grove," offered Tom. "Tim's wandered off somewheres down the Fork. Kids are with the women."

"It's all right, for now," Jesse answered. "There's nothing to worry about from those Injuns, right off. Their braves are all down the Black Fork running buffalo." The men nodded apathetically, and Jesse continued. "But I want a guard posted just the same. The four of you keep your eyes peeled. If you see any mounted Injuns coming into that camp, or riding out of it, come running for me. I've been riding all night and I'm tuckered. Right now I'm going back to the slough and wash off. Catch me a catnap, too, most likely. Remember. If you see anything, fetch me, instanter. You got that?"

More nods and a half-hearted assurance from Tom Yarbrough had to do for his answer. Heading into the grove and glancing back to see what the men were doing about his warning, he noted that Tom was talking to the others, apparently assigning them their guard spots. They, in turn, seemed to be arguing back. Jesse shrugged, turning his back on them. There was one stock of goods God never ran low on, and that was fools.

At the slough he shucked out of his buckskins and had his dip. The backwater was soft and soapy like all the mountain water. It let a man's muscles down and lowered his eyelids.

Crawling out on the same bar where he had surprised Lacey O'Mara, he stretched, bare belly down, on the drowsy sand. It seemed that with his nose to the warm bank he could almost smell where she had been spread out. Stretching again, he squirmed his legs, flexing his corded arms. Be damned, he wished he had her there, right now! Just the way he had seen her. . . .

Jesse came awake with something very wrong with his rear end. He'd had the same feeling once many years ago when he and Waniyetula (Winter Boy, Jesse's particular brother among the Minniconjou) had been out arrow-hunting snow hares. Winter Boy had jumped one of the big white bunnies and the tricky devil had doubled back to run right between the legs of Tokeya, the Red Fox—who just happened to be looking the other way. Full eye for the chase and none at all for his companion's backside, the Sioux youth had let drive with his hunting bow. Winter Boy had managed to assuage the ordeal of pulling the arrow out of his friend's posterior by assuring his brother, Tokeya, that he was now the only fox in the Sioux nation with two butt holes.

When that little arrow had come out, it had felt like whatever was wrong with Jesse's rear end at the present moment. The mountain man came up off the sandbank, grabbing and fanning all at the same time. Tender investigation showed no apparent damage and Jesse was about to admit he'd been bitten by a snake dream, when his eye mirrored a foreign sun flash from the shade of a nearby brush clump. One headlong dive into the suspect cover retrieved two affectionately related articles: a pint-sized, carrot-topped boy of seven, and an outsize, pocket magnifying glass.

With his trophies, the one kicking and squealing his innocence of the operation and end effects of concentrating the sun's energy to pinpoint heat via the focusing powers of a hand glass, and the other still warm from its loving labors in the toasting of Jesse's tailpiece, the naked mountain man returned to the sand spit. Depositing the boy on a down log, the slightly singed Mr. Callahan entered into exploratory peace talk.

"What's your name, young 'un?"

For answer, the boy slipped off the log and was away through the brush. Jesse dove after him, scooped him up, repaired to the log.

"We'll try it again." He nodded pleasantly. "What do they call you?"

"You ain't the boss of me!"

The boy's claim, neither defiant nor surly, was just plain statement. Jesse liked the way the kid said it and he liked the way he looked at a man while he was saying it.

"I ain't the boss of nobody." The mountain man grinned. "I *work* for my living."

"You do?" Apparently the boy hadn't known any-one in this category. His round, blue eyes ceased searching for a way off the log, started going over Jesse's powerful body. "Gee, you really got the mus-cles, ain't you, mister?"

"Name's Jesse, boy," he said, grinning. "I don't cotton to 'mister'. Makes it sound like you didn't take to a man."

The big-eyed sprout was not to be so lightly swung from the principal attraction of the moment. "What kind of work do you do, mister? My golly, I ain't never seed so many muscles!"

"You ain't seed much, then, young 'un." Jesse was displaying no false modesty, many of the men in his profession possessing frames of a heft that would shame a boar grizzly. "I'm a mountain man. What do *you* do?"

"Huh!" The youngster's snort was as wide open as his admiring gaze. "You ain't no such thing. Mountain men wear buckskin shirts with fringes all on the arms and things."

"I allow they do," agreed Jesse, stepping over the log and bringing his Sioux hunting shirt to view. The boy watched him breathlessly, as he hauled on the shirt, legged into the fringed leggings, toed-on the beaded moccasins. Eying the youth slyly, he asked: "Now then, what do you say?"

"Where's your gun? And your hunting knife?" The skepticism, still on its feet, was wobbling badly.

"Yonder's the holy iron," averred Jesse, pointing to the rifle where he had crotched it in a convenient cottonwood, "and here's the knife."

With the latter phrase, he whipped the Green River skinning blade out from under the buckskin shirt in a lightning belly draw Waniyetula had bequeathed him, whirled, and threw it with an underhanded wrist flip nobody had given him. The razored steel drove into the log between the boy's spread legs, vibrated there like a tail-wounded copperhead.

"What you say, boy?" the mountain man asked quietly.

Mouth and eyes falling still farther open in the frankest of salutes, the red-headed youngster looked up at the narrow-eyed Jesse and announced, admiringly: "I say you're a mountain man, sure as my name's Johnny O'Mara!"

"I might've knowed it." The dark-faced mountain man nodded thoughtfully.

"Knowed what?" the youngster queried, puzzled.

"That you was Lacey O'Mara's son. You've got your mother's eyes, boy."

"Gosh, do you know my mother?"

"No, I just seen her in camp when I was talking with your folks, back yonder," Jesse lied. "I don't recall seeing you, though, boy."

"Well, I seen you"—Johnny grinned—"but I didn't think you was a *real* mountain man. Tim said you was a squawman, and that you lived with the Injuns and liked them a heap better than you did your own white people. He said none of your kind was to be trusted on account you was red clean through to the middle once you'd lived with the Injuns. That's why I snuck after you when I seed you coming out here. I reckon most folks hates Injuns, but I love 'em. I mean to fight 'em and sneak after 'em and smoke the peace pipe and things like that."

"I allow every boy loves Injuns," said Jesse

soberly. "I know I sure do, and I was raised amongst them. Leastways, more or less, I was."

"Naw! You wasn't!" Johnny's denial was incredulous. It wasn't possible to imagine anybody being that lucky, to be raised up and to run around with real Indians.

"Hell I wasn't," the mountain man countered. "The Sioux got me when I was a cub not much bigger'n you."

"Gee! How'd it happen, huh, Jesse . . . ?" Johnny O'Mara, as would have been any Eastern boy of like years, was purely fascinated by the wild look of the long-haired, buckskinned figure beside him, and with the thought that here was a real, live white man who had lived with the hostiles and was still around to tell about it. The youngster's eager voice trailed off disappointedly, as he failed to see his own excitement mirrored in the mountain man's quiet face. "Gosh, I reckon you wouldn't tell anybody about it. Not just a little kid, anyways."

"Shucks, boy." Jesse grinned. "Not much to tell. I never had no mother, leastways not to remember, and the Sioux done my daddy in when they grabbed me. . . ."

"Gee, that's turrible, Jesse. I . . ."

"Not so much, young 'un," his companion interrupted. "I reckon my old man wasn't so good as all that. Way I recall it, he wasn't against larruping me rosy-butted whenever he could take the time to get his nose outen the jug to do it. Raising a boy up without no mother can be a tolerable problem, I allow. It sure was to my daddy, at any rate. I was fixing to run off, regardless, when the Sioux jumped our post and saved me the trouble. When you look at it long and short, I figure some growed-up men can give a kid more trouble than he can properly handle. I was coming twelve when them Hunkpapas killed my daddy. That's old enough to remember that I didn't shed no tears about it."

The mountain man's wide mouth had lost its ready smile during the brief running back of memory's track, and, when he had finished, the boy beside him, taking his cue from the grim set of the dark jaw, was silent. But youth isn't constructed to hold a quiet very long when the topic on the table happens to be Indians. Shortly Johnny gave in to his growing curiosity.

"Was them the Sioux what brung you up, Jesse? Them Hunkpapas? The ones that kilt your pap?"

"Nope, they wasn't, young 'un." The smile was back now, the rim frost gone from the blue eyes. "I was a puny-looking squirt, sort of on your cut. And them Hunkpapas is great traders. They knowed a white boy was worth somewhat amongst the Injuns, more'n dang' near anything, far as that goes. But their medicine man done looked me over and told them I wasn't going to make it through the winter. Said that come the new grass . . . that's the spring-time, boy . . . I'd be done-in as a froze buffalo calf. So them Hunkpapa up and traded me off to Long Chin's Dakota Minniconjous, and they was the ones brung me up. That's the whole gospel, Johnny. Them Minniconjous took to me like they was my own folks, only a mortal lot better, you can lay."

"Gosh all hemlocks!"

"Sure. They give me an Injun name and everything."

"Honest Injun?"

"*Wowicake,* boy. Honest Injun"

"Was that your name? Wowwy-Cake?

"Naw, naw. That means I'm telling the truth. Their name for me was Tokeya Sha."

"What's that mean? In American, I mean."

"Red Fox."

"Gee! How come them to call you that?"

Two reasons, boy," chuckled the mountain man. "First off, it was the red hair, see? That made the red part of it easy. Then they hung the fox part onto that after I fooled them all by growing up. Old Long Chin, he said that any boy who could look as mangy and raunchy and slat-ribbed as I did, and could even manage to stay alive, let alone grow any, must be smarter than the sly brother . . . that's the fox, boy . . . himself. So they wound up giving me that name."

"Boy."

"Well, I guess. Say, young 'un, how'd you like an Injun name? One you can be knowed by amongst us Sioux?"

"Shucks, I couldn't never have no Injun name. I don't even know any Injuns."

"Cripes, boy, you know me, and I'm the biggest redskin in the business."

"Golly, maybe you *could* give me a name, then. Just a little one, not too much. Nothing they'd ever miss."

"Why, dammit boy, we'll give you a real tongue-twister. A chief's name. Regular Minniconjou, too. None of your cussed tame Injuns. How's that?"

"Aw, you never would . . . ," said Johnny, embarrassed by this windfall of good fortune, not yet ready to believe any emigrant boy like him could be as lucky as all this.

"Well, let's see"—Jesse deliberately ignored his small companion's doubts—"what'll it be? You want

Little Dog? . . . or Short Calf? . . . or maybe White Pony? Say, boy," the mountain man interrupted himself with a flash of his quick smile, "how about Red Eagle? You know, after that red hair of yours, like the Minniconjous started my name. That's a real Sioux monicker, too."

"Red Eagle." The boy breathed the name like he was tailing off a prayer. "Red Eagle, the Minniconjou. The brother of Tokeya Sha, Red Fox. Oh, boy!"

"Ain't nothing to it." Red Eagle's new brother smiled. "Let's get a move on back to camp, partner. My wagons'll be rolling in pretty quick."

Tagging along, his freckled hand in Jesse's dangling paw, the boy kept quiet for twenty steps, finally found the courage to ask it.

"Say, Jesse, you know that Tim O'Mara? He savvies a lot about Injuns, too. 'Most as much as you do, I reckon."

"Yeah, boy." Jesse looked down at Johnny suspiciously, wondering what tricky side stream the freckle-faced fingerling was figuring to wiggle up this time. "I 'spose maybe he does. What about him?"

"Well," the youngster's query shuffled the feet of its delivery a little uncertainly, "he said that, when the Sioux Injuns give a name to a young warrior, they always give him a weapon to go along with it. He said it was a regular ceremony, called Cañon Kissy-cuppy. Leastways, something like that. I ain't saying it's so, mind you. But that's what Tim O'Mara, he said."

Jesse eyed the boy narrowly, caught his wistful blue eyes wandering enviously to the soft-tanned leather thong upon which, hidden beneath the greasy buckskin shirt front, dangled the mountain man's razor-edged skinning knife. His slow answer, not matching the quick twinkle in his lake-blue eyes, was a miracle of Sioux soberness.

"Tim told you right, young 'un. The Sioux call that ceremony *Canounye Kicicupi*. That means The-Giving-of-the-War-Weapons. You reckon you're ready for a full-size weapon, boy?"

"Yes, sir!" Johnny's answer was prompt, his eyes still fastened determinedly on Jesse's shirt front.

"I allow you are, at that." The mountain man nodded, easing the gleaming blade into view. "You know the Sioux most generally starts a young 'un off with a knife. Reckon you'd see your way to settling for this one? It's a genuine Green River, boy."

The boy's hands were on the blade's shaft almost before Jesse could move to skin the thong free of his neck. Watching the youngster stow the weapon fumblingly inside his own hickory shirt, the mountain man took him by his thin shoulders, warned him with the gravest of mock seriousness. "Now, listen here, Johnny . . . that blade's a Sioux secret 'twixt you and me. See that you keep it hid inside your shirt, same as I did, and don't you never tell nobody about it. Nobody. Not ever. You got that?"

"Cross my heart, Jesse. I won't never tell nobody. I'll keep it so well hid not even a Injun could find it on me. Gosh . . . !"

Beyond a wide grin to show he was soaking up his full share of the sprout's enjoyment, Jesse Callahan paid the pledge and the return promise no more heed. Three days later, he was to know he had just made the biggest dicker of his entire hard life.

Chapter 4

Andy Hobbs rolled the wagons in shortly before sundown, promptly put them in a tight box alongside the old fort ruins. Jesse pitched in with the parking, seeing no more of the newly christened Red Eagle, or of his sleeky blonde mother. By twilight everything was snug.

Waiting for the coffee water to boil up, he had his talk with Choteau & Company's wagon master.

Leading off, Andy Hobbs sucked noisily on his pipe, spat in the direction of the Arapaho camp. "What you make of them Arapaho lodges? Purty big bunch of them, I'd say."

"You'd say right." The mountain man's frown deepened. "Bigger than you think, likely."

"How big?"

"Black Coyote big."

"The hell!"

"The hell, yes. . . ."

"How you figure?"

"Number of lodges comes out right."

"That ain't no real clincher. Anything else?"

"Yeah. No warriors with them. Nothing over there but squaws and kids and old people."

"You been over?"

"Halfway."

"They stop you?"

"Yeah. Wouldn't let me into the camp. Claimed it was Heavy Otter's village. Said the braves was all downstream running buffalo. The big chief with them, naturally."

"Well, hell, it could be. That's sure as sin buffalo country down there and this here's the time of year all the tribes is running their winter beef. Country's like as not crawling with Arapaho hunting parties from here to the Powder. I don't see how you're so certain this is Black Coyote's bunch, thinking of it thataway. Did you ask them about him?"

"Nope."

"How come not?"

"Wasn't ready. Saving that for tonight."

"We going over there?"

"They're coming over here."

"Why, dammit? You know I don't cotton to letting a big bunch like that prowl my wagon camp."

"I asked them. Wanted to give you a look at them. And maybeso throw a scare into this here emigrant outfit. The clodhopper fools want to head back down the trail for Kansas. I'm aiming to talk them outen it, one way or another. Going to try and get them to tag us into Gabe's and then wait for a strong outfit to roll East with. And don't get your roach bristled about those Injuns. I told them only the head men and chiefs was to come. No squaws and no rag-tag."

"What's the matter that this emigrant bunch heading back?"

Jesse shrugged. "Dead broke. Food's near gone. Most of them old folks that ought never to have left Shawnee. Just like all these idjuts what starts for Californy with a brokedown string of played-out bulls and a slew of slat-bed wagons. God damn it, they ain't fit to crawl into the next county, let alone cover two thousand miles of cactus and riled-up Injuns."

"Hell's fire, Jesse. You been on or along this Medicine Road for better'n twenty years. You've seed a hundred and ten outfits like this one, and danged if I ever heard you offering to wet-suck none of them, before. What's chawing you, boy? You got yourself a piece spied out amongst them?"

"Not percisely, Andy, I just. . . ."

"Listen, Jesse. I got a dozen wagons of bad-needed trade stuff, not to mention that cussed Du Pont, to get into Gabe's ahead of the Mormon push. That's the way Choteau writ the orders and, by damn, I ain't figuring to tote along no ragged-tail batch of splay-foot dirt farmers while I'm doing it. Besides, they've got the best idee of what to do, as it is. If they're short on grub and plumb stony, they'd best get on down the trail for home."

"What about Black Coyote and that big Arapaho camp over yonder?"

"That don't mean a thing to me. We putten a crimp in Black Coyote's tail that'll keep his bung puckered for a month. He's going to be too busy explaining how you beat him around Jackpine Slash to bother with any farmers like these here. Why, what the tarnal hell's he got to bother them about? The Crows done got their spare cattle, already. There ain't a thing left to take offen the poor bastards. Look at them, boy! Cripes, even a Taos Pueblo wouldn't trouble to stop them to spit on. You mean

to tell me a big medicine trail-raiding Injun of old
Watonga's class is going to jump these here roupy
Kansas jaybirds? Wake up, Jesse. Get back on the job
that Gabe hired you for!"

Jesse took the tongue lacing and backed off. Hang
it, the old man was right. Figuring it the way he
talked, there wasn't a Mexican's chance in Texas
that Black Coyote would bother the emigrants. The
way Andy saw it made Jesse look like a pure ninny.
But then, the old coot hadn't seen Lacey O'Mara
with her clothes off! Nor played with her gopher-
faced kid and made a Sioux chief out of him!

"I allow you're right, Andy. Guess having them
Arapahoes dogging our wagon ruts ever since Fort
Laramie has got me smelling them where they don't
stink."

"I reckon, boy. You just forget it. You go ahead and
tend to this gal and you'll feel better."

"There ain't no gal, you damned old salt tail!"

"Hoss apples!" snapped the older man, turning
to poke up the fire. When he looked back up, Jesse
caught the quick drop in his voice. "Oh, oh. Shine
up your Indian lingo, boy. Yonder comes your three
friends. And then some, by God."

Following the wagon master's gesture, Jesse
made out a considerable line of Indians bearing
down on the wagon corral, foremost among them
the three old chiefs he had palavered with earlier.

"Get them emigrants over here, Andy." The
mountain man grunted the words hurriedly. "And
have Morgan wrangle that little red mule outen the
loose herd. That's the one what went lame on him
back to the North Platte crossing. Have him bring
her up here. I promised them chiefs a mule roast."

The wagon master started to leave, paused,

squinting hard at the incoming Indians. Jesse, following the older man's gaze, narrowed his own eyes. The dancing yellow blotches of the cook fires carried outward, splashing and dappling the approaching visitors with their shifting light. Behind the three old chiefs rode a tall, extremely dark-visaged Indian. This rider sat, stick-straight, naked legs dangling, body enveloped from shoulder to mid-thigh in a coal-black buffalo robe. Even in the uncertain light, the hawk-featured face showed savagely handsome.

"I dunno, Jesse. . . ." Andy Hobbs peered more intently before turning to go. "Maybeso you're right. Happen they *are* bringing only the chiefs and head men, like you told them. But, mister, if that big, mean-looking buck in the black robe ain't a squaw, I'll kiss your ruby-red rear feathers!"

Jesse fell flat on his scowling face in the powwow that followed with the visiting chiefs. Were they sure their tongues were straight? Did they call their real chief Heavy Otter with their hearts true when they said it? *Aii-ee!* Their tongues were straight as war arrows. Straight as a Kangi Wicasi lancehaft. That straight. Not a shimmer in the grain of the shaftwood. All right, then. The red-haired *Wasicun* had another name for them. Black Coyote. Had they heard that name? Watonga. Black Coyote?

Wagh! Had they heard that name! To be sure, to be sure. What Arapaho hadn't? A great raider, Watonga. One of the best. *Woyuonihan*, respect him. Respect Watonga. *H'g'un!* And, say, had the *Wasicun* not heard that Black Coyote was down along the Medicine Road this season? Had he not met him along the trail just now? Had the red-haired goddam guide not seen Watonga? He should have seen him, if his tongue was straight. If he was telling his red brothers the truth about just having brought those twelve goddams all the way from Fort Laramie. No? The *Wasicun* had not seen Black Coyote? *Aii-eee!* The red-haired one was lucky. The goddams were lucky. All the Arapahoes knew Watonga had come south very early this summer. *Wowicake, owatanla.* It was a true thing.

Andy Hobbs had looked across at Jesse, enjoying seeing the slick oldsters hamstring the big cub. These old chiefs were so plumb innocent and straight-out it made the mountain man look awk-ward as a 600-pound cinnamon bear backing down a smooth-bark sycamore.

The emigrants, too, bought the Arapaho yarn, whole skein. After their bad luck brush with the skulking Crows, these tall, handsome Indians with their quiet dignity, impeccable manners, and plausi-ble intent to be the white man's best friends struck just the right note of assurance. Watching the nods and smiles of the gray-faced farmers, Jesse nearly puked.

The damned addle-pate ostriches. You never took an Indian at his word. The minute you did, you had as good as given him a root-hold grip on your hair. And Andy Hobbs! By God, *he* ought to know better. Yet, there he was, head-chucking and empty-grinning with the rest of them, like as if he'd spent the last twenty years plowing corn in Kentucky, in place of wading beaver streams and watching scalp dances.

Even Morgan Bates, that aged-in-the-rawhide trail rough, sat, fat and stupid, with his ears uncov-ered, enjoying the orations and handshakes of the Arapaho head men as if this was his first trip up the

Medicine Road! Sneering at the whole business, the wonder was to Jesse that ever a wagon got to Salt Lake, or a train to California.

An hour after the Indians rode in, they departed, leading Morgan Bates's little red mule and waved on their way by the good wishes of everybody in the white camp—with the notable exception of one very disgruntled red-headed mountain man. During the palaver, Jesse hadn't noticed the tall, black-robed buck Andy Hobbs had spotted for a squaw, had assumed she had been hunkered down in the shadows back of the outer rank of chiefs, where a squaw belonged. Now, counting the Indians carefully out of camp, (a prairie practice designed to prevent any red visitors being left behind to hide and spring a surprise attack), he missed the squaw again.

Well, probably nothing to that. She was undoubtedly the absent head chief's woman. That would explain how come she'd gotten to tag along in the first place. Now she had evidently wandered off to poke and beg around among the emigrant women while her men folk palavered with the *Wasicun*.

Looking around the fire, he decided the muleskinners and farmers would squat around another hour swapping lies before turning in. Andy Hobbs was talking to Tim O'Mara and Tom Yarbrough. Morgan Bates was spinning a milehigh Missouri yarn for the remainder of the listening flat hats.

Jesse eased away from the group without troubling to make a speech about it. One minute he was leaning against a wagon wheel listening with the best of them, the next the wagon wheel was listening all alone. That damned six-foot squaw was loose somewhere in camp, and Jesse meant to find where. Of course, while he was looking for her, he would keep his eyeballs skinned for any other squaws that might be wandering around loose. Like, say, real light-colored ones. With maybe yellow hair. And, for sure, blue eyes.

To make certain he got started properly on his search, putting the interests of the emigrant folk ahead of his own wagon crew, as was only noble and just, the mountain man headed for the little flicker of fires over amongst the Kansas wagons. Skirting the other vehicles, he drifted up on Tim O'Mara's old Pittsburgh, paused back of a dwarf cottonwood about thirty feet out.

Tim had rigged a sort of flysheet of Osnaburg sheeting to make a shelter against the scalding suns and drenching dews of the upland prairies. This ran out from the wagon's tailgate, and under it, as Jesse moved in, crouched what he was looking for—both of it: the coffee-skinned Arapaho squaw and the creamy, gold-haired Lacey O'Mara.

The mountain man had no more than begun to scowl his disappointment at so quickly finding what he'd told himself he was looking for (especially at finding it in the company of what he actually was looking for) than he had something really unexpected to fret about. Between the two women, laid down on a bundle of mangy cowhides, was a small child. At first, in the weaving firelight, Jesse thought it was the boy, Johnny, but as his eyes adjusted to the dark he could see this kid was much smaller and had long curls. It was for sure a girl and a white kid, and it must be Lacey's!

Cripes. He hadn't figured on her having a whole setting of chicks. Just that smart pants little red-headed cockerel, that was fine. But, hell. It kind of shook a man to think a girl as slick and slim as

Lacey would have herself a whole batch of young ones. For the first time he began to wonder how old she was, and how long she'd been married to Tim. And, damn it all, how many other fuzz-head kids were stowed away under that rickety Pittsburgh.

While his mind wandered disconsolately, his eye watched professionally. And what it watched was the tall black-skin squaw. The Arapaho woman was making medicine signs and crooning some sort of an Elk Dreamer song over the kid on the cowhides. When she went to prying the tike's mouth open and dumping some kind of powdered junk down it, Jesse figured he'd best make his walk up.

He made it nice and quiet, as came natural to a Minniconjou. Neither of the women saw him until his sharp-growled—*"Hau!"*—startled them.

He didn't miss the flash of anger in the squaw's scowl, or the unexpected brightness of Lacey's look. He kept his voice down, deliberately ignoring the Indian.

"What's the matter, ma'am? The kid ailing?"

"Oh, hello, Mister Callahan. Yes, the baby's sick."

"How long's she been thisaway, ma'am?"

"A long time." Lacey's voice sounded dull, hopeless. "It's the main reason I came out with Tim. The doctor in Kansas City said she ought to be where it's high and dry."

The mountain man looked at the wasted cheeks, pasty color, flush spots over the tiny cheek bones. One look was plenty. The kid had lung fever. She was a goner, sure.

"Yours?" he grunted softly, feeling dumb for asking it, wanting, somehow, to hear her say it wasn't. Knowing, of course, it was.

"Yes."

"God A'mighty, she's a purty little thing. How old is she?"

"Three."

"Don't look it, poor little devil. What you call her?"

"Kathy."

"I know your other kid . . . uh, one of them, anyways. Little carrot-top about five. Buckteeth like a cub gopher. Him and me, we . . ."

"Johnny's seven, Mister Callahan. And there's no others, just him and Kathy. He told me about how you were the past president of the Sioux nation and that you were so smart and mean that, when the other Indians saw you coming, they all ran screaming . . . 'Run for your lives, it's the great Red Fox!' Really, Mister Callahan . . . !"

"Shucks, that's nothing." Jesse's grin spread, ear to ear, interrupting her threatened reprimand. "You should have heard about the time I tangled rear ends with Watonga, the king of the Arapahoes!"

The raw-boned squaw bent farther over the sick child. Eye tailing her a glance, Jesse caught the bounce of the fire's flicker in the lynx-bright eyes. Under cover of her pretended hovering over the child, the squaw was watching him like a wing-hung hawk.

"Yep, that was the time, ma'am," his voice hurried on, wanting to beat the question framing on Lacey's full lips. "Just happened down the Medicine Road a ways. Not two days gone."

The squaw glued her eyes to the child, not letting herself grab any of Jesse's bait.

"Old Black Coyote, that's Watonga, ma'am, he set a trap for me. But Tokeya Sha, that's me, ma'am, I was a mite too fancy for him. Tokeya, he jumped up and ran around Watonga while he was a-setting watching his trap. The shame of getting himself out-foxed thataway like to kilt the old chief. Him and his best hundred braves. Last I seen of them, those braves was thinking about making me chief, and running old Black . . ."

"Mister Callahan"—the blonde girl's break-in showed she was through monkeying—"Tim will be along any minute. If you want something here, say so and be moving on. Tim will never forget your hitting him, believe me. You'd best not be around when he shows up. He'll . . ."

"He'll do nothing," purred the mountain man, blue eyes whacking into the emigrant girl like a thrown knife. "And I do want something here, Lacey O'Mara. I want you."

Lacey's mouth dropped as her eyes went big. Before she could start to sputter, Jesse cut her down.

"Not like you're thinking, ma'am. I don't mean that. But I do want to tell you how I *do* mean it. I'm slow with talk, but when it's in me to come out, I got to say it. And I got to say it to you, gal. Alone."

"You can't see me alone. Tim would kill both of us, sure. And I don't care what you mean and I don't want to hear what you've got to say. I don't want to see you, I can't see you. I don't want anything to do with you. Is that clear, Mister Callahan? I've got more trouble than I can bear now. I can't do anything about you. Oh, go away, Jesse! I . . ."

The use of his name slipped out awkwardly, interrupting the rambling flow of her words. To hear her say it put a hot push to spreading up Jesse's spine fit to choke his wind off. To have said it caused Lacey to wallow, blushingly, in her own confusion. Eyes dropped, she turned her head away, stood, fist-clenched, uncertain, angry. The picture of her in the fire glow, flushed, excited, tight-strung, did nothing to dim the memory of that cat's grace and strength of beauty that had first hit the mountain man's eye without any clothes over it.

"You'll see me, Lacey." He nailed her soft blue eyes on the cross of his narrow, hard ones. "Make it as soon as you get the little 'un quiet, and that clabberhead, Tim, bedded down. I'll be down there on this end of the slough where I seed you this morning. I got to see you and say what's in me. I won't touch you, without you want it. You'll see me, won't you, gal?"

"Go away, please. I don't want to see you. I *can't* see you!"

"Meeting's breaking up, over yonder"—the mountain man's warning carried Lacey's eyes to the group by the distant freight corral—"and I got to skeedaddle. I'll be where I said, down by the slough. And I'll be waiting for you, Lacey."

She didn't answer but Jesse didn't miss the way her white teeth bit into her lower lip, or how the dark blood came into her face, thick and fast. A man could be wrong, and a good many had stood in the rain all night to find out they were, but Jesse didn't allow he would waste his time at the slough.

Come an hour from now, and happen Tim got himself off to sleep without making any fuss, him and that gold-haired girl would have their talk down there!

Chapter 5

Jesse, leaning his broad back against the big cotton-wood log, sucked absently at his stone pipe. The pipe had been out for ten minutes but a man's mind will run a back track as good on a cold pipe as it will on a hot one—providing that track's as warm as the one the mountain man's thoughts were on. And Jesse Callahan's mind was really running. A man could scout a trail just so far, then he had to sit down and tote up the sign he'd seen. The sign Jesse had seen so far, had been mostly *red*.

One way or another, he couldn't get Watonga out of his head. First off, he had figured that after the failure at Jackpine Slash, the Arapaho chief would give up and go home. That had been before he'd discovered Washakie's story about a white man's being along with Watonga was true. When he had found the Arapahoes did have a strange white man with them, he'd had to refigure that part of it.

Even so, he hadn't been too worried until he'd run into this emigrant bunch with Lacey O'Mara among them and with the big Arapaho camp squatting hard on them, and with that bad case Tim O'Mara riding guide for them. Right away he hadn't liked the looks of all that. Then, when he'd found the village empty of warriors and just of a size to match up to Watonga's number of war-party bucks, he'd really started to sniff his back tracks to see where he'd missed a sign he shouldn't have. And he knew full well he had, too. For one thing, there was something about Tim, beyond his being Lacey's man and a stand-out settlement tough, that fretted him considerably. For another, that strapping-big squaw with her raw-boned build and bold-out approach kept hitting a memory bell that wouldn't ring. For a third, his "Sioux blood" kept gingering him about leaving the emigrants to head East on the Medicine Road.

Just because that bat-blind Choteau & Company bunch of red-necked Missouri mule heads had joshed and rough-joked him off his hunch didn't stop that hunch from working. You don't spend twenty-two years eating half-raw dog and smoking yourself over a buffalo-chip blaze without you building up some trace of what every *red* Indian is born with—a sixth-sense nose, touchy as a blistered heel, for impending disaster.

The mountain man came out of his thinking spell, head sharp-cocked. "That you, Lacey?" His soft question went to the willow brush across the sandbar from the log. "Lacey, you hear me?" he repeated quickly.

He got his answer from a couple of tree frogs and the chorus of water peepers in the slough fringe grass.

Waiting five breaths, he eased off the log, went

fox-stepping through the dark. There was nothing in the willows save the wisp of night breeze that should have been there.

Could have been the wind, he mused doubtfully. *Man gets edgy setting up for something like her to show.*

The hour he had given her was gone. Not alone that hour, but a grudging and nervous half of the next one. Now he had to admit she'd likely meant what she'd said. Either that or she hadn't been able to dodge Tim. Well, if that was the way it was going to be, he would have to brace himself to seeing her in the morning. That, or forget the whole thing. Which, all things considered, wouldn't be a far piece from a good idea. But where was there anybody around to tell a man how he went about forgetting something like Lacey O'Mara? Something with a top-cream body like that, and eyes that went deeper into a man than a broad-head buffalo arrow?

She came out of the darkness as Jesse moved back out of the willow brush. Standing there in the starlight, motionless at the edge of the black filigree of the trees, she didn't offer to move or speak. Not even the tree dark or the pale star shine could hide the poised grace of that figure. When Jesse came up to her, she looked down and away, as though she didn't want to see him.

"Hello, Lacey. I'm certain glad you come. I was beginning to think you wouldn't."

"I didn't aim to. . . ." The voice was strained. "Please don't talk, yet. I . . ."

The mountain man took her arm, feeling the way it went tense under his fingers. "Come on over here, Lacey. We can set on that old log where you had your clothes this morning. Don't be feared, gal.

Ain't no call to be, I allow." With the words, his hand tightened on her arm, urging her gently.

She pulled away from him at once, and he let her go, sensing the bow-string tautness running through her, knowing that the wrong word or move could set her off, for good.

"Come on," he repeated easily, turning to lead the way, not looking to see if she followed, "it ain't going to harm us none to talk."

At the log, he turned to find her at his elbow. "Set down, ma'am." He made the words sound as calm as they could, coming from a man that was as tendon-loose as a bull elk with a strange cow ramping up to his nose sniffs. "I'll give it to you, straight out."

She sank to the warm sand beside the log, saying nothing, still not letting herself look at him. Jesse followed her down, careful that he left plenty of sand between them.

"It'll save time if we don't whale around the brush now," he began nervously. "I never been in love with a gal in my life, Lacey. Now, I reckon I am. I want you to come on to Californy with me. . . ."

"Jesse!"

"Don't break in on me!" The mountain man's order was rough. "I got it all in mind what I want to say. All I ask is that you set still and give it a listen. After that, you can have your own whack at it. How about it, gal?"

"All right. . . ." The answer was so low that it almost took a Minniconjou ear to hear it. But it came without hesitation, and Jesse marked that.

"We'll take the kids and go. Now. Tonight. You don't take nothing but them. Last I seed of Tim, he was killing a gallon jug with Andy Hobbs. I reckon the way he's asleep now, a mule could stand hipshot atop him, without Tim missing a snore." He paused, side-eying her before hurrying on. "That little gal of yours has got the lung fever. I seen it too many times in Injun kids to miss calling it. Best chance she's got is to get where it's mile-high and skin-dry. Your doctor told you that and, by damn, Californy is full of places to fit that prescription. As for Johnny, he's cut to size for my kind of cub. Coming to you, Lacey, God help me, I can't tell you how it is. I got it in me so strong I can taste it. I want to go on tasting it from here till the lantern goes out. That's all, gal. I can't say it no better."

The silence that mushroomed up was so thick Jesse thought he'd strangle of it. Still, when she spoke, the halting, soft way of it let him know he hadn't read her eyes wrong.

"You don't have to say it any better, Jesse. You've said it beautiful. I've never been in love, either, Jesse. I don't even know that I am, now. I only know how it feels when you look at me and how it squeezes here inside when I look at you. I've never felt it that way, before. But, Jesse, the whole thing's crazy. All of it. If it wasn't for Kathy, I might see it, might go with you. I . . ."

"What about Kathy?" Jesse interrupted harshly. "What's she got to do with it, Lacey?"

"She's got to get back to a doctor, Jesse. I'm afraid Kathy's going to die! And I've got to get her there. Give her that chance. She's got to have that chance, Jesse . . ."—the girl's voice trailed off helplessly, her words as dead as the hope within them—"and I guess you know where the nearest doctor is."

"Yeah. The Army surgeon at Fort Laramie"—he tried to give it to her softly—"and she'll never make it. That baby's going to die, Lacey. I allow you know that."

"Jesse! Kathy's got to have a doctor . . . !"

The mountain man said nothing, knowing that where a mother's got a dying child she's rightfully got her mind flowed-over for anything else. After a long minute he asked the question that had been on his mind from the moment she had told him she was Mrs. O'Mara. "How about you and Tim, Lacey gal?"

The emigrant woman hesitated with her reply. When it came, it was low-voiced with awkwardness. "Tim near hates me, I guess. I've not given him the kind of love a man has a right to expect from his woman. That bitters a man like nothing else. . . ." The girl paused, her voice dropping lower still. "Tim's not the children's father, Jesse. I married Tim only to get Kathy out here. Their real father, my first husband, died three years ago in the settlements. Scraping around back there to feed the children those three years, with the baby sick and all . . ."—another pause to let the embarrassment creep, thick and heavy, into the emigrant woman's voice before she concluded haltingly—"oh, I'm so ashamed, Jesse!"

The mountain man said nothing, waiting for her to continue. After a moment, she did.

"Well, when Tim told me he was taking this train as far west as Salt Lake and offered to take me along if I'd marry him, I just shut my eyes and said yes. Tim's a Mormon, you know, and I thought he would at least be good to us. But, oh, Jesse, it's just been hell! The whole shameful thing of it. So, when he refused to guide these folks back, I stayed with them to get Kathy back to the doctor like I told you. That's the whole story, Jesse. Of course, I never loved Tim, and, now that he's back, I'm terrified of him. Jesse, he's up to something, I know he is. I can feel it, and I'm scared to death!"

The mountain man waited while his hard-galloping thoughts raced to catch up with the half relief, half alarm created by the girl's astonishing outburst. At the moment he was too concerned with Lacey's and his own emotions to sort out the peculiar significance in her remarks about Tim O'Mara. And when his question came, it was deliberately and carefully off trail. "How old are you, Lacey?"

Her laugh was low, but not that low it hid the hardness in it. "Thirty-one, Jesse. 'Most thirty-two."

He had asked her only to change the subject, hadn't expected that heavy an answer. "God A'mighty, honey, a body'd never guess it. You look eighteen."

"I don't feel eighteen, Jesse, and that's another thing." The bitterness was gone now, in its place a sort of dull acceptance. "You look thirty and probably aren't a day over twenty-five. That's a lot of difference when it's on the woman's side."

He started to tell her he was a full thirty-three, trapped the admission with a snap of his white teeth, sealed it in with one of his quick grins. "Hell, Lacey, I not alone look thirty, I feel fifty. I've been night-sleeping the prairie by my lonesome for so damn' long it feels like I been waiting for a woman the past twenty years. Lacey, I reckon it ain't going to save you if you're forty. I aimed to make me a stake outen this trip and I got that stake more'n made, honey. I'll clear a thousand dollars on the peltries I brought down from Three Forks alone. Then I got a five-hundred-dollar bonus coming for getting some gunpowder through to Jim Bridger up to the fort. Cripes, we'll have more money than ticks on a sick elk!"

She kept quiet a long time then. Finally her words were thought out, careful. "I've had a bad life, Jesse. I guess you can tell that. I've not had a man the real way. I feel I could have you that way, Jesse, and I want to think we'd find the best kind of love together. But the way it is, I just can't quite dare myself into believing it. Jesse, I just *can't!*" After a moment, she went on. "I don't know anything we can do, either. My folks have got to travel on, tomorrow. Your train has got to keep going to Fort Bridger. We're just moving in opposite directions, Jesse. . . ."

"Lacey, will you leave Tim if I come back to Laramie for you?"

"Jesse! *Please* don't talk to me like that!"

The sudden fierceness shooting through her words narrowed the mountain man's eyes, put the blood, thick and hammering, into his throat. His great hands took her arms, high up, burrowing their hard talons into the warm hollows of her armpits, his mouth, wide and cruel as any Sioux's, smashing her soft lips apart, writhing and thirsting for the sweetness of them.

She threw her head, fiercely breaking the bruising kiss, surging back from him. Instantly his arms were behind her, trapping her against him, the swift hands flashing down to seize and crush her into him. She came to him then, her lips finding his, her round arms circling his cording neck, her body coming up to meet his, frantically hungry for a thing it had never known.

The lumpy, three-quarter moon, loppy and tired as a cantaloupe that has lain too long on the vine, took a polite yawn and went sliding into the hills across the Black Fork. The peepers in the fringe grass lowered their wracking song to a drowsy hum. Somewhere down the slough, a plover raised his plaintive night song. Out on the prairie, beyond the river, a sage hen muttered sleepily.

In the creeping shadow of the cottonwood log, other voices paced the slowing rhythm of the prairie night.

"Getting late, Lacey honey."

"Yes, I know. . . ."

"I allow we'd best be moving back."

"Yes. . . ."

Jesse rolled up on one elbow, lay there looking down on her, the last wanness of the dropping moon dappling them with its pale glow. Lacey lay quietly, one arm thrown across her eyes, the other slipping around the mountain man's bare shoulder. Her fingers moved over the carved sinews, lingered wonderingly along the swelling curve of the bicep. There was no heat in the fingers now, no frantic urgency. Their slow coolness felt like nothing Jesse had ever felt on him. He came into their touch, easing his body back down until it lay again against Lacey's.

The freshness and fragrance of her washed over him once more, but now, long and lazy, like lowering your body into mossy spring water. He pillowed his head in the crook of her arm, pressing his dark cheek gratefully into the moving swell of her cool breast.

"Lacey. . . ."

"Yes, Jesse?"

"You remember all we said?"

"I remember. . . ."

The peepers took over, filling the little silence.

"We'll leave it that way, honey. Like we last said."

"Yes, Jesse."

"You'll go on with Tim and your folks, back to Laramie. I allow you'll make it without no trouble from the Injuns. And I'll be back for you real sudden. We'll all of us, the kids and you and me, strike out for Californy. You'd like that, wouldn't you, Lacey? Taking up where your folks left off, going on out to the Californy coast?"

"Yes, oh, yes, I would, Jesse. And I'll go with you."

"Sure, honey. We know how we feel, now. That's the biggest part of it."

"It's the whole part, Jesse. You're the only man I've ever loved like this. I want that, Jesse. I want it for the rest of my life."

"Me, too, Lacey gal."

He rolled back with the tense whisper, letting her come into him, the wide mouth seeking under the yellow hair, finding the lobe of the small ear, a muttered phrase of endearment coming with the kiss—long-drawn, fierce, relentless.

The stream of Lacey O'Mara's mind had tumbled in a millrace of confusion from the moment she had looked up to meet Jesse's level stare across Paiute Slough. From the first of the dry tears canonizing the crude couch of the settlement wedding night, her life had dropped into that half-dead hell to which so many frontier women found themselves delivered twenty-four hours after some circuit-riding God-talker had hustled through the holy words to drop the Good Book and run for the whiskey barrel.

Looking up to see the red-haired mountain man

and the smoke-gray Sioux mare across that prairie bathing pool, the picture innermost in any love-cheated woman's mind had slotted into its golden frame—just as true and clear as ever that of any olden captive and despairing princess in storied ivory tower. That rat-tailed, mud-dirty snare with her popped eyes, rack-of-bone ribbing, and hipshot stance was the milkiest of white steeds. And most certainly that split-oak post of a rider, lantern jaw, lank hair, grimy Sioux moccasins and all, was the knightliest of armored errants.

Now, gliding toward the cherry glow of the wagon fire, her heart high with the excitement of the promise she had just concluded with Jesse, Lacey was suddenly terrified. The crouching figure hovering near the fire, its shadow bulking man-big against the rough boards of the wagon's tailgate, shoulder-shot her running dreams, dead center. Tim! God in heaven! Somehow he had missed her, somehow been aroused from his sodden sleep, was hunkered there, waiting for her. For a crazy moment she thought of turning back, finding Jesse, facing the whole thing out, here and now. A child's restless whimpering caught up the skirt of her impulse, sharpened her wide eyes.

The figure by the fire turned to reveal its craggy hawk's face, the small bundle clutched to her breast. The squaw! The big Arapaho squaw. Thank God. She was still there.

Lacey came to the fire, sinking down by the Indian woman, holding her finger to her lips, nodding toward the wagon bed and the rising snores of its occupant. The tall squaw nodded back, with a quick smile held forth the figure of the sleeping Kathy, close-wrapped in the pile of the black buffalo robe.

"Baby much better. Baby good now." The stilted words came in a grunt as deep as any brave's.

Lacey glanced at the child, noting the half smile on the little face, the peaceful, easy pace of her breathing. Dear God, she did look better. For the first time in weeks, Lacey O'Mara felt the sudden jump of mother hope. Her bright return smile to the Arapaho woman conveyed that hope.

"*Hau*," grunted the squaw, carefully shouldering out of the heavy robe, bundling the child in it, placing her gently by the fire. Under the robe, the squaw was garbed in a slipover of tanned doeskin. From the breast of this she now drew a small doll, a strangely ugly thing, its warped features and small, twisted limbs fashioned entirely of dried buffalo hide.

"*Hanpospu hoksicala*," said the Indian woman. "Holy doll, Sioux medicine doll. Very big medicine."

With the words, she placed the crude figurine in the robe with Kathy. The child turned in her sleep, smiled, snuggled the grotesque image in her thin arms. The squaw stared at the infant a moment, raised her narrow eyes to Lacey.

"Me go, now. Come back soon. Come back with the light. With the sun."

"Oh, thank you," the emigrant woman's gratitude hurried out, "but you can't! I mean it won't do any good. You see, we're leaving in the morning. We're going to travel on. My wagons are going away then, you see? But I do thank you . . . uh. . . ." The white girl paused, wanting to use the name of her new companion.

"Elk Woman. My name Elk Woman."

The squaw extended her hands across the fire, smiling. Lacey seized them impulsively.

"God bless you, Elk Woman. I know my baby is

better. Oh, thank you so much!" Her eyes falling on the buffalo-hide doll, Lacey added anxiously: "Can she keep the little doll, Elk Woman? See how she cuddles it already."

"*Hau,*" grunted the squaw, easing to her feet, "she keep. Me come back. Go, now."

"But . . ." Lacey started to repeat her explanation of the emigrant departure, only for the Indian woman to hold up both hands, palms out, asking for silence.

"Me come back with sun. Stay with baby. She get well."

"But, Elk Woman . . ."—it was clear the Indian had failed to grasp the content of Lacey's straight-spoken English, did not understand the camp was moving—"we are leaving. We go tomorrow. See? You can't stay with us."

"Me travel with you." The big squaw shrugged simply. "Go get medicine leaves now. Come back and travel with *Wasicun* goddams. Baby get strong."

"You mean you'll stay with us? Travel along with the wagons? Nurse the baby?"

"*Hau.*" The squaw nodded vigorously. "My braves downriver hunting buffalo. Maybe six, seven suns. Me go that far. Meet braves. Baby well, then."

"Oh, you'll stay with us till we meet your warriors. They're hunting down the trail. *Hau!*" The white woman used her first Indian word with awkward hopefulness.

"*Hau! Hau!*"

"It would be wonderful! How can I ever thank you, Elk Woman?"

Lacey's eyes were shining, her face high-flushed with color. When a person's luck turned, it seemed to turn all at once. Surely Lacey O'Mara's had turned today, for the first time in three long years. It had turned with the arrival of the lean, red-haired mountain man, and with the dramatic appearance of this tall, black-skinned Indian woman. God bless both of them!

"You no thank Elk Woman," answered the squaw. "Me love baby. All baby!"

With her statement, her sharp eyes shifted to the shadows near the back of the canvas tailgate shelter. Stepping past Lacey, she bent over the sleeping form of Johnny O'Mara. Lovingly the Indian woman tucked the threadbare blankets around the youngster. When she had them just right, she placed her right hand on the boy's forehead, whispering intently:

"Han mani wolkota, Ya Slo. Hdiyotanka!"

And with that, she was gone, fading into the outer darkness with all the noise of a cut-throat trout sliding out of a sun dapple into deep water.

Lacey looked after her, smiling happily.

For the sake of that smile, it was the Lord's blessing the white girl was ignorant of the Arapaho tongue. All Lacey understood was that Elk Woman loved all children, and had paused to say an Indian blessing over little Johnny. Well, maybe it was a sort of a blessing, at that. Johnny O'Mara had a cheery whistle, practiced its art more or less constantly. With true Indian direction Elk Woman had taken the habit and made a name for the *Wasicun* boy. She had used this name in muttering what Lacey so trustingly imagined to be her parting blessing to him. Could Jesse Callahan have heard it, every hair on his red head would have rattled in its root socket. *Han mani wolkota, Ya Slo. Hdiyotanka!* "Walk in the night with peace, Little Whistler. Soon you are going away with me!"

*   *   *

Jesse got back to the Choteau company wagons about 1:00 A.M., rolled into his blankets, slept like a shot soldier until 4:00.

Rousing at that hour, he padded through the dark toward the looming shadow of the lead wagon. He waited a second, adjusting his eyes to the gloom, bent quickly over the wagon master's huddled form, touched the tight-wrapped blankets lightly.

The old man came scrambling awake, fumbling sleepily in the blackness for his rifle. The mountain man put a bony knee in his belly, pinning him back on his blankets.

"Hold on, you old catamount! I told you it was me."

"It's you who? Who the hell is it? God damn it, what's going on around here?"

"Shut up! It's Jesse. What in hell's the matter with you?"

"The matter with me, you chucklehead? Don't you know better at your age than to go around grabbing a man outen his sound sleep in Injun country? I mighten've shot your leggings off!"

"You mighten," allowed the mountain man, "happen I hadn't've taken your gun out from under you before I shook you up. Leave off your grousing for a shake and pay attention. We're rolling outen here."

"You crazy, boy? What hour be it?"

"Four."

"What's the idee? You know I never holler catch up before five-thirty."

"I want to be moving before broad light. That'll be maybe an hour. There'll be light enough to catch up by in fifteen, twenty minutes."

"I asked you what's the idee?"

"God damn it, you got a contract for hauling gunpowder and supplies to Fort Bridger. And I get a bonus for seeing that you do it without losing any of it. We're back of time on account of that mangy Black Coyote and his damn' deal with Brigham Young. I'm thinking we'll have to roll soon's there's light to see, and to keep rolling far and fast from here on in. That is, providing we don't aim to let Watonga get set for us again."

Up to this point, the mountain man had been making a very good case for himself, almost convincing Andy Hobbs he meant every word of his tirade. But as usual, when things are going too easy for man, Jesse overreached himself. Clearing his throat, self-righteously he delivered what was designed as the *coup-de-grâce.*

"But, mostly, Andy, old salt, I'm wanting to get outen here before them hang-dog emigrants come awake. I'm feared they might change-up their minds and decide to tag onto us. And it's like you said yourself. We just ain't got no damn' time to mess with them. Come on, rustle your tail, old hoss. Roust the boys out!"

The white-bearded wagon master cleared his own throat in turn, spat contemptuously. "It's like I said, all right, young 'un. But you ain't quite quoting the part of it I'm thinking about. If ever I heard a young stud whickering over a bellyful of sour oats, it's you."

"What the hell you mean, you bent-prod old steer?"

"I mean it's sand-bottom clear that you tooken your whack at that piece you had sighted amongst them emigrants. It's just as clear that you missed it, clean. Now you're peed about it and you're getting the hell away before you have to face up to her in the daylight, or maybeso her old man. Sure funny how a man'll get hisself all hot for something till she turns him down. Minute she does, he lets on like she smelled worse than a clabbered cheese bag to him the whole time. You know what I think, boy? Hoss apples, that's what."

"We going to roll early or ain't we?"

Jesse put the question sullenly, ignoring the oldster's center shot.

"Five's earlier than I like, let alone four. I'll split the difference with you, Jesse. We'll toll at five."

"Thanks for nothing," muttered the mountain man. "I'll see you at ten of."

"Going somewheres, meantime?"

"Reckon I'll sneak over and eye those Arapahoes. Make sure they ain't moving out early, too."

"Make sure they don't trap you at it, Dan'l Boone," cautioned the old man. "I don't hate you so purely that I'd want to find your thick head stuck in the Medicine Road on a sharp stake."

"I'll step soft," promised Jesse. "Just got me a four-bit hunch that something's stirring over there."

At that, there wasn't a thing in the world wrong with the mountain man's suspicion—save that it was a little more than somewhat late. Long hours gone, Tall Elk had sent her hastily instructed messengers down the back trail toward Wild Horse Bend and the waiting Watonga.

Chapter 6

Riding the head of the wagon line, Jesse tried keeping his mind on the remaining road to Fort Bridger, and his eyes on the hills around it. In the path of the lumbering Conestogas now lay the old familiar landmarks: Squaw Creek, Sioux Lick, Paiute Butte, Black Timbers, fair enough places, all, to harbor a red-hued reception committee eager to readjust that little matter of the Jackpine Slash detour. Try as he would, however, the mountain man couldn't hold his thinking to what hostile possibilities might lie off the bows of his axle-squealing prairie schooners.

Time and again, as the interminable morning wore away, his Indian hunch kept herding his thoughts back to the emigrant camp at Paiute Crossing. Damn a man's mind, anyway. He still knew he had fumbled something back there, and it wasn't anything about Lacey, or even about Tim O'Mara. It was something with those accursed Arapahoes—most particularly that hawk-faced squaw. There

had been something about her he should have tumbled to. Some one, shifty thing that kept skipping
around the back of his head and wouldn't stand
still long enough for a man to get a membranous
look at it.

An hour after noon halt, with the wagons rolling
steadily over the hard-packed going, and with him
and Andy Hobbs out-riding the lead Conestoga, the
wagon master suddenly remembered something.

"Thunderation, Jesse! I just thunk of something.
Here . . ." The old man dug inside his shirt, bringing
forth a wadded scrap of yellow paper. "I was supposed to give you this. That emigrant boss's woman,
the purty gal with the yellow hair, she brung it over
while you was sneaking around that Arapaho camp
this morning. I ain't read it."

Jesse took the paper, unfolding it, and studying
the enclosed writing, the frown ridges building up
heavier by the second.

"What's the trouble, boy, bad news?"

"I dunno," answered Jesse sullenly.

"What the Sam Hill you mean, you dunno? You
can read, cain't you? What's she say?"

"No," gruffed the mountain man shortly.

"Well, hell! That's nothing. Lots of women have
said no. Don't let that throw you. It's their favorite
three-letter word."

The mountain man handed the paper back to
Andy Hobbs. "I didn't mean she said no," he mumbled, flushing. "I meant, no, I cain't read."

"Oh." The old man took the paper, spreading it
proudly on his saddle horn. "Well, that's nothing,
neither. I allow there ain't nobody in this here train
what can, saving me. Let's see, here. . . . Uh, 'Jesse,
darling' . . . that's the way she begins it. *Hmmm,* now

how does it go? Let's see, here . . . say!" The oldster broke off, eyeing Jesse suspiciously. "God damn you, did you get that piece, or didn't you? Jesse, darling! *Hmpfhh!* You sneaky bastard. And all the time here I was feeling sorry for you. Allowing you'd got your ears slapped back. Why, you ungrateful . . ."

"Read the letter, you horny old goat! Never mind if I whapped the gal or not."

Andy Hobbs, glancing at the mountain man, took due note of the way his blue eyes were darkening, decided to read on with strict attention to Lacey O'Mara's ideas, foregoing his own with commendable good taste—and faultless good judgment.

> *Jesse, darling—*
> *I wanted to see you to tell you that I'll be waiting for you at Fort Laramie. It's funny how everything seems to brighten up at once.*
> *When I got back to the fire, that Indian woman was still there and she had made little Kathy much better. And then, guess what, Jesse! She said she would travel with me and take care of the baby until my folks met up with hers. Her tribesmen are buffalo hunting somewhere down on the Black Fork.*
> *Isn't that wonderful? I know that when you see us in Laramie, Kathy will be fine and strong.*
> *I love you, Jesse darling. Remember me.*
> *Lacey*
> *P.S. Be careful of Tim when you come. He left camp early this morning after waking me up to tell me he knew all about you and me and that he was going to fix it so no white man would ever want me. He couldn't know about us and he has always been a bad talker. I'm afraid of him, Jesse, but I know I won't need to be once you're back with me.*

The wagon master handed the crumpled note to the mountain man, along with a tentative grin. "Boy, I'm sorry I razzled you. You're fixing to marry that yellow-haired gal, ain't you?"

Jesse accepted the note and the apology. "Yeah, Andy, I allow I am. We're plumb in love and she ain't got no use for Tim O'Mara."

"Well, she's a looker." His companion nodded. "And that little boy of hers is cuter'n a fuzz-tail buffalo calf. I allow you'll be right happy, providing you can work around that lunkhead, Tim."

"He don't bother me no more'n a mule marble in a wagon corral," the mountain man muttered. "What gets my nanny is that slant-eye squaw. She's been bothering me right along and now this damn' fool gal of mine has to go and leave the red slut suck in and tag along with her and the kids. Damn it, for some reason I can't help fretting about that squaw."

"Cain't say as I blame you, young 'un. But I allow it's just the look of her that's got you breaking bother wind. Hell, she just plain looks bad. That six-foot build. Them wild eyes. That slit-ear mouth. Why, even the twisting way she limps around is enough to spook a tame steer."

Andy Hobbs's rambling words sprung the trap of Jesse's reaching mind. That god-damned Arapaho squaw! The one that'd been sucking around Lacey. That one. He'd never seen her walking. Only riding in on her pony, then squatting at Lacey's fire. And now Andy said she walked crooked. What was it his Sioux foster folk had used to call Black Coyote's wife? Wasn't it Ousta? Hell, that was it. Ousta. The Sioux name for One-Who-Limps. The Limper. The Lame One. *Aii-eee!*

He threw Heyoka on her haunches with a hackamore twist that nearly wrenched her head off at the withers. Wheeling on the advancing Conestogas, he dug his heels in. Going for the wagons, with the mare belly-flat, he stood in the stirrups, roaring like an arrow-shot bear.

"Hold up! Hold up! Corral! Corral!"

By the time Andy Hobbs got his breath and kicked his old gelding to follow the mountain man, Jesse had the lead vehicles circling.

With the corral made, the red-haired trapper talked, and hard. The astonished muleskinners just sat their seat boxes and gaped. You couldn't even get your mouth half open, let alone spit a word sideways out of it, the wild-eyed mountain son was barking his orders that fast.

"Boys, we got us some tall riding to do. And, happen you like the sound of it, I reckon some high fighting. Get all this and get it straight. There ain't going to be no repeats."

Caught up by the big-shouldered mountain man's intensity, the Missouri teamsters nodded mutely, none thinking to interrupt the hard gallop of words that followed.

"That big buck squaw which rode into our camp with them old chiefs last night was Watonga's wife. That village is Black Coyote's!"

Morgan Bates, as usual the first to put tongue to what went on in his head, drawled his challenge, tight-mouthed: "Well, what of it, Jesse?"

"Just this!" Jesse jumped his answer. "Andy remembered something a minute ago. He handed me a note from that yellow-haired gal that was with them emigrants. That's the one with the little redhead boy. That note said this here squaw . . . Black Coyote's wife, now, mind you . . . was traveling with the emigrants. She give the yellow-hair gal a yarn about tagging along to take care of her other little kid, the one that's puny, the little dark-hair gal. I allow you can all figure what's coming. Them red scuts will sandbag that bunch of farmers sure as we're standing here picking our noses. I allow the squaw is aiming to grab that red-head boy. Her and Watonga can't have no kids of their own. I remember that from hearing it camp-talked when I was amongst the Sioux. Watonga, he's dying to have a son. And, boys, that hard-face squaw ain't against dying to give him one!"

"I reckon there'll be more dying than her," vouchsafed Morgan Bates, "less'n we put a hump in our butts. How you aim to work it, Jesse?"

"Leave Andy and two men here with the wagons. You and me takes the other ten. Maybeso we can catch them emigrant folks before Black Coyote does. It ain't no secret I got more stake in that train than just saving them farmers. I'm saying that, right now, and asking any of you boys what don't want to go, to sing out. Nobody ain't going to hold nothing against you, neither. You ain't getting paid for shooting coyotes."

"Hell, I'm tired of muleskinning." Morgan Bates's careless shrug picked up a following of quick grins around the listening circle. "Happen we can peel a coyote for variety, I'm for it."

"Let's ride," snapped another of the Missouri hardcases. "We ain't catching no emigrant wagons standing here."

The saddle herd was run in, each man making his own hurried catch-up. Twenty minutes after Andy Hobbs had mentioned the Arapaho squaw's limp, Jesse's coyote skinners were on their way.

Sitting the high-loping Heyoka in the midst of his little band, the mountain man nodded grimly. A man had to be proud of his color, sometimes. There wouldn't be a manjack of these boys worth his salt by settlement standards. They were, every one of them, ignorant as pigs and dirtier than a Ute's scalp. But where else would a man find a dozen bucks as ready to slap on a saddle and ride their bottoms raw just for the privilege of swapping shots with 100 touchy Arapaho hostiles?

When Jesse's dust-bearded riders rounded Little Willow Bend of the Black Fork, to gallop into cross-meadow view of the mile-distant loop of Wild Horse Bend, the damage was already done. Not that they hadn't known it would be, damn the red devils. Five miles back on the Cut-Off they'd seen the grease-black smoke of the burning wagons snaking skyward. Now, breaking across the meadow in their headlong, yelling charge, they got the whole picture.

Two wagons had somehow made it to the fork, and from behind them and a convenient shelf bank of the river the handful of white survivors were standing the Arapahoes off. The other wagons, amid a shambles of dead and dying oxen, were burning freely in mid-meadow.

Jesse led his aroused muleskinners down on the still circling Arapahoes, trapping them against the half-moon curve of the riverbank. Had the odds been a little less overwhelming in Black Coyote's favor, the saga of the Wind River Arapahoes might have come to a much more abrupt and satisfactory end. And even as it was, for all the beautiful strategy with which Watonga split his forces and broke them out both horns of the half moon, the Arapaho chief left behind no less than ten of his slit-eyed followers. The injured among these, on Jesse's short-barked order, were shot through the head, the white rescuers then setting quickly about pulling the terror-stricken emigrants together.

By the way the hostiles had broken and fled rather than making a fight of it, Jesse knew, even before he slid Heyoka in among the shocked survivors, that Watonga had already gotten what he'd come after—whatever that might prove to be. And what it proved to be was his own hunch: Lacey O'Mara's red-headed son, Johnny.

He got the entire tragedy from the compressed lips of the strangely composed Lacey. While she told it, Morgan Bates put his muleskinners to helping the emigrants bury their dead and tend their wounded. Lacey's story went tough and straight and short.

Approaching Wild Horse Bend, just after the wagons had passed a high spur of sand hills, the Arapaho squaw had come leaping out of the O'Mara wagon in which she had been riding with Kathy. The squaw had shouted that the child was dying and that the wagons must halt at once.

Tim, with peculiar alacrity and total carelessness about the train's exposed position in the open meadow, had stopped the train at once. The squaw had then disappeared back into the wagon to return in a moment clutching the blanketed form of little Kathy. She had at once begun to cry out that water must be brought from the river, without delay.

Three of the men, on Tim's orders, had grabbed water skins and run for the river, on foot. The instant they had left, Elk Woman had lifted Johnny up on her pony, saying: "Bad him see sick child. Child die, boy no see."

Lacey, taking Kathy's bundled form from the Indian woman, had nodded, thinking the squaw meant to divert Johnny's attention from the fact of his little sister's condition. A second later she had looked up, horrified to see Elk Woman riding like the wind toward the spur of low hills, Johnny kicking and yelling across the withers of her racing pony.

The next moment they had all been startled to see Tim leap on his saddle gelding and take out after the Indian woman. From his shouts and yells, they had assumed he was dashing off on an instant and brave attempt to catch the squaw before she could reach the sanctuary of the hills. But then, even as they were voicing their confused admiration for Tim's act, and before any thought of an organized pursuit of the squaw could be formed, the hills had belched out a cloud of screaming red warriors. Elk Woman and Johnny, followed by the hapless Tim, had disappeared into the belly of this cloud that then swept on unchecked, to surround the strung-out wagons.

The three men who had gone for water had been shot down immediately, cut off as they tried making it back to the train from the stream. Most of the wagons had been overturned and fired before the first white shots were gotten off. Only the fact Tom Yarbrough's two wagons were mule-drawn had allowed any of the emigrants to escape. These survivors of the first Arapaho rush had managed to get into the two mule wagons and make a dash for the riverbed, Lacey, still clutching Kathy, among them.

They had reached the river ten minutes before Jesse's arrival. In those ten minutes the Arapahoes had pulled off toward the hills, evidently being undecided about continuing the assault. Their chief's towering figure, unmistakable under its sinister, eight-foot war-bonnet trademark, had been plainly visible as he rode the front of the packed warrior ranks, exhorting them to return to the attack.

Then, as the hostiles had hesitated, an even more sinister figure moved out of their ranks to join Watonga in haranguing them to wipe out the rest of the white party. Not a member of the emigrant group had failed to identify this latter figure. None of them would ever forget the shock accompanying the identification. Beyond all reasonable doubt of distance or over-wrought nerves, it was the hulking, bearthick form of Tim O'Mara. The renegade's oratory, text unknown, had been quickly fruitful, the whooping savages having just launched their second charge as Jesse and his muleskinners rode around the bend.

The mountain man and the dry-eyed emigrant woman had been crouching against the shelf bank while she told her story, Jesse not touching her or interrupting her, knowing the least sign from him might precipitate the breakdown he could see building behind her staring eyes. All through the stumbling recital, she had clutched the huddled form of her daughter, hard against her, not looking at the child, not even seeming to know she held her. When she had finished, she remained crouching against the caving sandbank, looking, glassy-eyed, right through the listening mountain man.

Jesse reached over, then, taking the pitiful bundle from her. A glance at the eggshell crush of the small face, blood-smeared and wide-eyed, showed him the squaw must have heel-swung the child's head against the inner sideboards of the wagon bed. His low-growled mutter went to the stony-calm mother.

"She's dead, Lacey gal." The emigrant woman did

not appear to hear him and he touched her on the shoulder. "Lacey, I said she's dead. Kathy's done for, honey."

Lacey nodded dully, her eyes contracting as her face muscles pulled her lips up into the blank smile. "Dead," was all she said, before starting to laugh.

Jesse dropped the child, leaped for her mother. Seizing her by the dress front, he swung his hand, hard and dry as a cedar chunk, across her mouth.

"Shut up, Lacey! Shut up!"

He shook her like a bear with a range colt in his jaws. The laugh kept coming. Harsh. High. Crazy.

Stepping back, Jesse sighted the writhing mouth, smashed one short, right-hand jolt up under the slack chin. Lacey's head flipped back, dropped, sagging forward, the mountain man moving in and catching her as she fell. Easing her slumped form down beside that of the dead child, he legged it up the sandbank.

Minutes later, the shocked survivors of Watonga's raid were being loaded into the two mule wagons.

"We put the bodies in that water cut over yonder." Morgan Bates pointed out the shallow grave to Jesse. "We heaved some loose sand and rocks over them . . . enough to hold off the buffalo wolves. Ain't much else we could do."

"How many dead?"

"Six. Five men and one old woman. Any back of the riverbank where you was?"

"Just the little gal," Jesse answered.

"Well, that makes seven, all told," said the boss muleskinner. "I checked them three that was cut off trying to get back from the stream. They're so full of feathers they'd fly if you launched 'em."

"All right, then"—the mountain man nodded—"you're set to roll. You oughtn't to have no trouble making it back to the company wagons."

"What you mean, *we* oughtn't? Ain't you coming?" Morgan Bates eyed Jesse, waiting with his fellow muleskinners, for the mountain man's answer.

"Nope, reckon not. The sons grabbed that little redhead boy the same as I figured they would. I got a stake in that kid and I mean to look after it. And another thing, too . . ."—Jesse paused while his blue eyes swept their faces—"I owe the pot a few dollars for not pegging that damn' Tim O'Mara, right off. He's the white son-of-a-bitch that's working for Brigham Young in this deal. Cripes, I've been dumb as a Mexican mule. He's a Mormon, he ditched this train to go on up to Salt Lake, he shows up again right along with Watonga's village, he gets it from the squaw about me taking his woman away from him . . . hell! The whole damn' mess is my fault, and, boys, I aim to clean it up. Beginning with Johnny and ending with that lousy Tim!"

"Talk's cheap," Joplin Smith, one of the Missouri hardcases, broke in acidly. "How you aim to get the kid back? Hell, they probably knocked his brains out the minute they got him behind them hills."

"By God, I don't know how I'm going to do it." Jesse scowled. "But one thing I do know. They ain't harmed the kid, and they won't. Not short of us getting him away from them, they won't." The mountain man paused, regarding the silent men with his strange, quiet eyes before continuing. "That big squaw is barren and she's set on getting a son for Watonga. Well, she's got him now. She sure ain't going to club him. I know how them hostiles are with boy kids. Happen they knock over a settler outfit, they'll near always scalp the little gals and hoist the boys. They're locoed on boy kids. If they wasn't, I wouldn't be here to know about it. I was grabbed outen a Injun burn-out like this one when I wasn't much more'n Johnny O'Mara's age. And I know what they'll do with that kid." There was another eye-sweeping pause then, and the mountain man concluded harshly: "The boy's mine now, and I ain't hankering to have no son of mine brung up Arapaho-style."

"You're rocking your head-hobbles, Jesse." Morgan Bates shook his head stubbornly. "You can't get that kid away from them. If you manage to get close to doing it, they'll kill him. Allowing they're the same about it as the Comanches and Kiowas down along the Santa Fé, they will."

"They ain't no different, Morgan. That's what's sweating me, too. Right off, I ain't got no ready answer for you, neither. But we, all of us, have got to do what we can."

"Such as what?" the dry-voiced Joplin Smith wanted to know.

"Well," the mountain man's answer rapped out unhesitatingly, "you boys get this emigrant bunch moving for our wagons. When you get there, tell Andy to hit for Gabe's fort, instanter. At the fort you can gather up some help and come along after me. Happen I can track Watonga till you get back with that help, maybe we can figure some way to snatch the kid."

"How the hell you expect us to find you?" The boss muleskinner's demand was short. "Even providing we can get a bunch together what's willing to try?"

"That ain't so hard as it might appear, right off. I

figure them Arapahoes to head north, pretty much
following the main line of the Medicine Road for
quite a spell. They're looking for buffalo, and, when
a northern Injun looks for buffalo, he don't look no
place quicker'n he does Cheyenne Mesa. That's over
west of the main road, and the road's the cleanest
trail to take to there from this part of the country."
The mountain man's narrowed eyes pounced on the
boss muleskinner's laconic opinion like a skinny cat
on a fat mouse. "God damn it, Morgan, that's it! The
powder! I know the stuff ain't mine to trade, but under the circumstances I allow old Gabe'll give me
the loan of half of it against that stack of peltries I
brung down from the Three Forks. And, by damn,
Watonga would give his left stone to get even half of
that Du Pont, wouldn't he?"

"By God, man!" the lank Joplin exploded admiringly. "You mean to swap him the powder for the
kid?"

"Why sure! I don't see how the tarnal hell we can
miss. Happen you and Morgan and the boys can get
them emigrants on up to Gabe's, pick up some help
there, and come along up the main trail with that
Pittsburgh and a dozen kegs of that Du Pont, and do
it all fast enough, we got that boy back sure as the
last drop drips. . . ." The mountain man broke his
words, the blue eyes leaping to Morgan Bates with
sudden intensity. "Not forgetting, Morgan, that
along with that powder I want you should bring me
a good, stiff coil of touch-off medicine . . . just in
case!"

Breaking out his wolf grin, the lean boss muleskinner nodded his understanding of the final,
cryptic instruction, expressed his agreement with
the general plan reservedly: "There's a chance, all

right. Allowing you can keep the trail without being caught at it, the Injuns follow the Medicine Road like you figure, you can open your dicker with them without they get jumpy and brain the kid, and that even with the powder you can get that red bitch to leave go of the boy . . . them and about forty other maybes I can think of."

"We got to gobble them maybes. What you say, boys? You all game for it?"

"I reckon." Joplin shrugged, saying it like he thought it, not giving a damn either way. His laconic agreement was hacked by a wave of sober nods from his fellow muleskinners, Morgan Bates putting the official company signature on the hasty contract with his slow-drawled grin.

"Me, I ain't got nothing to lose but a few days' pay and a scalp that ain't been washed since last July. Besides, I ain't never felt right about us crooking poor old Black Coyote outen his honest deal with Brigham Young and his blessed little Saints. I dearly love them Mormon bastards and anything I can do to prove it to them, I aim to get done. I got a daddy and two brothers was kilt in them saintly riots around Nauvoo back in 'Forty-Four, and I reckon they'd want me to make it up to old Brigham. Jesse . . ."—the black-bearded Missourian's grin, although opening another wide notch, failed, somehow, to match the beaded intentness of his dark eyes—"if you aim to finish delivery of that Du Pont to Watonga, I'll skin your red-wheeled wagon for you!"

"You'll get your pay"—Jesse Callahan's blue eyes were snapping—"and hold onto your hair, too. And finishing delivery of that Du Pont is what I aim. After all, old Brigham's a white man, no matter what

you Christian Gentiles think. And he's give his
bounden word that Watonga's to get that powder.
Outen my own great love and respect for my red
brothers, I got to see that the straight-give word of us
whites ain't allowed to green up with no tarnish!"

Many a center shot is fired for a hard joke. Unknowingly the wide-mouthed mountain man had
got his slug of cynical lead square in behind the left
shoulder of immediately future fact. He found the
bullet hole a sight quicker than he was looking to.

Chapter 7

Jesse made no effort to follow Watonga's war ponies. Instead, he headed back for Paiute Crossing. He knew Tall Elk would have ordered the village to knock down the teepees and pull out as soon as the emigrants left, knew, also, that it was a mort easier to track a 1,500-head horse herd and a passel of old men and squaws than to stick to 100 high-traveling trail raiders like Watonga's war party. He was more right than rockets on the day after the 3rd of July.

The village track lay north and west, just as it ought, to cut the Medicine Road like he'd figured, and it lay, broad and clear, as a bull's bottom in a Sharps' sight. A blind squaw could have followed it backward in a fog thicker than boiled-dog soup.

Jesse Callahan was far from dim-sighted, and the weather was clearer than a first-prize glass eye. He caught the village just as the long prairie twilight was playing out to pure black. Next morning, he gave them an hour's start, then set off dogging them, keeping to the west and well back. He expected to have some company from the east soon, and wanted to give them ample room to move in peacefully. Watonga should swing out of the tumbled hills to the mountain man's right before very long now, to join up with the moving village. That is, he should if Jesse had things figured right.

He had. Black Coyote's bunch, with Johnny, Tim, and Tall Elk, cut into the village track ahead of Jesse, about 10:00 A.M., passing so close to the granite outcropping back of which Jesse and Heyoka were hiding that in spite of her severe training along such lines the mountain man nearly had to strangle the little Sioux mare to prevent her whickering a lethal welcome to the nose-close Indian ponies.

Jesse got a real, big-eye look at the whole flashy parade. Watonga, looking bigger and blacker than ever in the clean morning sun, rode first, impressively haloed by the eight-foot aura of his white-eagle war bonnet, the gargoyle-faced Tall Elk jogging, hard-eyed, at his side. Between them, in a place of honor that would have dazzled any frontier boy of seven, and whistling free and easy as though he'd been delivered of an Arapaho squaw in the first place, Johnny O'Mara trotted proudly on a beautiful little calico pony. Jesse couldn't help grinning at the cheeky little sprout, sitting there on that sawed-off paint, chipper as a jay bird in a berry bush. Either the kid was dumber than all get out, or he was smart enough to play it happy. Whichever way, it made no difference. What counted was that he was well and frisky and showing more spunk than a spit-face kitten.

Back of this honor group cantered Black Coyote's high command: Gray Bear, Elk Runner, Yellow Leg, Blood Face, and the canine-jawed Dog Head—

preciously remembered faces, all of them, to the tensely watching Jesse. Behind the sub-chiefs, atop a wheezing pack pony, came Tim O'Mara, and the way that he came spread Jesse's blue eyes wide with justifiable surprise. Where the mountain man would have guessed the Indians would have been escorting the renegade Mormon like an honored guest, they had him laced onto that pony's back tighter than a wood tick on a wolf's tail.

Before Jesse could begin to guess at the possible reason for Tim's captivity, the renegade had ridden on past, closely followed by his special and delighted guard, the perpetually grinning Skull. Regardless of his puzzlement, the mountain man knew that the ropes binding Tim's feet beneath his mount's potbelly must have an explanation that very probably concerned Jesse, most personally. As Skull and the captive white man passed, Jesse knew that his first problem had just been put—the discovery of what lay behind Tim's fall from grace.

Strung out for a quarter mile back of the white man and his leering guard, eating the rising gray trail dust of the others, straggled the main pack of Watonga's flea-bitten coyotes. Watching the last of them disappear over the top of a mile-distant rise, Jesse let out his breath, eased off on Heyoka's nose wrap.

"By God, old clown," he muttered feelingly, "they're riding just right . . . heading to hook up with the village and not a scout or out-rider in the lot of them. *Hookahey*, Heyoka! Let's get out of here!"

The mountain man spent the first part of that night on a hogback ridge 600 feet above the fully rejoined Arapaho village. The lodge fires were lit early and Jesse could see from the distant movement of the tiny figures toward Watonga's central teepee that a powwow of some kind was coming up. To get closer to this he decided to risk a roundabout sneak up on the council gathering. There was never any telling what a Sioux-reared man could make out from sight-reading the fluent Indian hand signs and keeping an ear cocked for the louder bursts of Indian oratory. Providing he could get in close enough, he might learn plenty.

He had good luck. A spur of the very ridge he was on clearly ran down into the campsite, being close to twenty feet high where it ended in among the teepees and heavily covered with low brush. He was able to get up to within fifteen yards of Black Coyote's open-air Indian forum. Watonga and his six sub-chiefs were squatted around a blazing fir, chewing the last of the pemmican and discussing such varied topics as the lack of heavy buffalo sign, the best way to boil a fat dog, the comparative merits of the teepee techniques of the Arapahoes as against the Sioux and Cheyenne women, and, naturally, the legal status and problematical future hunting grounds of an erstwhile friendly white man suspect of having turned traitor in the small matter of the recent abortion of the attempt to wipe out the emigrant train. Jesse held his breath at this mention of Tim, waiting shadow-quiet for Watonga to proceed.

Presently the chief spoke to Gray Bear. "Go and get him, now."

Gray Bear nodded to Elk Runner and the two friends departed to return in a moment with the bound but glowering Tim O'Mara stalking between them. A quick look around the fire changed the renegade's expression from one of anger to one of uneasy apprehension. And with excellent reason.

Yellow Leg was there and he was a reassuring sight, his shriveled parchment face, snake's eyes, and dwarfed leg toting up to a sum of rare comfort. Blood Face squatted next to him, a still pleasanter vision, the birthmark that gave him his name spreading its sick stain from his forehead well past his loose, purple lips. Dog Head was pretty, too, and well named. His jaw and nose were long, with a mouth that began up by his ears and featured four hand-filed canines that glistened attractively whenever he chose to smile—which was about once every three years. Toad was equally winning, his bloated body, neckless head, and thick, warted skin giving ample evidence of the logic behind his name. The last and in size, least, of Watonga's head men was the most cheerful of the lot. Not, in rank, one of the sub-chiefs, this brave squatted well back from the others, only the handful of dry twigs that Yellow Leg threw on the fire at the approach of Tim O'Mara flaring to reveal his heretofore unnoticed presence to Jesse. His tall, elegantly proportioned comrades called him simply Skull. Very short for an Arapaho, Skull's continual wracking cough was the clue to the dread white man's plague that accounted for his skeleton-like emaciation. The broad, Mongol structure of his face, from whence, obviously, came his name, wore a perpetual, delighted grin. The fact that this expression was the result of jaw muscles contorted in their healing from a Comanche lance slash did nothing to detract from Skull's bright outlook. He appeared incapable of harming a weanling mouse—and would open his mother's guts for a fair horse or a handful of good powder. Skull was a war-raid orphan, adopted by Watonga himself. He was only nineteen, the best tracker and bloodiest knife fighter in the band, and Black Coyote's court favorite.

There were no introductions as Tim's guardians stepped back to give him the fire-lit central stage.

"What has Big Face to say?"

In his hiding place, Jesse marked the fact the Indians had a familiar name for the renegade, judging from this that Brigham Young's mission was not his first work among them.

"We trusted you," Watonga was continuing, "and you betrayed us. Do you deny it?"

The Arapaho chief had addressed his questions in Sioux, the common language of all the plains tribes, and to the hidden Jesse's continuing education Tim answered them in the pure, fluent tongue. Evidently little Johnny O'Mara had known what he was talking about when he had told Jesse that Tim knew as much about Indians as he did.

"*Wonunicun*," answered the renegade, using the Sioux apology word. "A mistake has been made. I don't even know what you are talking about."

"Then you shall," said Watonga. "Now, listen to this. You came among us bearing the word from the Mormon chief, telling of the gunpowder in Big Throat's goddam." (Big Throat was one of the Sioux names for Jim Bridger.) "Big Throat's friend, Tokeya Sha, he was too smart for us and the powder got away. That was not your fault. But then you came again, telling us you would show us how to get the powder in return for our helping you to attack the shabby white goddams and kill your woman. You even agreed that Tall Elk was to have the red-headed boy into the bargain. We agreed and we attacked. And, as we attacked, here came that cursed Tokeya Sha and nearly killed us all. Ten good warriors were left there in the Grass of the Wild Horse. Now then, answer this. How did Tokeya know about that attack?"

Jesse could see that Tim was as stunned by the turn of events as Jesse was, by hearing the full charge of the renegade's treachery. Tim looked help- lessly about him, began stumblingly to talk. Surely the chiefs could see that he had no way to prove he knew nothing of how that red-haired friend of Big Throat's had learned about the attack on the emi- grants. They would just have to believe that Big Face's tongue was straight, as it had always been with his red brothers. As to the new plan for seizing the gunpowder, he had really had one. But then Wa- tonga had seized him and made him prisoner and would not let him talk of it.

As the cornered renegade went along, his red fel- lows began nodding and grunting pleasantly. Tim took heart. It was clear that he was still the old mas- ter at befuddling these red half-wits. Hell, they were all as simple-minded as so many settlement goofs. All a man had to do was have guts and a gift of gab. Tim had guts enough to stuff a bear, with maybe a handful left over. As for gab, he never ran out of that. It was plain that he still had the gullible buz- zards firmly in hand. Secure in this belief, he wound up his speech abruptly.

When he had finished, Watonga took one step. Right out of that hand. "Well, well. Now that you have spoken, here is what I think. Big Face stinks like a sick dog."

Tim had time to gasp and that was all.

"Let us understand one another, brother," Black Coyote continued softly. "I say that you never had another plan for seizing the powder and that you plotted with Tokeya Sha to trap us in that meadow so that you could take all the powder and supplies for yourselves. I say that. . . ."

"Black Coyote is an idiot!" Tim's words burst angrily. "Where is the sense in such a plan? This Tokeya has stolen my woman. He is a faithful friend of Big Throat's. I have been well paid by the Mormon chief. I . . ."

Watonga interrupted the interrupter. "Who can make sense out of the ways of white men? We think Big Face is a liar, and we no longer trust him. I think we will kill him, too."

"How will we do it?" asked Skull happily.

"I'd like to burn his feet, first," suggested Yellow Leg amicably. "Like the Utes did to this leg of mine."

"No, no," Blood Face put in hurriedly. "Too simple. There is no art in burning like that."

"That's right," Dog Head agreed. "No art in that."

"How about just taking the tongue out?" asked Elk Runner. "I mean before the other things, of course. That always feels good."

"Yes," his friend, Gray Bear, sided in earnestly. "And we could flay the tongue first. You remember how that Kiowa showed us last summer. You heat the hot grease until it is blue, and then. . . ."

"Enough!" snapped Watonga. "We'll leave it to my woman, Tall Elk. She'll know how to deal with a white brother who gives our plans away and lets us be trapped like wet-nosed children. Tall Elk has a head for such things. That squaw's a real artist. She'll know how to do it best."

"Yes, nobody like Tall Elk for fun. I'm thinking that, too." Skull was trying to be helpful.

"No matter what you think," barked Black Coyote. "Any of you. It will be as I say. We will leave here tomorrow and go on after the buffalo. After we have found a herd and made our winter meat, we'll have a dance with this *sunke. Nohetto,* that's all."

Jesse didn't need Black Coyote's final word to tell him that Tim was flayed closer than a newly skinned skunk. When the Arapahoes got their buffalo hunting done, they would set up a scalp dance, a real *Pekocan sunpi wacipi.* It was the season for such affairs. And when the last ceremony was over, Tim would have tripped the light fantastic right on through the front ballroom of *Wanagi Yata,* the Indian Land of the Final Shadow. As for Tim, the former wagon guide for the Kansas emigrants and sometime Mormon jack-of-all-dirty-trades was thinking of how he had never learned to dance, and of how he would hate like tarnal sin to take his first lesson from Watonga and his Wind River Arapahoes.

All the next day, Jesse trailed the slow-moving village, the welcome shade of twilight bringing him and his Indian quarry out onto the main Medicine Road. As he watched the scattered caravan crowd out of the rough country and line out on the broad, wheel-rutted track of the Oregon Trail, the new direction of the hostile line of march together with the leisurely trail gait with which they headed into it brought a grunt of satisfaction from the mountain man.

Scanning the dusty southward reach of the trail behind the Arapaho cavalcade, he caught the distant glimmer of the jagged Green River range that marked the site of Fort Bridger. *Wagh!* Plenty good, by damn. Gabe's peaks. Everything was smack-dab on the schedule he had given Morgan Bates and his Missouri muleskinners. It brought a good feeling inside a man to find his tricky Indian arithmetic come toting up to a sure-fire sum. The red buzzards were heading north, taking the wide-open Medicine Road while they were about it, and traveling plumb slow. And at this point they weren't three days' mule drive above Gabe's fort!

Later that evening, Jesse, shivering in the night cold of his fireless hiding place above the Indian camp, had time for a little more frontier sum toting. The answer came out that, if Andy Hobbs had hammered his mules from first light to late dark, every day since Morgan and the boys had gotten back to him with the emigrant survivors, he might now be at Fort Bridger. That would put the arrival of the powder wagon at Jesse's present position at about four, probably five, days away. Cripes! A man would need some luck now.

If Watonga headed up the Medicine Road by regular marches, even not hurrying his present pace any, the powder wagon *still* could miss ever catching up to him. And if he headed west, into the goat-wild tangle of the Wasatches, it *sure* never would. It was a spot for some big luck and fast figuring. Depending on what action daylight brought from Black Coyote, Jesse might have to move on in and make his lone-hand stab at snatching Lacey's boy away from him.

What daylight did bring was neither of the things the mountain man feared—it was worse than both of them. With sunup, the nerve-strung trapper saw all the lodges, save one, come tumbling down. By eight o'clock, the main village had departed, moving straight up the Medicine Road in long marching order. Left behind were Watonga's starkly black hunting teepee and his 100 hard-core warriors.

These war-painted remainders made no move to travel, lolling around the deserted camp until close to high noon. Jesse had not been able to see Johnny among the multi-ponied panoply of the departing village but an hour ago he had spotted Tall Elk coming out of the chief's lodge and had guessed from this, with a sense of vast relief, that the boy hadn't left with the main tribe.

With the sun directly overhead, things picked up down below, Watonga appearing in full hunting garb to lead his restless pack through the yelling ceremony of a short buffalo stomp. Jesse's interest perked, at once. By damn, this was more like it. Evidently this was a picked group of hunters, hanging back while the main bunch drifted to the Wind River winter camp. He should have guessed as much from the fact they kept no lodges, and from the hefty size of the horse herd that stayed with them. You needed plenty of ponies to run buffalo and tote meat, happen you got into a good bunch of young cows.

Now, if the sons would only lay around camp a couple of days to give the powder wagon a chance to get up from Fort Bridger. . . . They didn't.

The mountain man had no more than put the wish that they would into his head, than he saw Watonga's black lodge coming down. Minutes later, the whole passel of them was streaming off west, nearly square away from the Medicine Road, into a country where a wagon could go easily—providing it could fly

Jesse knew this country. The track led up toward Portola Springs, through Carson's Cañon by way of Rockpile Meadow. It was the direct route to Coulter's Meadow (the hostiles' Cheyenne Mesa), the famed North Park of the Rockies, where buffalo could be found when they weren't any place else in the Indian world.

Riding hard, the mountain man got uptrail of the savage column, tied Heyoka in an alder clump, bellied his way up over the trail where it squeezed through a narrow granite defile leading into Carson's Cañon. Here, he could all but spit on the braves as they filed past beneath him. Plenty close, anyway, to check for certain sure if they had Johnny with them. He had to *know* that. He couldn't just guess at it.

Ten minutes later, Watonga's lump-jawed face came bobbing over a ridge top 100 yards away. The chief topped out on the ridge, started haunch-sliding his pony down into the declivity above which Jesse lay. After him, piled the grim train of his followers headed by Tall Elk and Johnny O'Mara. When the woman and the boy passed below him, Jesse noted the youngster was drawn-looking, no longer chipper and whistling. Looking at the brute faces of his Arapaho escort, the mountain man could understand the change. The kid might be spunky enough, but the first excitement was gone. No doubt he had expected his white folks to catch the Indians and get him away from them long before this. More specifically, he probably had looked for Tokeya, the Minniconjou to come thundering out of the sunset and kill the hell out of these mangy red dogs, releasing Red Eagle amid a withering hail of gunfire and high-pressure Sioux screaming. Now three days of hard trailing through a lonely wilderness, with no sign of a conquering white hero any place, had silenced the boy. He was a pinched-faced, scared-looking kid when he jogged

past below Jesse on the little spotted pony. The
mountain man's heart turned over in him with a
heavy tug that lumped his throat proper. By God, if
he didn't get that boy away from Watonga and his
slate-faced wife, it wouldn't be for not trying!

Waiting for the Arapahoes to get on past, Jesse got
his second jolt. At the tail of the bunch, flanked by
Yellow Leg and Dog Head, followed by the grinning
Skull, came the bound and scowling Tim O'Mara.
The captive renegade, eyes red from spending his
nights laced, upright, against a tree, a long week's
trail dust blurring his slab face, buckskins dirt-
stinking from not having been off of him in six suns,
looked about as happy as a short-haired hound in a
bluestone hailstorm.

Raising his head and shifting his body to get a
better look, Jesse's hand moved a fraction. A walnut-
sized pebble rattled over the edge of the rimrock,
fell toward the passing Indians. At the first rattle,
Tim's nervous eyes snapped upward, the slit
glances of his red companions following swiftly.

Jesse jerked his head back down, lay, tense and
eartuned. A cat couldn't have been any more strung
up to jump. God damn it, why did a man have to get
careless just when his chances were nearly snowed
anyway? Tim had seen him, sure as hell was hot,
and likely the rest of the cussed slant eyes, too. The
guttural questions barked up from below did nothing to loosen the bite of the mountain man's nails in
the scaly granite of the rimrock.

"What was that?" Yellow Leg's challenge burst
growlingly.

"I heard nothing," said Skull. "Only a pebble rattling down. A lizard, maybe. Who would know?"

"I would!" snapped Dog Head. "I thought I saw

something get back of that rock up there. It was bright, like hair. I'm going up there."

Jesse's belly shrank and the slime dried in his mouth. He gathered himself to leap and run for it. Tim, bass voice sneering, spared him the jump. "Sure it was hair. I saw it. An old boar marmot. Very bright color, almost red. Big as a man's head. He went right behind that rock, like Dog Head says. That one you are pointing at, there, Dog Head. Didn't you see it, cousin?"

"I don't know. It looked too red, not gray enough for a whistle dog."

Dog Head was obdurate, inspiring Jesse to give Tim's surprising co-operation a gentle boost. He hadn't tried the trick since he was a boy with Waniyetula, but there'd been a time not even Winter Boy, that prairie magician of animal imitations, could beat Tokeya at whistling-up marmots. Pouching his taut cheeks, he brought the breath high and jerky through his clenched teeth.

"Ho, ho! You hear that, you dogface, you?" Yellow Leg was laughing at his comrade. "It is even as Big Face said. An old dog whistler, nothing more. Come on, we fall too far back. Watonga wants to pitch his lodge at those springs tonight. *Hopo. Hookahey!*"

"All right," Dog Head gave in grumblingly. "*Hopo.* It was too red, though. Much too red."

When they had gone, Jesse rolled back off the rimrock, legged it for Heyoka. Mounting up, he raced the gray mare back toward the Medicine Road and the previous night's Indian camp.

There, twenty minutes' work with his knife and some cook fire charcoal on the back of his buckskin shirt, and he had done all he could to steer Morgan Bates and the hoped-for muleskinners. When he swung back up on Heyoka, kicking her around for Carson's Cañon again, the shirt stayed behind, flapping on a cottonwood stake jammed into the broad trace of the main Medicine Road. Happen a stray gang of Indians didn't wander along to tear it down, meantime a pack of white teamsters from Fort Bridger, providing they moseyed this way and could read Sioux sign scratching, might get the idea that at this point in the Medicine Road Tokeya the Minniconjou had lit out toward Rockpile Meadow, hot on the tracks of a big black coyote and a very small red eagle.

Chapter 8

Tim O'Mara, the renegade Mormon, was well born into a bad trade. Strong as a buffalo, tough as a range bull, tricky as a fox in a farmer's barnyard, moral as a stray dog, Tim was bred to get fat grazing trouble's lean pasture. You get yourself a bad lot like that snubbed up to where his string is shorter than a broken crotch-cloth lace, and you can dig your toes in for some fast shuffles. In the case of the "old boar marmot" diving behind that rock back there on the cañon rim, Tim had seen enough to know that Dog Head had been right. That marmot had been way too bright-colored. Too bright-colored and red-haired. Too narrow-eyed and sunburned. Too wide-mouthed and human-looking.

Tim's first impulse had been to yell out and put Jesse Callahan out of business for good. His second thought, plugging his big-lipped mouth tighter than the bung in a powder barrel, had been that the hidden white man represented what might be his last link with the world of safety, a world that was cur-

rently falling behind Tim's scalp-itch-inspired reha-
bilitation at a shuffling pony gait of thirty miles a
day. At the moment Tim had no idea how he was going to profit by his knowledge that Jim Bridger's
red-headed wagon guide was trailing Black Coyote's buffalo hunters, but the dry breast of necessity
always has a mouthful of milk for the nurser who
sucks hard enough. By the time the Arapahoes had
stopped to give their ponies a noon rest in Rockpile
Meadow, he had it figured pretty closely.

There could be only one reason for the mountain
man's presence. He meant, somehow, to sneak in
and release that damned brat of Lacey's. That gave
Tim his idea. The idea was a revolutionary one for a
totally bad man, but Tim O'Mara was a born revolu-
tionist. If he could some way beat Jesse Callahan to
that triumph, could in some way manage to free the
boy and return him to the white settlements, he
would then be in a position to share in some of the
hump fat of heroism that would undoubtedly reward that rescue.

The hog's bulk of Tim's body was free of the fat of
sentiment. The Mormon hireling would as quickly
have shot the boy as saved him, providing the pay
was better that way. As it was, if he could get the
captive boy out of the Arapaho camp, Tim would be
as welcome in the white settlements as salt in a thin
stew, and not just welcomed but in all likelihood
pardoned for his apparent part in the Wild Horse
Bend massacre. As far as his own bulging neck went,
Tim was gambling less than nothing in any attempt
he might make to free Lacey's boy. His Arapaho
brothers were carrying him along only until they
might find the time to serve him up in style—the Indian taste for traitor meat being what it was. On this

score the captive white man had no illusions, nor was the worry attendant on that score any great problem. The only problem in Tim's whole, sly world at the moment was how to break away with that little red-haired drip-nose of Lacey's. Come sundown that afternoon at Portola Springs that problem would be taken care of, too, and along this latter line the Mormon had some particular ideas.

Skull, his constant guard, had always had a sort of mutual rascal's admiration for the squat renegade. In matters of tactical execution—the business of how best to incise a scalp skin for the neatest removal of the hair; how, most cleanly, to cut a live victim's tongue out, or burn his toes off while not damaging the main foot in the least; how, with the greatest efficiency, to open an opponent's bowels in dark-of-the-moon knife fighting, and such other little vital niceties of frontier survival—in such matters the settlement-bred Big Face was an acknowledged genius. In his youthful, fresh way, Skull looked up to Tim. His was the clean-cut, clear-eyed, inspired admiration of the ambitious tyro for the finished master butcher.

Of late, this touching admiration of Skull's had taken the course of allowing his bull-shouldered charge camp freedom at the end of the day's ride. At the same time. Tim was not entirely dazzled by this generous treatment. To the student of red psychology of Tim's rank, the motives of Watonga's protégé in this apparent kindly action must bear yet a bit more probing. There was always the matter of counting the big coup. Bored with the routine dullness of mothering a doomed captive, helpless and with his feet tied, the young brave had begun turning Tim loose in the hope the desperate white man might make a break for freedom. Although it went by the name of Comanche charity among the plains tribes, *ley de fuga* by any other name was the same law. A prisoner ran—he got shot. And *nohetto*, there you were. Oh, maybe not shot. Maybe knifed, or lanced, or skull clubbed. Whatever looked like the most fun at the moment. Anyway, killed. And with that, *wagh!* You had your coup. Always remembering that where the guard was a young man without particular reputation, and the prisoner was a rascal of Big Face's considerable record, it wasn't just an ordinary one. It was the big coup.

The Arapahoes surprised the captive emigrant guide by halting early, five miles short of Portola Springs, surprised and delighted him. An advance scout party had ridden back from Crow Mesa, a high, barren grassland that formed one wing of Coulter's Meadow, with the news of a fine herd. Watonga had ordered his lodge up on the spot, called an immediate council. After a brief session with his sub-chiefs, it was decided not to try for the buffalo until tomorrow. Meat and powder were both too low. No chances of a hurried or careless stalk were to be considered.

Gray Bear and Elk Runner, the senior hunters, were sent out to tail the herd and figure the best plan for tomorrow's hunt. The rest of the camp busied itself readying weapons, cutting favored ponies out of the horse herd, staking them close in to the cooking fires for quick use in the morning. Old *pte* was best hunted in the misty hours, and from the backs of fresh, strong ponies.

The unexpected confusion of preparation wasn't the only smile fortune had ready for the hapless Tim. Johnny O'Mara was kept pretty much to Watonga's lodge, within hand's reach of his fierce red foster mother. In this camp, the chief's lodge had been pitched against a heavy fringe of cedar timber—timber that stretched, unbroken, along the cañon's floor for the back four miles of trail. And, now, Tall Elk was hustling overtime, completely busy with the dressing of the last of the meat and the heating of the *tunkes* (red-hot stones, dropped in the paunch skin cooking bags to heat the water for boiling meat) for the pre-hunt feast.

There was but a short half hour of weak daylight remaining. If Tim could elude Skull, snatch Johnny out of Black Coyote's lodge, and get into the dark timber, it might go many minutes before either fugitive was missed. Minutes in which fast horses could be snaked out of the pony herd. Snaked out and scrambled astride of. Scrambled astride of and kicked in the rump. And quirted for their scrubby lives down the back trail.

Given twenty minutes' start, full night would come before any considerable pursuit could catch up mounts and get on the trail. Given full night and two fast ponies, Tim would smile about his chances of keeping Watonga's coyotes from cornering him and Lacey's kid. He was a real lad, Tim O'Mara. One with a big head. The marrow fat in those sly skull bones had greased his way out of more than one narrow squeak in his twenty-odd years of dealing with such as Black Coyote. *Woyuonihan!* Tim respected himself.

With daylight, once well away from his pursuers, he and Johnny could hole up, riding nights only. Or even walking, if it came to that. In any event, making it safely into old Bridger's fort with the cursed kid alive and unharmed. If they should encounter

Jesse Callahan along the escape trail, all right. If they didn't, all right, too. Either way, the desperate long bow that the renegade had drawn on his chance to avoid certain destruction at the hands of his former red fellows and to win a haven of safety and forgiveness with the frontier whites at Fort Bridger would bury its arrow to the fletching in the fleeting and tricky target of complete success. *Hum-hun-he!* Pay the brave honors to Tim O'Mara, you red *heyokas*. There was a real chief, that Big Face. Even if he had to say it himself!

The condemned Mormon could see the holes in the blanket of his plan quite easily. They were as plain as the pock pits on a Pawnee's nose. Even so, a man in Tim O'Mara's position couldn't look too closely at a plot's complexion. Given one was dealing with captors like Tall Elk and Watonga, his best chance in a year of waiting wouldn't pile any higher than two bone-dry buffalo chips.

When Skull finally untied him to let him off the pony, Tim put on a good act of being mortally weary. Crawling weakly over to it, he collapsed beside a down log whose butt lay hidden in the fringing woods not thirty paces from Black Coyote's lodge. In turning around three times, like a choosy dog before lying down, the captive was careful to select a final spot where his outflung right hand lay less than inches away from a broken cedar snag, thick as a man's wrist, two feet long, sun-dried to iron hardness.

Skull, lance-scar grin going full blast, idled over and slumped on the far side of the log. A great actor, Skull. One of the best. In twenty seconds his snores were rattling the cones off half the cedars in the forest. Back of the snores, his pouchy eyes showed a hairline slit of glittering pupil between the heavy-closed lids. *Wagh*, what the hell? Skull always slept with the eyes a little open.

To Tim, lying panther-tight on the far side of the log, it made no difference if Skull were really asleep or not. He would be in a minute.

The renegade's eyes flicked left, out across the busy camp, right, over to the chief's deserted lodge, back again to the cedar chunk at his slack fingertips. Skull had time to pop his eyes open—if not his mouth. The cedar chunk bounced off his parchment-wrinkled temple, backed by an arm and shoulder of bear-like power and weight. Skull went down behind the log, scarred grin working widely and loosely, empty eyes staring straight up, dead as a water rat in a blacksnake's belly.

Tim shaded thirty seconds getting over that log, grabbing Skull's trade musket and knife. Bellying into the cedar tangle, he cat-footed his way up to the back of Watonga's lodge. Once there, the business of slitting the rear skins and popping through into the lodge's interior added another five seconds.

"*Psstt*. Shut up, Johnny," he hissed at the startled boy. "It's me, Tim. Come on, boy. You and me are getting outen here. You grab my shirt tail and foller along. Jump it now, and no noise!"

Johnny, rolling up off the pile of buffalo robes he'd been lying on, started crawling toward the waiting Tim. Halfway he stopped, felt inside the front of his faded shirt, started crawling back toward the robes.

Tim was after him like a light streak, nailing him as he reached the furry pile. "You damn' little louse head. What're you up to? One damn' peep outen you, boy, and I'll brain you."

"I ain't going to peep, Tim," the boy whispered. "I got to get something. It must've slid out of my shirt. . . ." He was rummaging in the robes as he talked, coming up shortly with a bright Green River skinning blade. "Here it is, Tim. See?"

"Come on, boy. Crawl after me. And, remember, you make a sound and we're both shot and scalped."

Johnny nodded, big-eyed, scrambling across the lodge floor to follow his rescuer through the knife slit. His feet were just disappearing through it when the teepee entrance behind him grew black against the graying twilight.

In Tall Elk's hand was a short stone maul used in pounding the dried buffalo beef before throwing it into the paunch skin to boil. Indian-wise, the squaw made no outcry, slipped back out the front flap of the lodge and on around its side, gliding soundlessly as some monstrous black ferret.

The Arapaho woman had not seen Tim, expected only to startle the white boy in a clumsy escape try. The training of a chief's son could not begin too early. Ya Slo must be taught that a good warrior always looked to his rear the last thing. She came powder-stepping around the lodge as the Mormon, meaning to carry the excited boy the first part of the way, was swinging Johnny over his shoulder.

With the game in full sight, Tall Elk broke her silence. The first hint Tim had that his scheme had lost the blessing of Wakan Tanka was the explosive grizzly snarl of the Arapaho war challenge. This cry, patterned after the coughing roar of the wounded silvertip, short, harsh, deep bass, was like no other sound on the plains. Hearing it, the white renegade wheeled in time to see the immense squaw towering over him, buffalo maul back swung for the real coup.

Tim O'Mara's erratic mind was faulty only on the longer hauls. In short spells it worked like gun grease in a dry barrel. Rolling backward, he twitted the slight form of the boy between himself and the striking squaw. Tall Elk, swerving her falling arm to avoid braining Johnny, was thrown off balance.

Instantly the burly Mormon had her locked in a bear grip, the two of them rolling and growling in the flying cedar needles with all the fury of fighting dogs. Johnny, scudding free of the tangle, dove for the sanctuary of the teepee slit, making it just as Watonga and a dozen braves swept around the lodge.

Their arrival saved nobody's skin but Tim O'Mara's. Unable to unsheath the knife he had stolen from Skull, he had lost his own grip on Tall Elk's maul arm. The raging squaw was on the point of pulverizing the renegade's head when Black Coyote and his warriors piled into the mêlée.

It took a good half of the braves to seize and subdue Tall Elk, the remaining half surrounding the recumbent Tim. The white man lay where he was, making noble effort not to twitch an eye, knowing the least move might put his trigger-nerved, erstwhile business associates on top of him.

The squaw was raving out her story to Watonga, and, when she had finished, the huge chief nodded to the Mormon.

"You heard the woman, Big Face. But you tell great stories, too. Good for a laugh, always. So talk now. Now it is your turn. A laugh is never bad before food. Go on. Our ears are uncovered. Let the braves have a laugh before they put their lances through your liver."

Tim ran his eyes around his audience, found it creepily attentive. Licking his thick lips, he arose and stepped forward, raising his right arm in the gesture used to request polite listening.

The glitter-eyed circle laughed, nodding the one to the other. *Waste*, good. Old Big Face was all right. He wasn't going to cheat them. He was a real talker. You had to admit that. A real windbag. And no *can'l wanka*, no coward. Not Big Face. *H'g'un*, courage, Big Face! Go on.

In the moment of silence before he began talking, the Mormon traitor made his gamble and played it. It was dark now. Skull's death might well go unnoticed until morning. He had cached his guardian's gun back in the timber, had his knife hidden under his shirt. *Wagh!* Short odds, sure. So what? All a man had left now was his mouth.

"I grew lonely with only Skull to be with. None of you, my true cousins, would talk to me. A lonely man longs for talk. And then I thought of the boy in the teepee. My heart is big for a man child, like any Arapaho's. That big. This Tall Elk will let no one near the boy. And as you know this boy is the son of my white squaw. I thought the boy would want to talk, too, to hear his own tongue. Skull left me, saying he was going back in the timber and make a buffalo dream for tomorrow. Skull honors me. You all know that. So I gave him my honor word. But I was lonely. So I came to the boy. The squaw was working in front so I had to come in the back. *Nohetto*, there you are."

The braves looked at one another, scowling their disappointment. *Iho!* Well, well! Big Face was failing in his old age. No laugh here. Just a straight tongue. Too simple. No imagination. Any man could get lonely around that cursed Skull. Naturally. They shifted their gazes to Black Coyote, awaiting his word.

"Where is Skull?" asked the chief presently.

"Off in the trees, like I said." The renegade shrugged. "He was going to make dirt first. Then go make his dream. He said he would stay in the trees until first light, making a big dream. He said the need for meat was that bad. That he thought Black Coyote needed a real dream for tomorrow's hunt."

Tim paused, assaying the effect of his tale on the blank-faced braves. Apparently the assay ran a little short. Clearly feeling this, the Mormon nervously fattened it up a bit.

"Oh, and yes. Skull was going to see to his ponies. Going to bring them up from the herd for tomorrow. Right after the dream he was going to do that."

It was a good try, worthy of the politician's brain bequeathed Tim by his Hibernean forebears, and it had several of the braves nodding their understanding of such a serious business. Dreams were big things. Very important. Perhaps Black Coyote should reconsider his decision to let Tall Elk put this Big Face on the red holy pole. After all, the need for meat *was* great. And if Skull's dreams were successful . . .

The nods had barely started when Dog Head's long jaw opened to snap them into instant motionlessness. "He had already brought his ponies up. I helped him."

"Go get Skull," ordered Watonga, his eyes studying the way the white man's skin was going gray under its travel-dust cover while the little silence born of Dog Head's laconic statement was living its brief moment, and dying. "We will leave it to Skull. But be careful. If he is truly in a dream, don't wake him. He can talk later."

Yellow Leg and Dog Head were back in less than a minute.

"Skull won't talk for a long time," vouchsafed the former. "Not for a very long time."

"Not for any time," added the latter succinctly.

"Where did you find him?" asked Black Coyote softly.

"Back of the log where he lay down with Big Face," explained Yellow Leg. "He won't need all those ponies he brought up now. Just one."

"His best one," agreed Dog Head reverently, "that the journey to *Wanagi Yata* may be swift and pleasant."

"*Aii-eee!*" Watonga's sibilant answering hiss wasn't so low but what the pain in it was evident. Skull, for all his consumptive shortcomings, had been the light of the chief's fierce eye. "Anything else?"

"His gun was gone. The knife, too. You know that knife? The one with the white handle and the black skull burned on it? I always wanted that knife. . . ." Yellow Leg's suspended words took the eyes of all to the putty-faced Tim O'Mara.

By this time, the rest of the braves had come up from the cooking fires to crowd soundlessly behind the Mormon's accusers. In the silence Watonga stepped forward, put his hand inside the white man's hunting shirt, stepped back to hold aloft the bone-handled, skull-emblazoned signature on Tim's death warrant.

His words spilled like glacier water down the rigid channel of the Mormon's spine. "We will give him to Tall Elk now. She caught him."

This was all he said, but as to the manner and immediacy of Tim's demise he couldn't have said more had he orated all night. The squaw, who had retrieved Johnny O'Mara from the teepee, handed the child to Watonga, shifted the blunt-stoned maul to her right hand, stepped toward the waiting white captive. The braves pulled silently back, making a lance-studded circle.

Halfway across this circle, the crouching Tall Elk hesitated, interrupted by a commotion in the back rank of watching braves. The outer warriors parted to admit a newcomer, all eyes flicking in his direction.

Blood Face was excited, his silence-gesture sweeping dramatically with the barking—"*A-ah!*"— that announced his arrival. It was the tribal warning word of sudden danger and it commanded precedence over even a traitor-killing.

"I was tracking Mato, Kicking Bear, my best buffalo pony. He wandered back along the cañon trail from whence we came today. The light was going bad and so were the tracks. But I saw those other tracks. The light wasn't that bad."

"What other tracks?" Watonga's question was instant and intense.

"Arapaho moccasin. Toed-in."

"Snake!" the name burst from a dozen slit-mouths, labeling the enemy people, the Shoshone.

"No, Shoshone!" Blood Face's contradiction was harsh. "Minniconjou! I know that track. I have studied it well. Do not forget, I was the last scout, before Toad, to leave that red-wheeled goddam's trail before the Water Road of the Pines."

"Tokeya Sha!" Tall Elk snarled the hated name into the quick silence.

"Aye," nodded Blood Face. "Tokeya Sha, the Minniconjou."

Turning to await Watonga's word on Blood Face's

startling discovery, the braves were interested to see
the chief's huge jaw spreading the frost of a slow
smile across his coarse features. "*Waste*," growled
the hulking savage. "Good, good."

Blood Face had expected more than this out of the
drama of his revelation, showed his irritation immediately. "How is this? I bring Watonga news of his
great enemy. I tell him that Tokeya Sha is following
him. And he does no more than stand there grinning like a dog coyote smelling bitch-heat blood!"

"I just thought of something," answered Watonga, letting the grin spread, unchecked. "Let me
ask you. Who gets the first rules of *woyuonihan*?
Even above the best friend?"

"The worst enemy." Blood Face frowned. "Any
heyoka knows that."

"All right, then. We owe this Tokeya Sha hard
courtesy rules. Am I talking straight?"

His answer was a wave of scowling nods. Erasing
his slack smile, Watonga added his own scowl to the
others.

"So, then. Who gave us this white mongrel in the
first place? Who was it attacked our ambush in the
Bend of the Wild Horses, thus letting us know of
Big Face's treachery?" The chief's repeated questions were accompanied by glowering thumb stabs
at the cornered Mormon.

"Tokeya Sha, who else?" admitted Blood Face.

"Even so," Watonga nodded. "And is the Sioux
Fox to outdo the Arapaho Coyote in the matter of
simple *woyuonihan*?"

By now, the listening braves were beginning to
swing into the drift of their chief's shifty thinking,
their big mouths slackening into a splattering of
loose-lipped grins.

"Truly, it must not happen that way," said Yellow Leg seriously. "Clearly we cannot avoid this matter of courtesy. It must be as Watonga is thinking."

"Well?" Blood Face's growl showed all the resentment of the slow mind left behind by swifter ones. "What in *pte*'s name *is* Watonga thinking? I am lost as a blind wolf whelp six feet from a hind tit."

Watonga's deep gutturals boomed out, giving the answer to them all. "When this stinking Big Face betrayed us for the first time, Tokeya Sha attacked us and so warned us of the betrayal. Now Big Face has betrayed us for the second time. He has tried to steal my little white son, Ya Slo. *Nohetto*, there you are. This time Watonga will leave Big Face in the middle of the trail for Tokeya Sha. It is *woyuonihan*, courtesy rules, that's all."

Chapter 9

Jesse, moving as close on Watonga's backside as a man dared in shut-in country, cast a worried eye skyward. Above the overhanging cañon escarpments, the sun glow was cooling out. Already the gray of early evening was blurring the hostile pony tracks. Another five minutes and a cat couldn't see that trail, with glasses.

As it was, Jesse had to follow it afoot the last mile. And being off his horse, with the cussed Heyoka tied in a cedar clump a mile back there, didn't add to a man's easy breathing, either. Due to the brush-choked nature of the cañon, he'd had to hang farther back than he liked, too. In more open country a man could see to take his chances. In here, with the scrub and all, you had to tread mighty light and far back. One thing, anyway, he had plenty of room now.

The Arapahoes would surely make Portola Springs their camp for tonight—were, no doubt, already there. That gave him a good six miles to play with. He'd sneak those miles plenty quickly, once dark shut down. Be right on top of old Watonga when he broke camp next morning.

Rounding a blind corner in the narrow track, he nearly knocked heads with the fact he wouldn't have to wait until morning for Black Coyote. He was on top of him, right now.

The grazing Indian pony threw up his head, stood staring, prick-eared, nostrils flaring. The mountain man knew another second would bring the nervous animal the hated *Wasicun* scent, start him to whistling out the warning-whicker.

"Waste, sunke wakan. Waste, waste." Jesse muttered the Indian words like a prayer, slipped back into the screening brush as he did so, crouched, breath held, awaiting the little beast's reaction.

Confused by the familiar, gut-deep tongue, the pony hesitated, snuffled curiously, forgot its momentary alarm, fell to grazing again.

Seconds later, Blood Face trotted down the trail.

"Ho, there, Mato! May Wakan Tanka curse you with spavins and stringhalt. An hour in camp, and here you are two miles along the back trail!" The pony moved a few yards away from Blood Face, as the sub-chief came sidling up to seize its trailing halter rope. "Next time Watonga finds a herd of buffalo and calls an early camp, I'll stake you so close to the . . ."

The brave's voice broke in mid-threat, his eyes going quickly to the thick dust of the trail a few paces beyond the pony. Only a second he hesitated, before swinging up on Mato and turning him for camp. After all, when you're one of the best trackers on the short grass, you don't need more than a second to single out a Sioux moccasin stamp from 400 barefoot pony prints.

In his piñon scrub cover, Jesse cursed. Had the

red son seen his tracks, or hadn't he? Chances were, he hadn't. The light was nearly gone and, besides, what the hell difference did it make? A man ought to be thanking Wakan Tanka that the Arapahoes hadn't seen *him*, not fretting about whether he'd spotted his moccasin prints. As a matter of calm fact, the brave probably hadn't even seen those. Anyway, Jesse sure as sin hoped he hadn't. It was quirky enough trailing 100 pucker-bung hostiles without they were onto your being after them.

Piecing together what he knew of the Carson's Cañon trail, with what the Arapaho sub-chief had growled at his wandering pony, the mountain man figured Watonga must be camped in Carson's Creek Flats, two miles ahead, five short of Portola Springs. Also that the reason for the halt had been the discovery of buffalo ahead. Blood Face had said so, and the sub-chief's word was good enough for Jesse. Now, any sizable herd would not be down in the cañon but up on Coulter's Meadow, somewhere beyond the springs. That was a ten-mile trot from Watonga's present camp. The sons would have to leave in the dark, tomorrow, probably about four, to get up on the herd by daylight.

The more he thought of it, the better it shaped up. The Indians would no doubt make their hunting camp at Portola Springs, leave Johnny and the squaw there to get ready for the meat dressing. The hunters would likely be gone the best part of the day. Cripes, a man couldn't ask for a much better shot than looked to be coming up—a near-deserted camp, heavy timber, one squaw to handle, and ten hours to handle her in! If a Minniconjou-trained gambler couldn't make a hand like that pay off, he'd just as well forget the whole game.

When Jesse snaked out of the brush to go dog-trotting back toward the hidden Heyoka, the set of his mouth and eyes were those of a man who had just drawn three cards to an inside straight—and made it.

Carson's Creek Flats lay like the bulge of a paunch skin in the slender channel of the cañon, the narrowed neck pointing toward Jesse. In this regard, the mountain man's approach to the Indian camp site, cautiously made about 5:00 A.M., was necessarily a blind one. There was no way to see into the flats save to follow the main trail squarely on into them. Sneaking around the last turn in that trail, hand-leading Heyoka, Jesse's eyes widened.

The Indians were completely gone, all right, but they had left a little something behind for Tokeya Sha, the Minniconjou. Its name was Tim O'Mara and it was rawhide-bound, hand and foot, to a four-inch sapling stump in the center of the deserted clearing, and stark naked.

The first flash that tightened the trapper's tenderloins was that Watonga had built a *wick-munke* for him, using Tim as bait. Then, given a little thought, the idea of a trap didn't hold up too well. Even if Watonga knew he was after him, he had ought to know better than to try and bait Jesse with Tim. Or to bait him at all, after falling into Jesse's trap at Jackpine Slash. By cripes, there was something fishier here than Friday in St. Patrick's parish. In a spot like this, there was only one sure thing to do: circle the whole flats and make dead certain there wasn't a pack of Arapahoes ambushed to jump him the minute he moseyed out to sniff around Tim.

Considering this longhead action, the preciousness of time forced him to chuck it out. Carson's Creek Gorge cut into the main cañon here at the flats, from the east, its own cañon being nearly a quarter mile wide at the junction. If a man circled the flats, he would have to feel up that side cañon half a mile or so, too. By the time he'd got that done, he'd have shot two hours he didn't have to spare. And likely for nothing, at that.

Chances were nearly gut-cinched that the Arapahoes had gone on, had tied Tim out naked with the idea of having him sun bake and thirst to death. It surely wasn't any accident that the bubbling thread of Carson's Creek ran past just inches beyond the staked-out renegade's feet.

Crouching back in the trail-fringe brush, the mountain man calculated his next move. When a man had run a ten-to-one track into an odds-on stymie like this, he might as well chuck in the rest of his poke. No use standing there, picking his seat about it. Leaving Heyoka in the brush, Jesse chucked his in.

Swiftly he went, gliding out into mid-clearing, bearing down on the waiting Tim like a mountain cat coming up on a tied-out colt. Eastward, the sun was just rimming the mesa, tumbling its red flood down the cedar-black gullet of Carson's Creek Gorge.

The hostiles had rigged Tim with what Jesse's Sioux folks called an Arapaho halter. This was an inch-wide strip of green rawhide, passed through the mouth, cinched down on the tongue and tied fast back of the skull base. What this crude bit, shrinking slowly in the sun, did to discourage a man's urge to converse was six shades stiffer than considerable. Even after Jesse had slashed it out of his mouth, Tim couldn't make anything but deaf-mute mumbles for a full minute. Then he got his tongue going.

"Listen, Callahan . . ."—delivered in hoarsely earnest tones, the Mormon renegade's plea broke out desperately—"and for Gawd's sake, believe me!"

"Go on," snapped Jesse, blue eyes swinging an apprehensive circle around the flats.

Now that he was out in the open, the mountain man's Indian hunch was hammering at him again, telling him he had likely been right, first off, thinking this thing was a hostile trap. Tim's rushing speech stumbled in, harsh and heavy, on his red-haired companion's rising instincts.

"They left me haltered like this for trying to get the kid away. I killed that lousy Skull, grabbed the boy, and run for it. The squaw nailed me and would have killed me but for Black Coyote busting in. He thought it would be funny as hell to leave me tied up for you to finish off. . . ."

"What the hell are you trying to give me, O'Mara?" Jesse's interruption was ignited by the quick flash of the narrowed eyes behind it.

"Listen, I'm telling you. You know how them red scuts are for their damn' courtesy rules. Well, they somehow figured I had tipped you off to that ambush in Wild Hoss Bend. They give you credit for letting them know I'd crossed them up. So Watonga he says . . . '*Wagh!* We'll leave Big Face' . . . that's me, see . . . 'in the trail as a courtesy gift for Tokeya Sha.'"

"Well?" Jesse's challenge froze the perspiration beading Tim's scowling gaze.

"Well, hell! They figured you'd kill me account of

them grabbing me when I took out after the squaw in Wild Hoss Bend and making it look like I was mixed up in the ambush."

"You know something, O'Mara"—the mountain man's break-in was deceptively quiet—"they figured right."

"My Gawd, Callahan, you don't mean that! We're white men. Listen. Didn't I steer them offen you when you knocked that pebble off the cliff? Didn't I try to—?"

Jesse's answer came with the flashing knife blade that whipped out to sever Tim's bonds. "I'm cutting you loose. You get ten seconds to loosen up your arms and legs. Then I'm going to kill you, mister. With my hands."

Flexing his thick shoulders, the renegade shot a side glance at the waiting mountain man, decided to make one more try. "Callahan, I ain't lost no more love for you than you have for me. But unless I can have a hand in getting that kid of Lacey's back from them scuts, I ain't got a chance in the settlements. Leave me throw in with you. There's nobody in the camp up yonder but the kid and the squaw. The braves are all up on the mesa running buffalo. I swear I ain't had nothing to do with this whole deal. As for Lacey, hell, you can have her. You got her, anyway. Me, I just don't want them red buzzards sticking me full of cedar needles and burning my hide off. What do you say, Callahan?"

If there was a time Jesse would have felt any kinship with the white man in front of him, it was long gone. He wasn't seeing Tim O'Mara's sweaty face, nor hearing his hoarsely growled words. He was seeing the sodden-blanketed eggshell crush of little Kathy's head, and hearing the dull, sick mon-

otone of her shocked mother's low-voiced cry:
Dead. Dead.

"I say you're a god-damned liar, O'Mara. And
that your ten seconds have come and gone."

"Callahan!"

"Save it," grated Jesse. "I was in that brush spur
over Watonga's lodge when the sub-chiefs voted you
down. It was a still night, mister, and none of you
was whispering."

Jesse was backing off with his words, placing his
Hawken and knife belt carefully out of reach on a
shelf-high rock ledge. He saw the dark light shoot
Tim's sudden scowl at his flat challenge. Didn't miss
the following blankness that spread like pond ice
over the big Irishman's slab face. Knew, without
anybody having to write him a letter about it, that
he had made his match—and met it.

"You came after me once, O'Mara," was all he
said. "Now I'm coming after you."

Tim's answer was to glide away from the mountain man's crouching advance, his light-stepping,
easy way of going, as though his feet had better eyes
in them than his head, letting Jesse know he had a
fighting man on his hands. And, in the breath-held
seconds of the first wary circling, a man had that
strange, timeless pause that goes ahead of any
hand-to-hand encounter where the announced
stakes are life itself, to study just how much of a
fighting man!

Tim O'Mara was big. Six foot two, anyway, and as
thick-set and well-balanced as a boar grizzly. His
massive, fleshy head was set on a neck that seemed
to be nothing more than a foot-wide continuation of
the sloping, ropy-muscled shoulders. His eyes, tiny
and close-set as any bear's, appeared lost in the re-

ceding shadow cast over them by the protruding
Neanderthal brow ridge. His wide, blunt jaw, slack
now under the looseness of the thick lips above it,
had the look and cut of base rock. A keg-chested,
heavy-waisted man, his wide hips and thick legs
were a grotesquely bulky foundation for the support
and movement of the gross muscularity of the great
trunk above them.

Crouching now, moving lightly, stripped to the
gee-string as the Arapahoes had left him, nearly the
whole of his hulking figure overlain with a coarse
mat of black body hair, Tim O'Mara looked brute
enough to give any fellow human ample pause.
Across from him moved a man of different cut.
Nearly as tall as Tim, lean, supple, graceful, Jesse
Callahan was the renegade's diametric physical opposite: the kind of a spare, unimposing-looking
man an opponent would be likely to dismiss, at first
glance, as ordinary. Then, if that opponent were a
seasoned frontier rough like Tim, he would take another look, as Tim was taking now, and figure
maybe this mountain jasper wasn't so ordinary, after all.

Where he looked on the slight side for a trade that
ran to big men, he had a spread of shoulders you
could lay an axe haft across and a set of hands sizable enough to span a horse pistol without stretching, and dangling on arms as long and thick as
split-oak posts. What 190 pounds there was to the
rest of him was pure, dry muscle and dense, big
bone. He handled himself in a way that made you
watch him, two feet moving as softly as though
there were nothing but summer wind under his moccasin soles. Huge hands and forearms flexing and
unflexing in that slow, rhythmic way that told you

you'd better get in close to this one. Close and bear hug-tight. Where he couldn't wind up that rock-sized fist and throw it with that mule-muscled shoulder back of it. Just about when you had settled your mind to that, you found yourself looking into the quietest face you'd ever seen on a man, and, back of the face, into the chilliest pair of blue-dark eyes this side of two chunks of lake ice. And then you didn't know what to think. You just kept on moving in your circle. Moving and watching. Watching and moving.

Five eternity-long seconds dragged away as Jesse deliberately closed the circle. He was within six feet of his man now. Another step and it was five. Then four. And still the big Mormon waited.

Jesse hesitated. Tim O'Mara matched his pause, seeming not to look at him, not to know he was there, tiny eyes appearing to watch everything within the mountain arena except his opponent. It was a bad trick, this thing of a man not looking at you when you were trying to get in on him. You couldn't see his eyes. And when you couldn't see a man's eyes, you couldn't read his body. Jesse cursed, wavered, took a half step backward, finding himself confused, uncertain, for the first time in his life afraid.

As the mountain man's retreating foot felt behind him for a safe and solid setting, he was necessarily and for the least fraction of split time off balance. Tim struck instantly. Whirling to roll with the lunge, Jesse's pivot foot struck a loose, fist-sized boulder. He felt the searing pain of the ankle turn as the leg spun on out from under him, knew he was falling even before Tim's huge weight bombarded into him.

Where it should have cost him his life, the awkward fall saved it. Tim's leap, thrown off time by his adversary's collapse, carried the burly Mormon's body on over its intended target, causing the thick grasp of the circling arms to miss their intended bear hug, close, instead, on the mountain man's desperately upflung arms. The next instant Jesse's drawn-up thighs had straightened, driving his bony knees up and into the twin pits of Tim's groin. With the groin thrust, Jesse balled his body, rolled sideways to his hands and knees as Tim, ten feet away, came scrambling to his feet. It was now the Mormon's turn to hesitate, slowed by the intense pain of the double blow in his groin.

It was a hesitation that sent Jesse leaping toward him, big fists clubbed. But the first surge of that leap sent a hot knife of sickening weakness up the calf of the mountain man's left leg, bringing him to a staggering halt five feet from the waiting renegade. White-faced, Jesse tested the foot, found it would just bear his weight. And no more. The fight was ten seconds old, unjoined as yet, and he was going into it with a sprained ankle!

As the injured Jesse halted his rush, Tim wheeled and came at him, his headlong attack indicating a sudden disregard of caution and maneuver. The indication was only apparent. The big Mormon was one of those occasional humans whose instincts to kill or be killed had survived 10,000 years of civilized veneering. He came down on Jesse now, as one wolf would on another, sensing the fact of the mountain man's distress without knowing its nature. Without knowing and without caring, his animal-sharp extra-sensory perception telling him as accurately as any certain knowledge that he had wounded his foe and had him going down. Jesse did what he could, and it was not enough.

As the charging renegade leaped in, he set himself back on his good right leg and drove his right fist fully into the snarling face. At the instant of the blow's delivery, Tim tucked his chin for the classic frontier brawler's diving head-butt. Jesse's whitened knuckles smashed into the matted hair and iron-hard bone of the Mormon's skull top, the wrenching shock of the collision spearing up his straightened forearm and bicep to explode with rocket-bursting force in the spasmed muscles of his shoulder. He felt the rupturing impact of the bull's head-butt bury itself in the pit of his belly and knew he was falling again.

He had no sensation of striking the ground, his next memory being the perfectly clear one of an interval during which he could not breathe or move. The same clear, helpless consciousness told him that Tim had him in an armlocked bear hug and was crushing the literal life out of him. His breath, reflexing from the solar-plexus smash of Tim's head, came bursting back with its swift, familiar burgeoning of fresh strength. Twisting to free his arms so that he could get his hands into Tim's face, he found his numbed right arm would not respond, while his left was pinned by the double prison of his own and his opponent's weights. At the same time he found the Mormon's great hips and legs had his own long limbs hopelessly wedged beneath them.

With the cool dimness of coming unconsciousness spreading its grateful shade before him, he forced his mind to work and his eyes to see. What they saw was an ear. A thick-lobed, protruding, dirt-crusted human ear. It was attached to a big round head that was buried, grunting and straining, against the giving crack of his upper ribs. That was undoubtedly Tim O'Mara's head and the ear was undoubtedly Tim O'Mara's ear. With all of consciousness and strength that remained to him, Jesse flashed his white teeth down and into that ear.

He felt the grating of the parting cartilage as his jaws clamped crazily home, sensed the spasmodic, wild recoil of Tim's whole body, heard the animal pain in his hoarse cry. Then he was free. Standing clear. His feet under him once more. His mind and vision glass clear.

Tim was waiting across from him, dull face contorted, hairy left paw just coming away from the side of his head. Tim brought the hand down. Stared at it wonderingly. Jesse's eyes followed the Mormon's, seeing the hand and the bright blood.

For a long five seconds the two stood silently, feet wide-braced, breaths close-held, the Mormon letting his eyes come slowly up from the bloody hand to lock and hold with Jesse's only after what seemed an eternity to the waiting mountain man. Tim was muttering now, like an angry, crazed beast, and backing away from Jesse to begin the circle again. The guarded maneuver narrowed the mountain man's eye, quickened his thinking.

With the leg gone, Jesse knew he had one chance: to keep Tim from guessing he was crippled and to make the hulking Mormon come to him. Slowly he moved on in, white with the pain of the ankle, yet making himself walk on it. Tim fell back into his circle, moving and looking away from the mountain man. In Jesse's mind the plan was forming. It had worked once by accident. It might work twice by intent.

He feinted a quick step forward, taking the weight on his good leg. Tim spun with the feint, and, as he spun, Jesse spun with him, half slipping to one knee. Tim took the bait, his diving leap coming with a rush and a grunt that dazed Jesse with its speed. But this time the mountain man was in under it, and he had his feet under him. He felt his shoulder drive into the crush of the Mormon's hairy belly, got his palms against the great chest in the same instant. Coming erect, he straightened his long arms, the knotting shoulder muscles cracking with the sudden, snapping heave.

Tim's huge body appeared to hang in mid-air for a full second, the arc of its pause a good seven feet from the rocky ground. Then it was in the rocks, flat-sprawled, the contact force of its falling seeming to jar the very earth under Jesse's running limp. It was a fall that should have broken a strong man's spine but Tim rolled away from it and found his feet before Jesse could get to him. Stunned, bleeding, half blind from the rock dust and pine needles that matted his broad face, the Mormon came, groping and muttering, toward the crouching Jesse.

The awkwardness of that limping run toward the fallen Tim had cost the mountain man a precious advantage, but it had brought him something equally dear. The turned ankle was strengthening, would take its share of the weight now, felt stronger by the second. A man could work with his feet under him. Could set himself to use those club-hard hands and swinging shoulders. And more. Now was the time to use them.

Tim's last clear memory was of seeing the grim white face across from him suddenly ease into a

wide-mouthed trace of a grin. Then he was reaching
for his man and storming him under. The face was
gone and the grin with it. There was nothing there,
then, and his ears were ringing and he was coughing with the blood that was bleeding back from his
nose and into his throat. Head swinging, eyes blurring, the renegade found his man again. Now he
was only a gray shadow, without face or arms or
legs. And he was moving against a flatness and an
emptiness that was as gray as his shadow. But he
was moving, and Tim could see that. Jesse set himself once more as Tim came weaving in, sighted the
bloody mouth and nose, swung his aim three inches
below them for the blunt chin. Again a last moment
lurch of the dazed Mormon steered the blow away
from the hanging jaw, landing it with a tearing side
slash across the right eye and cheek bone. Tim's
whole body twisted to the force of the smash, falling
past Jesse to land with a tooth-setting wrench on his
left side and shoulder.

From some ageless, dim, atavistic well of primal
instinct, Tim O'Mara drew the last bucket of brute
will. Somehow, unbelievably, he got his knees under
him. And then, incredibly, his feet. Turning with the
last, thrusting lurch that brought him up, the right
side of his face swung around, broadside, to Jesse.
The mountain man saw the dead white of the exposed bone beneath the damaged eye, the formless
mass of the closing flesh above it.

He knew, then, that instant, inner wash of cold
sickness that is the brave man's psychic rebellion
against destroying another, equally brave thing—be
it brute or human. And then the sickness was gone
and he was moving in on the sightless, whimpering
renegade. Moving in to do what he had to do. And

meaning to do it with every ounce of merciful strength that was in him.

Stooping, his groping fingers closed around the jagged, melon-sized rock, his weary arm drawing back and up as he straightened. For a long, slow breath the rock hung poised above the featureless pulp that had once been a fellow creature's face, then fell from the nerveless fingers to roll and bounce harmlessly in front of the knee-braced Tim O'Mara. Jesse was still standing over the slumped huddle of the Mormon's sagging body, his mind and jaw setting to fight down the sickness that was building in him again, when he heard it.

It was a deep voice. And pleasant. Not angry, and not English.

"*Woyuonihan!* Red Fox is a fighter. We respect him!"

The affable growl of the speech broke in a chain of high plains monosyllables that mounded Jesse's spine with gooseflesh. A man would never need to turn to guess that orator's identity. Still, it went against the mountain breed to take lead in the back without at least a farewell wave at what was undoubtedly getting ready to sling it there. Before he could move to face around, however, the voice was continuing its guttural, unhurried way.

"Now, wait, Fox. Just step back there, where you are. Only a little way."

Without hesitation, Jesse moved to obey, placing his moccasins carefully behind him for three slow, backward steps, knowing the dangerous shift of these red minds, not wanting to bring that coup shot any sooner than necessary. On the third step, the voice came again.

"That's enough, cousin. You were in the way of that crawling dog, there."

The laconic words were punctuated with a single, barking rifle shot.

Jesse heard the slug slap into the heaving chest of the still conscious Tim O'Mara, saw the big renegade's hands go jerking toward the spreading stain beneath the left nipple, watched them claw and knot briefly, before the thick body slid forward into the granite and lay still.

In the following quiet, Jesse turned, taking care that the movement was slow and steady. A man had to grant they looked beautiful standing over there in the throat of the creek gorge. Back of them the red morning sun bounced and gleamed off the rifle barrels and lance blades, the nervous pattern of their many war ponies making a motley-pied background for the eagle feathers and war grease that draped and splattered their bodies. 100 yards in their foreground, thirty from Jesse, his great size dwarfing the piebald stud horse he rode, the beautifully proportioned bulk of Watonga sat, black and stark, against the climbing sun.

"*Hau*," said Jesse. "We meet at last." Bowing slightly, he touched the tips of his left fingers to his brow. "*Woyuonihan*."

"*Woyuonihan*," responded Watonga, the near-black mask of his face cracking in a grotesque grin. "*Hohahe*, Tokeya Sha is welcome. Watonga has waited long for this pleasure."

"Tokeya is a fool!" replied Jesse, feigning a self-disgust that wasn't half a tone from bitterly real.

"*Iho!* Don't say that," begged the huge chief solicitously. "Even when you were a boy, Long Chin told my father you would one day be a chief. And now, look. Every Arapaho north of the Medicine Road knows of Red Fox. Tokeya Sha is a *real* chief! *Wagh!*"

"A real *heyoka*," insisted Jesse, stalling the precious seconds as his glance reckoned the distance to Heyoka's hiding place against the number of pony lengths between him and Black Coyote. "Were he not such a witless one, how could he have come so blindly to smell at this putrid bait?" He indicated the silent Tim with a contemptuous, backflung gesture of his thumb.

"Big Face was telling the truth. He did not know we came back here to catch you. He thought we had gone. He thought I left him here as a courtesy return to Tokeya. And so I did. *Oha!* Take him! Watonga gives him back to you. But do not say he lied. He didn't know we were hiding in Little Chief's Valley. Big Face didn't know that."

Jesse nodded, understanding that by Little Chief they meant Kit Carson. Damn. His hunch about looking up Carson's Creek Gorge had been dead right. As he hesitated thus, he saw the braves behind Watonga beginning to split and file around either side of the flats to hem and circle him in solidly. There was no move to harm him, no apparent hurry to surround him. The ponies just shuffled easily along the cedars' edges, their blank-faced riders sitting, slack and dead-eyed, not seeming even to look at the trapped goddam guide.

In another moment, the southern file of warriors would be between him and Heyoka. If he were going to make any break, now was the time. Still he hung back, fearing the odds, undecided, confused, as near to being stampeded as he had ever been. Finally it was a little thing that decided him. One of those strange, stray little thoughts that will flash through a man's mind at a time like this—the thought of Tall Elk, the dark-faced squaw. Fronted by 100 of the hardest-cut prairie warriors ever to swing astride a spotted pony, the Sioux-reared mountain man found himself thinking about one female squaw! And what he was thinking was that once these red sons got him back to camp and to that damned hawk-headed Tall Elk, there would be a sharp end to all this courtesy rules horseplay.

The Indian men were great for ceremony, always. Their women, never. With the squaws it was meat in the pot or a scalp on the drying rack, and the hell with the details of how it got there. All right, then, he would go now. He tensed his body for the leap that was going to start his sprint for Heyoka. If he could get to the cat-fast gray mare, he would give these red devils a ride they could lie to their grandchildren about for the next ten generations. The panther-scream war cry of the Minniconjou welled up in his throat, his legs straightening for the jump.

The leap never got started, the yell never out. A flashing burst of pain exploded in the back of his head. The red sun behind Watonga shattered and flew into a thousand pieces. The amber morning light went black as the nether pole. . . .

Tall Elk was still spraddled over the fallen body, raising her stone maul for another drive at the bright red head beneath her, when Black Coyote's heavy voice interrupted.

"*Hinhanka po*, that's enough!"

The chief's barking command stopped the final hammer blow, left the squaw staring up at her mate, broad mouth writhing like a sow bear that had just had her snout cuffed out of the hot bowels of a yearling doe.

"That red scalp is a fine one," growled Watonga irritably. "Why get it all gummed up with the brains?"

Chapter 10

When Jesse came awake, he was tied to a torture stake, twenty feet from the entrance flap of Watonga's lodge. This stake was a real *can wakan sha,* a real red holy pole. Fifteen feet high, dyed a brilliant scarlet with the juice of the *wica kanaska* berry, its vibrant color was no more evident than the forecast of the trapped mountain man's future contained in its raw pigment. All doubts a man might have had as to how the Arapahoes intended handling him were now pleasantly resolved. They aimed to barbecue him.

Down cañon, he could see the hanging ledge and rank fern dell of Portola Springs. Around him and Watonga's lodge was scattered the circle of ash-gray mushroom spots marking the early morning ceremonial fires made to induce the spirit of *pte* to co-operate in the upcoming slaughter of his four-legged patrons up on the mesa. The camp appeared deserted, the angle of the sun, squarely in Jesse's face, indicating about 10:00 A.M. He'd been *tela nun wela dead yet alive nearly four hours.* Testing the rawhide thongs, he was pleased to learn two things: his limbs were sound, his blood moving well. His head ached something sinful but his eyesight and mind were clear enough.

There was a considerable trick to stringing a man up so he would keep for hours in good condition, yet have no chance in God's back pasture of working himself loose. The Arapahoes proved they were onto this trick by the way they had him laced to that holy pole. Beyond testing the job he made no effort to loosen it. No point wasting good strength. These butchers knew how to hang their hogs.

The fact they had strung him up so carefully, leaving his leggings on, putting him in a nice shade clump, let him know they didn't aim to sweat him like they had figured for Tim. Nobody raised with the Miniconjous needed any more telling than that about their plans for him. The only time they took care to keep a prisoner good and alive was when they reckoned to take their sweet time getting him good and dead.

As to the precise manner of this prospect, the mountain man wasn't held long in question. Tall Elk came barging out of the cedars, noisy as a wind whisper in young grass. Her arms were loaded with straight-grain cedar chunks. Seeing Jesse's eyes on her, she nodded, displaying that curious Indian quirk that brought them to accept a condemned enemy as highly privileged.

"*Hau*, you have been walking in the shadows. *Hohahe*, welcome back."

"*Ha ho*," replied Jesse, straight-faced, "thank you. That is fine wood you have there. Hard and dry. The splinters will be excellent."

The big squaw nodded again, approving the *Wa-*

sicun's good guessing. "Indeed, nothing like dry cedar for a real roasting."

"*Hau*, it burns slow and long. The meat gets done right, that way."

The squaw grunted an agreement to Jesse's statement, squatting down in front of the lodge, beginning the loving work of splitting the foot-long burning-splinters off the seasoned cedar.

Jesse gave her a few minutes to get started, then inquired politely: "Where are all the men? Where is Watonga and Little Chief?"

"All gone," growled the squaw. "All gone to hunt. There is a fine herd up on the high grass. Gray Bear and Elk Runner found it there. Black Coyote took Ya Slo, his son, along that the boy might learn how a herd is properly approached."

And that, apparently, was the end of Tall Elk's conversational efforts for the day. To the mountain man's further inquiries, she was deaf as a limestone post, her only further contribution to the palaver being to come up off her haunches, move over to the captive trapper, and belt him in the mouth with one of the iron-hard cedar chunks, the blow being accompanied with a soft-grunted request: "Shut up now."

Jesse licked his split lip speculatively, spat his mouth clear of blood, and complied.

For a pleasant hour, then, he was entertained by his contemplative viewing of Watonga's wife at her ingenious best—displaying all the fascinating hand skill of the Plains Indians. The fact the Arapaho woman's prairie art craft was being devoted to fashioning the shapely little hardwood splinters that would, with nightfall, be illuminating various and tender portions of Jesse Callahan's swart skin was irrevelant. The woman was an artist.

Along about noon, business improved. First off, Watonga came riding down the mesa trail followed by Johnny O'Mara on his stubby paint pony. Jesse had time to sing out as the youngster spotted him.

"Hi, there, Johnny boy! Are you all right?"

The put-on cheerfulness missed its mark with the dirty-faced boy, his answer coming with childish direction, right to the point. "Gosh all hemlocks, Jesse! Am I glad to see you! Say, golly! What have they got you all tied up for? I'll bet they're going to torture you, Jesse. Gee, I . . . ."

Evidently the Indians hadn't let the little cuss see him when they had brought him into camp after Tall Elk had sneaked up behind him in the flats and floored him with that damned maul. Jesse was about to reassure Johnny that he was not in any danger, but before he could Tall Elk grabbed the boy off his pony and hustled him into the teepee.

From within the lodge, the mountain man could hear the squaw growling at him like a she-bear warning her cub. Hearing nothing from Johnny, Jesse called out, still putting his words light and easy: "Don't you worry none, Johnny! They ain't going to harm me none. You watch, now. The Arapahoes ain't been whelped what can handle us Minniconjous. *H'g'un*, in there, Wanbli Sha. Keep your heart big and your ears wide open!"

There was no answer from the teepee and shortly Tall Elk came out to join Watonga where the chief squatted by the lodge entrance. Looking at her mate frowningly, the squaw demanded: "What happened? Why did you return? Where are the braves?"

Black Coyote shrugged. "It was nothing. Such a thing as will happen no more. We got a bad change in wind and the buffalo smelled us. They began to

run before we could get around them. Yellow Leg
and the others went after them. I brought Ya Slo
back, that's all."

"*Waste*, it is good you did. Ya Slo should sleep.
Last night his eyes were open to the smoke hole as
long as the stars were there."

"*Hau*," rumbled Watonga, "mine, too. You can't
sleep much around that Tokeya Sha. I haven't had
my eyes closed right since he fooled me about that
gunpowder. Right now, I am tired. Like an old chief
with six young wives. Curse that red-haired *Wasicun* devil. Curse his red-wheeled goddam. Curse
that damn gunpowder!"

"Not the powder!" Tall Elk said quickly. "Don't
curse the powder. Don't put a bad dream on that.
Remember, we must get powder soon. Don't curse
it, then!"

The chief scowled the squaw down, snapped at
her irascibly: "That red-wheeled goddam is the
curse of my life. It has defeated me. It is a devil. An
evil thing. I would give much to have it in my hands.
Wagh! At least I have the *Wasicun* who guided it
against me. Who ruined my honor agreement with
the Mormon chief. Now we'll see. I'll kill him.
Maybe that will count as a coup against the goddam. Do you think so?"

"Oh, sure. But sleep now. Don't think about it.
Old Horse has dreamed that you will get the powder. Maybe the Mormon chief means to give it to
you after he has captured Big Throat's fort. Anyway,
Old Horse always dreams right. You will get that
powder. And soon."

Observing this conversation, Jesse was aware of
Johnny O'Mara's pinched face peering out from under the lodge's side skins, a few feet from the en-

trance flap. The boy looked about as drowsy as a tom kitten in an Airedale kennel. He caught the mountain man's eye at once, waved quickly, disappeared back under the side skins. Another second and his high voice was piping in defiant disregard of Tall Elk's warning to he quiet.

"Don't worry, Jesse. We'll get away all right!" The mountain man had no more than winced helplessly at this boyish optimism than Johnny's voice concluded with a bull's-eye shout that hit dead center of Jesse's bitter sun squint. "Shucks, we've still got our Sioux secret, ain't we?"

As the meaning of the boy's words struck into Jesse's thoughts, the big Arapaho squaw was inside the lodge, scolding the youngster angrily, cutting his words sharply off. But the mountain man had heard all he needed, and a heap more than he had expected or hoped for. Maybe it wasn't much, but a hidden Green River skinning knife was for sure a sight more of a something than the nothings Jesse had been able to think of for the past two hours. As this hope arose in the mountain man, Tall Elk came out of the lodge, standing aside for Black Coyote to enter.

"What have you done with Ya Slo inside there?" the chief demanded.

"He is quiet, tied by the leg to a lodgepole."

"*Waste*," replied her mate. "Now we will sleep. The hunters will be returning by the time Old Father *Wi* has traveled almost to the west. See that you have plenty of burning splinters by then, woman. I owe this Minniconjou Fox a real roasting."

"There will be plenty. I will make more while Watonga sleeps."

Jesse figured that Black Coyote, like any seasoned

soldier, would not need more than five minutes to be asleep. He gave him ten, then began anxiously hawkeying the side skins of his lodge where he'd last seen Johnny O'Mara's gopher face.

Another endless five minutes crawled by and the side skins hadn't even quivered. Well, hell. It had been a long shot, last chance, at best. Even if the gutsy cub had meant that he still had the knife Jesse had given him, he would never get the chance to use it with that cursed squaw squatting there splitting those damned splinters.

The mountain man's slant gaze swung away from the lodge, narrowed down on the busy squaw. She looked up, catching his eye, nodded grimly, held up one of the splinters for his approval. He nodded politely, and she fell again, loosely smiling, to the loving concentration required by her labors. The second her glance left him, Jesse caught an eye tail flash of light from the direction of the lodge.

Then he was looking at the three brightest spots any Arapaho-bound white man ever saw under the slightly raised side skins of a hostile Arapaho lodge: the lively sparkle of two Johnny O'Mara blue eyes and the sun bounce off the glittering blade of a Green River knife. Now, by God, if that horse-size squaw would somehow turn her back for twenty breaths. *Man Above! Wakan Tanka! Make her do it. Send her down something to do besides sitting there, hacking away at those burning splinters!*

The next second's reaction on Tall Elk nearly made an Indian Christian out of Jesse Callahan. As though in ordered obedience to the mountain man's fervent prayer, the Arapaho woman suddenly stood up. Glancing at the prisoner, she scowled, went limping off into the brush. Jesse could still see her as

she hoisted her deerskins and hunkered down, back
to him and out of sight, behind the screening brush.

Good old Wakan Tanka. Bless that Man Above.
Thank him for the clock-like regularity of the Plains
Indian bowel!

The next instant his warning, side-mouth hiss was
on its way toward the sleeping chief's lodge, and
Johnny O'Mara was popping out from under the
side skins, leaping across the open, racing, wide-
eyed, down upon the waiting mountain man.

"The hands first, boy. For God's sake slash those
thongs. Never mind if you get a little meat along
with them."

He felt the bite of the razored blade whacking into
the rawhide laces, felt them loosen and fall slackly.
Writhing, he seized the knife from the white-faced
boy, low-voiced his tense order.

"Back in the lodge, young 'un. Hop it before she
sees you."

Without waiting to see his harsh command
obeyed, Jesse bent forward, slashing at the intricate
knottings of the ankle rawhides. Another second,
now. Just one. Looking up to check the squaw, his
fingers frantically seeking out the twistings of the
thongs, the better to get the knife at them, he was in
time to see Tall Elk coming for him.

Passing the splinter pile, the long arm swept
down, scooping up the stone maul. Three more big-
cat leaps and she was on him, the grating grizzly
coughs of her people coming with her.

Jesse measured her diving drive, twisted as far
left as his bound feet would let him. The stone maul
missed, hissing by his ear an arrow's width away.
As it passed, Jesse shifted the knife to his left hand,
his right striking, snake-like, for the squaw's right

wrist. Striking and going home. Nailing the squaw's arm clean as a ten-penny spike. At the same instant, he put every ounce of the power in his tendon-tough muscles into a wrenching shoulder twist.

He felt the Indian woman's wrist bones turn and snap under his fingers, saw the falling stone maul leave the squaw's nerveless fingers. Simultaneously his free left hand whipped the skinning knife into her contorted back.

White mountain man, stone buffalo maul, and knifed Arapaho squaw all hit the ground together, Jesse's clawing right hand biting into the maul's haft as they did. Tall Elk flung herself to one side, surging to free her broken right wrist from the *Wasicun*'s grip, found that the hand brought up in the iron school of Minniconjou horse-breaking doesn't give worth a puny damn. The squaw had time to start one last, broken growl, and that was all.

With everything he had to offer, from his memories of little Kathy's crushed face onward, Jesse drove the stone maul squarely into the snarling face. The pop and splatter of the pulping bones, the way the maul broke in past the nose-bridge, suddenly soft and deep, let him know that Tall Elk, the wife of Watonga, had split her last burning splinter.

Twisting free of the squaw's body, Jesse came away from it as Black Coyote stumbled to the opening of the lodge. The chief's eyes, heavy with sleep, seized the situation a little slowly. When it came to him that the *Wasicun* was cutting himself free, Watonga wasted no breath in war whooping. Crouching for his leap at the still tethered white man, his knife flashed into his hand.

Jesse needed five seconds more. He got them by grace of Johnny O'Mara's quick-headed thinking.

As Watonga launched himself through the teepee flap, his own four-foot coup stick hanged itself between his bowed legs, knocking him as head over heels as a bear cub in a scuffle play. Before he could come clear of the ground, Jesse was on him.

Black Coyote got as far as his knees when the mountain man's size-eleven stomper took him dead in the crotch cloth. The bursting pain of the groin kick doubled the chief forward into the split-oak fist that followed the foot. Watonga jackknifed down into the dirt, his great jaw sagging. He rolled half over on his back, lay there, glaze-eyed as a pole-axed steer.

"We've got plenty of time." Jesse's reassuring nod went to Johnny O'Mara, where the nervous boy sat his paint pony fifty yards downtrail of Watonga's buffalo camp. "Just you set there and hold onto Heyoka and that stud hoss of the chief's. I'm going back to the camp a minute. I got me a message I want to pin on old Watonga."

He was gone, loping easily back toward the silent camp, before Johnny could put his nerves into words. White-faced, the boy sat his pony, dividing his frightened glances between keeping an eye out for Jesse's return, and seeing to the considerable business of holding onto Watonga's skittery piebald stallion.

Heyoka, the mountain man's indispensable but immoral mare, did her bit to heighten Johnny's trial by choosing to make the most of this, her first opportunity in months to be alone with a gentleman. The way she kept rumping up to the nostril-belled attentions of Black Coyote's best buffalo horse was likely to pull the boy's thin arms clean off.

Breaking out his manliest seven-year old oath, the

near-panicked youth belted the watch-eyed stud frantically across the nose. "Dang your mangy 'Rapaho hide! Leave that there mare alone! Jesse'll kill the both of us, happen you bust loose of me!"

Whether annoyed by Heyoka's delicate Minniconjou scent, or impressed by the plain audacity of a weanling *Wasicun* boy's gall in rope-swatting a chief's war mount, the ear-pinned stud backed off, cleared his offended nostrils disdainfully, quieted down.

Johnny, cinching down the grip of his stubby fingers on the two lead ropes and the bite of his best buckteeth on his quivering lower lip, swung his pinched face again toward the uptrail bend where Jesse had disappeared.

With true Sioux sense of the properly dramatic, the mountain man had, before leaving the camp with Johnny, strung the unconscious Watonga up on the holy pole from which he himself had just escaped. His only addition to the rawhide embroidery the hostiles had sewed him up with had been to clamp a snug Arapaho halter on the helpless chief.

Now, returning happily to the haltered Black Coyote, he had his message to leave with him. And he hadn't been keen on Lacey's boy seeing him deliver the little token of fond farewell, either. And for a very quickly evident cause. The fact Watonga had recovered consciousness when Jesse got back to him didn't dampen the mountain man's fine red enthusiasm one morsel. Whipping out Tall Elk's gutting knife, he took the awkward weapon by the back of the blade, holding it like a skin-painting stick. As the chief's expressionless eyes followed him, he brushed the flies off the sun-blackened chest, went carefully to carving his parting Minniconjou pictograph thereon.

Jesse was no artist by the exacting Plains Indian

standards, but when he had finished his tongue-screwed labors on Watonga's chest, the incisions hurriedly rubbed with a little salt and trade tobacco from the chief's own pouches, he had a readably good design.

Any Plains Indian cub of eight or ten could have told you it was an unmistakable Minniconjou Fox, leg-hoisted and urinating upon an equally undeniable Arapaho Coyote.

Chapter 11

Breaking around the trail head in a reaching dog-trot, Jesse loped up to the tearfully grateful Johnny O'Mara and grabbed the halter rope of Watonga's stud as the boy flung it hastily to him. Swinging up on the crouching stallion, he immediately balled one horny fist and drove it down between the nervous brute's ears with a force that came near knocking the ugly jughead off the scrawny neck. Watonga's war horse, establishing a record for losing all interest in the opposite sex and completely forgetting his own, left off his goosy crouching, went to standing as broken and gentle as a second-string travois pony.

With his borrowed charger properly chastised, the mountain man turned his attentions to the waiting Johnny O'Mara. "All quiet in the Land of the Coyote!" He grinned broadly, cocking his head back toward the Indian camp and giving his small red-headed companion a reassuring bear-paw thump on the shoulder. "I don't like to crow, boy, but when your Uncle Jesse quietens them down, they stay silent-like! You ain't going to hear no more Injun peeps today."

The brag was no sooner out than it tripped head-long on its own boast. From up on the mesa trail, no more than half a mile above Watonga's black lodge, it came. Long, low, weirdly beautiful, the hunting-song of the buffalo wolf.

"Son-of-a-bitch!" The curse snapped off Jesse's tongue like a shot bowstring. "Me and my big mouth."

"What's the matter, Jesse? What *was* that?"

"Scout signal," grunted the mountain man.

"Gee, it sounded more like a loafer howling, huh, Jesse?"

"Well, it was a kind of a loafer, boy. Like none you ever seed, I allow." His companion's agreement came acidly. "That loafer up there is near six foot tall and carries a smooth red coat with a sprouting of long eagle feathers around the skull."

"You mean Injuns, Jesse?"

"I don't mean field mice, young 'un. Shut up. You'll hear quick enough."

On top of his gruff order, Jesse threw his head back and howled dismally in reply to the Arapaho signal. The call had just time to echo up under the mesa rim before it was seized up and flung back from above, attended, this time, by a whole discor-dant symphony of assorted wolf howls.

"Gosh! It *is* Injuns!"

"You got it figured, boy. Come on, toss me Heyoka's lead rope. And get yourself set solid on that scrub paint. Those're Black Coyote's boys. They're back from the hunt somewhat sooner than I allowed. About six hours somewhat I'd say. *Aii-eee*, Johnny boy! We got us some big butt pounding to do now."

With all three horses hitting a flat gallop, Jesse set himself to figure a little Arapaho algebra. Well, one thing was easy, even before you started sweating. There wasn't any question of what trail to take. The first five miles back to Cedar Flats was as laid out and one way as a fairground racetrack. But that wasn't getting your figuring done. After Cedar Flats, it was another ten miles to Rockpile Meadow, and then another ten on out to the Medicine Road. If you ever got that far, you had a chance of running into some white pack outfit working between Fort Bridger and Laramie. That, or maybe Andy Hobbs and the muleskinners coming up from old Gabe's. That last chance was about as fat as a she-grizzly coming out of her winter sleep sucking six early cubs. But fat or lean, ribby or raunchy, just about your best chance, at that.

There could be no doubling back, no laying hidden out to let the hostiles run by you. The cañon, all the way, was so narrow a trade rat couldn't have stuck his big toe out from one side of it without some trailing Arapaho would stomp on it going by. Second place, there was no cut-off along the way. The only opening in the 100-foot cañon walls in the entire twenty-five miles was the mouth of Carson's Creek Gorge at Cedar Flats. As far as Jesse knew, that ran into a blind box three miles from the flats. It came squarely down to a stretch-out race, with the odds a 100 to two against him and the kid reaching the Medicine Road.

The biggest hitch was their horses. The mountain man had planned to rope a string of the best ponies out of the big Indian herd at the camp, lead and ride them in relays, thus giving him and the boy fresh, fast mounts the whole way into Fort Bridger. The unexpected return of the buffalo hunters had gutted that. They'd had to cut and run with only Johnny's short-legged paint, Watonga's spooky stud horse, and the good gray Heyoka.

On the stud horse he had slung two parfleches, one loaded with the pick of Black Coyote's possibles: a few pounds of jerked buffalo beef, a couple of pints of good powder, fifty galena pills, plus, hastily slung across the boy's saddle horn, Watonga's fancy old Hawken rifle; the other parfleche he had crammed with something his Indian eye had spotted in the chief's lodge and which his Sioux soul hadn't been able to resist—fifty pairs of beautifully worked Arapaho moccasins, the net proceeds of Tall Elk's long summer evenings, lovingly packed for the winter trade at Deseret. In the optimism of fresh horses and a six-hour start, Jesse had allowed he might as well turn that profit as not. Arapaho moccasins were the best on the plains, went whizzing at three dollars a brace anywhere a mountain man could get his paws on a pair. Too much the born trader, Jesse Callahan could not turn down a $150 gain for two minutes of extra packing! Not when he and Lacey and the boy would need every cent they could get to set up in California, anyway.

Now, with equal decision and eye for the future, the mountain man went out of the moccasin business. Slowing the galloping stallion, he seized the near parfleche, slashing the rawhide cross-strap through. The next second Johnny's pony and the trailing Heyoka were bucking through a $150 shower of handmade Arapaho foot skins, and Jesse was grimly lacing the remaining parfleche hard and fast to his saddle horn. Right now, the going price of two pints of powder and fifty rifle balls was higher than a fort full of fancy Indian footgear.

Looking back to check how Johnny had survived the moccasin spattering, the mountain man handed himself the luxury of a short grin. The damned sprout was all right. Grinning right back at him, there. Quirting his little pony along, busy as a monkey on a dog's back, and withal, hanging onto the cumbersome four-foot barrel of Watonga's elegant Hawken as though his life depended on it—which it sure as thunder might, come another five miles.

Jesse patted the worn butt wood of Old Sidewinder, his own treasured Hawken, hurriedly recovered from among the plunder in the chief's lodge. By God, if he went under, he'd take a few along with him. Given the boy to pour and prime, with two top guns to handle, he'd make the red sons come! Happen he could find the right spot to hole up when the time came, he'd throw a good part of them for keeps. This comforting plant had put down about half its first, tender root in Jesse's mind when it curled up and died, a-borning.

Back trail, a scant two miles, a yammer of Arapaho wolf howls blossomed high and sudden. Yellow Leg and the buffalo hunters had come home. Hearing the Indian howls, Johnny belabored his pony up even with Watonga's scrubby stallion.

"Hey, Jesse! Here they come, huh? That's them, ain't it?"

"That's them, boy. But they ain't coming just yet. Kick hell outen that pony, Johnny. We can win another mile, maybe two, before they cut the chief down and get lined out after us. They been running buffalo and they'll have to catch up and change

horses. That'll take five minutes. Ride, boy. You
ain't even trying. Whang your pony across the butt
with that gunstock. He'll go if you larrup him.
Hang on!"

With the shout, Jesse demonstrated his instructions by belting the boy's pony across the rump
with his own Hawken's butt. The little paint
squalled and jumped, churning his short legs.
Johnny hung on and kept up the belting.

For the next two miles they ate big trail. Then the
runt pony began to fade. Come the open of Cedar
Flats, he was done. The mountain man, figuring
they had four miles on the hostiles, shouted to
Johnny to pull up in mid-clearing. As the boy did so,
Jesse ran Heyoka up alongside the blowing pony.

"Pile over on Heyoka, boy. Hang onto that pine.
That's the idee. You all set?"

"Sure. Where we going now, Jesse?"

Never you mind"—the mountain man slapped
the stud horse with his rifle—"you jest burr onto
that saddle horn and leave the mare take her own
way. She'll follow me as long as there's a jump left
in her."

In the next fifteen minutes they made three of the
ten miles to Rockpile Meadow, were topping out on
Spanish Saddle. This cross ridge, the only considerable rise in the floor of Carson's Cañon, gave the
long view of the back trail offered in the full length
of the defile. From it, Jesse could look back and
down on the distant clearing of Cedar Flats.

He kicked Watonga's stud on over the crest of the
ridge, haunch-slid him to a stop on the far side.
Waving back to Johnny, he sang out: "Hi there, boy!
Get that mare down offen the skyline. Hurry on!"

As Johnny brought the mare slicing down the

trail, Jesse caught her cheek strap to keep her from
plunging on down the roof-steep decline.

"Here, young 'un. Set tight on the mare and clutch
this stud's lead rope. Keep it up short. Don't let him
get to smelling around Heyoka. She's apt to nip him
good and likely belt his ribs in, too. And we ain't in
no place to be putting on no two hoss courtship on
this here six-foot ledge. You get the idee?"

The boy peered over the trail edge at the thin
stream of Carson's Creek eighty feet below, gulped,
tried a laugh that came out a gurgle, reassured the
mountain man. "Yeah, sure, Jesse. All right. Where
you going now?"

"Back up on the ridge and take a belly flop. You
know. So's I can see the Injuns crossing Cedar Flats.
Our hosses have got to have a blow, too. They can
take it right here as good as the next place. This way
we'll get them a breather and give me a chance to
see how far back the hostiles are. We can't see them
again short of the Medicine Road. Hold them
hosses, now, boy!"

Slipping around the panting mounts, the mountain man backhanded the gray mare a sharp crack
on her sooty nose.

"Stay, Heyoka! You move a muscle toward that
stud, I'll hamstring you clean up to your croup."

Seconds later, the red-haired trapper was bellying
up on the ridge and squinting over its granite spine.
A half breath after that he was popping his eyes bigger than sourdough flapjacks. He had figured to
have close to fifteen minutes for the horses to blow
out before the pursuing Arapahoes would hit Cedar
Flats—and found he had the shag-tail end of one.
And he used part of that rolling down off the ridge
to leg it for Johnny and the horses.

Cripes! The last of the red buzzards had been slamming, hell-for-yellow-lather, across the clearing before he'd gotten his eyes over the lip of the ridge, had disappeared in a cloud of red dust and distance-thin wolf yammers before he could get his sight properly squinted.

"Last one away's a hind-tit pig!" he yelled at Johnny, crawling aboard Watonga's startled stud with the yell. "Hit the trail, boy. We're back in business!"

Johnny hadn't time to do anything but hold on. Heyoka was off down the narrow track pell-mell as a bitch hound with a razorback sow in tow. They rode now with nothing but the exploding grunts and paunch-water belly sounds of the straining horses making the conversation.

In two miles, with five yet to go to Rockpile Meadow, Watonga's stallion began to go under. Jesse felt the mean flutter of the big heart under the gaunt ribs, sensed the rhythm of the gallop going rough under him. Punctuating the discovery, a fresh burst of Arapaho howling broke out from the back trail. *Aii-eee!* If those redbirds hadn't made up nearly a mile on him and Johnny, he'd kiss a buffalo's behind.

Heyoka, snorting and chopping foam at the stud's rump, was still going smoothly as a hawk downwind. God bless the mud-ugly bitch! She was only getting to her bottom when two ordinary horses had already run clear through theirs.

"Johnny"—his back-flung shout brought an answering wave from the boy—"leave the mare come up alongside me when we hit that open ground yonder!"

With the command, the mountain man pulled the stud aside, letting the boy shoot Heyoka forward.

"Ease outen the saddle there!" he shouted, gesturing abruptly. "No, hell! Not up on her withers, boy! Back on the cantle. God damn it, get back there outen the way. Make room. I'm coming aboard with you!"

With the two horses running shoulder-to-shoulder, Jesse bellowed at the mare. "*Heeyahh!* Heyoka! *Waste, waste.* Bear in, gal. In, you muddy bitch! Shoulder in! C'mon here!"

The mare, eyes rolling, ears plastered flatter than a bear-grease haircut, crowded over into the faltering stallion. Jesse flung his off leg clear, letting her come in. The next second he was aboard her, bowed legs clamping her heaving barrel, lean arms snaking along her lathered neck to grab the loose-flying reins.

"Grab yourself a holt on that knife belt of mine, young 'un. Here we go. *Hii-yee-hahh!*"

The Minniconjou war cry echoed shrilly in the narrow cañon, putting another foot to the gray mare's reaching stride.

A mile. Four left now. Three miles. Two left. Still she ran. Not so smoothly then. Roughly. Raggedly rough. Lungs sobbing. Heart in spasm. Flared nostrils belling red as fresh blood. The hollow roar of windbreak building in the coughing gulps for air. A mile, then. One more mile. A mile to Rockpile Meadow. Rockpile Meadow? What the hell was Rockpile Meadow? Just a lousy name for a pile of horse-high boulders in the middle of a quarter-mile grass flat. Why the hell did it keep repeating itself in a man's mind as he rode the last jumps out of a dying horse? Rode with a weanling red-head kid pounding the cantle behind him.

Then, even as they went that last mile, the hostile wolf howls crawling up their rumps, two jumps for every one they were making, Jesse knew why. Knew why Rockpile Meadow had been hammering at his memory. His plan shaped, now, as they ran. Shaped to the breaking stagger of Heyoka's splaying hoofs. Shaped to that last-gasp name—Rockpile Meadow.

By damn, if he could make it into those boulders, he would carve that meadow name on a few Arapaho hides for keeps! He'd make them remember Rockpile Meadow, god damn them. He would if he and the boy could make it there.

And they made it.

What the hell difference that Heyoka went to her knees 100 yards out? Sent them sprawling, hard and headlong? Other men had run for other rocks off the buckled backs of downed horses. The main thing was—they made it. Made it with time for Jesse to kick the slobbering mare to her feet, hand-lead her in a weaving trot on into the boulder pile. Made it with time to slash the ammunition parfleche off the saddle, load and prime the two rifles while barking out the steps in the process for Johnny to watch and get the hang of.

Three minutes after they slid into the rocks the mountain man had Old Sidewinder poured, patched, rammed, and shouldered, its ugly brown snout leveled through a chin-high crevice in the rock fringe fronting the back-trail entrance into the meadow. And three and a half minutes after they had slid in, the Arapahoes bombarded out of the trail mouth and into the open meadow.

In their van, knife-cut blood still lacing his black chest in bright-red filigree, Watonga stood in his stirrups, cursing his second choice, blue-roan warhorse, frantically howling his followers on.

Jesse shoulder-nudged Old Sidewinder's butt,

shifting its thick muzzle three inches to the right, bringing the V-notch of the rear sight across the distant ripple of Black Coyote's belly muscles. 300 yards. *H'g'un.* 250 yards. *Hunhunhe.* Let them come on. Get it down to 200. *Hii-eee!* Now!

Finger squeezing off, both eyes open like any sharp shot's ought to be, Jesse suddenly hunched the rifle muzzle another two inches to the right, swerving the V-notch off Watonga's belly, filling it with the shorter Dog Head's throat base. With the recoil punching his jaw, the mountain man wondered why he'd done it. Why he'd pulled off his bead on the chief, put it on the hapless Dog Head.

The shot seemed to roll out slower than the subchief's answering scream. Jesse saw the red hands fly to the throat, and then there was open meadow in the sight's V-notch. Dog Head, fourth-line chief among the lodges of Watonga, was on his way to Wanagi Yata, his one-way lead ticket punched squarely and truly through the Adam's apple. With the blast of the hidden rifle and Dog Head's flopping dive, the following Indians checked their ponies, hard up, their followers, in turn, banging into them, piling the whole forepart of the pack into a confused tangle. Only a handful of the front-runners had marked the flash of Jesse's gun, the bulk of them not yet guessing the source of the sub-chief's ambush.

Jesse didn't keep them long in doubt.

"Gimme that gun, boy. Load this 'un. And see you take your time and do it right."

Grabbing Watonga's Hawken from the gaping youngster, he scuttled forty feet to the right, snapped an offhand shot into the maw of the milling pack. Two ponies reared, screaming, showing him he'd gotten a lucky one in, drilling the first horse to tap the second.

By now, the Arapahoes had counted two separate flashes, were beginning to break back for the meadow's edge, undecided.

The mountain man raced back past Johnny, snatching back his own Hawken as the boy finished pouring the powder. Diving behind a big boulder thirty feet to the left of his original shot, he spat the spare galena pill from his mouth into the muzzle, banging the stock on the ground to seat the charge, not having time to ram it home with the hickory wiping stick. For sure, it wouldn't do much damage when it got out there, but it would get out there. Right now the idea wasn't a center shot. It was just any old shot.

Blam! The third shot whanged across the open, taking Elk Runner's bay mare fairly under her flag, sending her pitching and squalling like she'd had a hay fork rammed up her.

That did it. *Hopo,* get out! *Hookahey,* back to the timber! *Wagh!* Where had the reinforcements come from? Who was out there in those rocks with Tokeya Sha and Ya Slo? Two shots—well, maybe the boy was shooting. But three? Who would know? *A-ah,* now was the time to look out. Something wrong here.

Back at the meadow's edge, the hostiles pow-wowed millingly. Shortly two groups began skirting the edge of the open grass, keeping back of the timber, one group each way around the meadow. They traveled slowly, eyes intent on the ground.

Watching them from the rock pile, Jesse spoke thoughtfully to Johnny O'Mara. "They're tracking us out, young 'un. Aiming to see did we get outen the meadow, or did somebody else get into it."

"Gee, what'll they do then, Jesse? Reckon they'll scalp us?"

"Not you, boy. You'll make out, happen I work it right. They'll come for us right sudden, now, though. When they meet up over there on the far side, they'll know it's just us and nobody else out here. Then we'll catch it, sure as Old Sidewinder shoots high and left."

"Say, looks to me like your piece held plumb center, Jesse. You sure nailed that old Dog Head right in the neck." Johnny was more impressed at the moment with the marksmanship of one white Minniconjou than with the threat of 100 red Arapahoes.

"It don't, though, boy. That's why I got it named Old Sidewinder. Strikes like a crotchety buzz tail. Hits on the up go and a trifle left of center."

"It sure hits for you! High, left, or anyways."

"They'll hit where you hold them, young 'un. Happen you know where to hold them. You . . ."

"Hey, look!" the excited youngster interrupted. "They're staying over there. Look at them waving their arms around!"

"Shut up," snapped the mountain man. "Leave me read them signs."

Chapter 12

For three minutes the Arapahoes talked back and forth over the heads of Jesse and Johnny, signaling with broad hand gestures and a series of barks and howling cries that sounded like nothing nearer than a loafer pack bickering over a division of buffalo guts. As they conversed across the quarter-mile bowl of grassland, Jesse translated for his big-eyed companion. He didn't call the signal barks like he was talking them for a seven-year-old, either. When a man reckons he's run his kite string to the winding stick, he talks. Happen he's one of two whites betwixt 100 red Indians, he does. And birthdays don't mean a damn. It's blood talking to blood, and the cleanest way to say it is to say it short. Leastways, if you mean it to be that you're saying good bye.

"That's Elk Runner over there, Johnny, and Gray Bear with him. I think that's Blood Face doing the signal calling. Must be, he's their head tracker. He's telling Watonga that no tracks come outen the meadow over there. Now he's waving that there ain't none coming in, neither. There he goes saying it must be only Tokeya Sha and Ya Slo out here in the rocks. That's it, boy."

The mountain man flicked his eyes to Watonga's group. "Now, you watch old Black Coyote. He'll give them their marching orders. This is where we come in. There he goes, see?"

The boy nodded, wide eyes pinned on the gracefully gesturing chief. "What's he telling them, Jesse? What's old Black Coyote saying to do?"

Jesse, watching the chief, tensed suddenly. Ignoring the boy's questions, he reached one long arm over to draw Johnny close to him. His voice was low, with no shred of excitement in it, but the narrowed eyes behind it burned fever-bright. "Boy, listen to me. They've caught up to old Jesse. They're going to rush us. Both sides against the middle. Now, get this"—the mountain man illustrated the flat lie with serious finger wags—"I can tell by their signs that they aim to take us alive. But when they bust into these rocks, ahossback, a little shaver like you might get stomped on, accidental-like. So here's how you play it. When they start for us, you head outen them rocks to the north there. Right through that opening. You mark the one I'm pointing?"

"Yes, sir. Gosh, Jesse, you mean you want me to run out there as soon as they come at us?"

"And keep running," the mountain man spoke sharply. "Scoot like a cottontail bunny with his flag on fire."

"What are you going to do?" The youngster eyed his companion suspiciously. "Stay here?"

"I'll be right behind you," Jesse assured him. "That'll give them a chance to come up on us in the open. Nobody'll get trompled, see?"

"Why'n't we just surrender now?"

The boy's direct question jolted Jesse's yarn, forced him to throw a thickening handful of pure slop into the thin soup he was ladling up. "Listen, boy. They'd figure it for a trick and ride right into us. This way they'll know we're giving in, straight. You do as I say and you'll see I'm right."

"Gee, I dunno. I . . ."

"Just do it, god damn you, boy. Don't argue."

"All right, Jesse, all right. I guess you know. . . ."

"You damned betcha. So long, boy." The mountain man wrapped the youngster in a bear hug that popped his trusting blue eyes. "You mark what old Jesse said. Run like hell when they start in for us. Don't look back for me. You might stumble and get yourself trompled, after all. Now, get over in them north rocks. Keep your eye on me, and, when I wave, you scoot!"

Johnny scuttled obediently over into the far rocks, crouched trembling fearfully, awaiting the mountain man's go sign.

Jesse hoped he had figured it halfway soundly. You could never tell about those flighty red devils, though. That was the trouble. However, if the kid had any chance, it was to get out in the clear as far away from Jesse Callahan as he could leg it. Watonga had Tokeya Sha where his hair was shorter than a scalded hog's. And the big black-skinned chief had blood in his small slant eye—Minniconjou blood.

Happen the boy got in the way of the Arapaho head man getting to that blood, he'd get hurt. Out in the open and running away, chances were near sure some buck would make a dead gallop scoop-up of him and lug him clear of the fracas. *Wagh!* There'd be plenty of honor in that. Grabbing Watonga's foster son right out from under the *Wasicun*'s magic holy iron. Scooping Ya Slo, unharmed, from under the very muzzle of Tokeya the Minniconjou's *mazawakan*. *Wagh,* indeed! Anyway, that was as close as a man could set it up for the boy. Johnny might make it, might not. He'd have his chance. *Nohetto.* A man did what he could, then let it lay.

Shrugging, the mountain man turned his rifle eye on his own prospects. Half a look was plenty. The Arapahoes, both sides of the meadow, were ready. On the up cañon side, Watonga was wheeling his roan gelding in front of the main force. Twenty yards down the waiting line, Yellow Leg pivoted his pony in imitation of the chief's revolving horsemanship. Across meadow, the thirty braves with Blood Face stood hooking their toes in their ponies' surcingles, hawkeying the gyrations of their chief and Yellow Leg.

In his rock pile, Jesse watched the weaving turns of the ponies with equal interest, if inferior anticipation. The Sioux-taught mountain man understood the pattern and purpose of that wheeling maneuver as well as an Arapaho within rifle shot. Watonga and Yellow Leg were riding the *icapsinpsineela.* The swallow, the circling signal ride that announced that the preliminaries were done—the final act coming on stage. When the tracks of their ponies crisscrossed, look out. When the hoof prints came together and divided like the forked tail of the wheeling swallow—*a-ah,* that was the time. *And the time was now.*

Watonga spun his blue roan, hard left, heeling him straight for Yellow Leg's mount. The sub-chief hauled his pony around to meet the approach of his chief. The two careening horses veered at the last moment, crossing each other in the lethal forked angle. The scaling red-granite float of the meadow floor churned to the hammer of 400 barefoot pony hoofs. Jesse whirled, flagging Johnny to run. The boy caught the signal, started to run, got out in the clear past the rocks, got his first look at the lance-streaming Indian charge.

Skidding to a stop, his childish cry wobbled back to the mountain man: "Come on, Jesse! Oh gosh, look at them come!"

"Go on, boy!" Curse the little devil's red-head hide. "Run, god damn it, Johnny, run!"

Johnny O'Mara hesitated half a second, turned, and ran. Ran like old Jesse had told him. Scooting like a singe-tail bunny. Straight back toward the mountain man.

Jesse threw his left arm, wide, hooking the sliding youngster to his side, cursing him while he hugged him, winking the first tear he could ever remember out of his ice-blue eyes, snarling at him like he'd heard Tall Elk snarling at him in that teepee, and thinking for the first time how the giant squaw must have felt about this freckle-face tadpole.

"God damn you, boy! I'll flay your bottom raw for you. I told you to run. What's the idea, Johnny?"

"You wasn't coming." Lacey's son was sobbing, now, the tears flooding Jesse's buckskins. "You said you was coming, and, when I looked, you wasn't. I got scared, Jesse. Honest Injun, *wowicake*. I'm sorry, Jesse. I . . ."

Jesse gritted his teeth. "Hit the dirt in there!" he yelled, shoving Johnny flat on his face between two jutting boulders. "If you so much as twitch, Johnny, I'll knock your goddamn' head off!"

Without waiting to see his command obeyed, the mountain man threw himself over a waist-high rock, leveled on the nearest hostile, the wild-riding Blood Face. That was the greatest single shot Jesse Callahan ever made. Not only Blood Face flew out of his saddle, but four of his braves out of theirs. And—even more remarkable—Yellow Leg and two of the big-mouth war whoopers in Watonga's backside charge grabbed their bellies and lost interest in their work.

Jesse was just as confounded as the Arapahoes. Gray Bear and Elk Runner swung the remaining braves in Blood Face's bunch wide of the rocks, hightailing it for Black Coyote's riders. Pudding proof of their panic and an almost unheard of action among Plains warriors, they left their fallen where they hit. In this case it was equal proof of their excellent judgment, too.

As they piled into Watonga's charge, checking and turning it with their warning shouts, the mystery of Jesse's great shot was blasted wide open. Black Coyote, unable to see clearly across the rocks, missed the loss of Blood Face and the four braves, had seen Yellow Leg grab his middle but figured that for the work of the hidden Tokeya. Jesse had seen the braves go down with no idea what sent them, had assumed that wild lead from Watonga's bucks had done the damage. The rag and tag of the galloping Indian pack, on both sides of the charge, simply had no idea what had hit them.

Watonga, Gray Bear, Elk Runner, and surviving company now got the second installment of Tokeya Sha's holy iron miracle. It came crashing from the elevated, rocky aperture of the down cañon trail head, the one toward the Medicine Road, and it set three more Arapaho ponies to carrying double. The smoke of that second volley, crawling up the cañon walls, raised the curtain on as fine a natural eyeful ever a surrounded mountain man took in. Ranging back of their granite breastworks, waving their rifles and whooping it up as woolly as any pack of braid-hair hostiles, Andy Hobbs, Morgan Bates, Joplin Smith, and the balance of the Choteau Company muleskinners hooted and catcalled the fleeing Arapahoes.

Jesse slumped down on a handy rock, feeling the sudden need for something harder than a handful of hot air under his seat. "All right, Johnny boy. Come on out. We got ourselves a breather."

The mountain man had to grin at the puny sound of his own voice. It wobbled out weaker than a ten-day kitten. By cripes, a man had to allow that when he'd been in a tight that cozy, he knew he'd been squeezed somewhat. And he knew more than that as soon as he'd gotten his wind and had himself a sick smile at Lacey's young one wiggling, tearful and dirty-faced, out of his crack in the rocks. He knew he wasn't yet home in bed. Not by forty miles and ninety-five howling-mad Arapahoes. He and Johnny were for sure in the middle of the plank. With both ends sawed off, short. The Arapahoes couldn't get at them without running the ambushing teamster's fire. The muleskinners couldn't get out to relieve them without exposing themselves to the rifles of Black Coyote's raiders. And both sides counted plenty of center shots in their ranks. When a man faced up to it, the Indians still had the top hand on the coup-stick handle.

In the mountain man's working mind, the fact

that Andy Hobbs and the boys had gotten up from old Gabe's so suddenly meant one of two things: either they hadn't brought the powder wagon at all, or they'd brought it part way and had to leave it down on the Medicine Road. From where Jesse squatted, cuddling Johnny and snatching looks at both trail heads between reassuring pats on the tousled red head, the whole thing looked like a clear stand-off.

Damn the luck. If Heyoka could still run, he'd chance a dash for it in half a shuck. But the mare was stove. If she could walk out of the meadow bareback, let alone getting up a gallop under double carry, it would be a mortal wonder. He had raveled the knit of their chances down this far when a commotion among the Arapahoes sent his eyes, following their excited pointings, swinging to the white side of the meadow. Jesse grabbed his look and got excited right along with the hostiles. *Son-of-a-bitch!*

Don't ask how that big leather-faced hardcase had done it. Don't question what skull work and back break had gone betwixt him and Andy Hobbs and the rest of the muleskinners to get it done. Don't say a god damned thing. Just squat there and run your ever loving eyes over her from her upswept prow to her high-tailed stern, from her glaring white Osnaburg top sheets to her circus-red wheels! Yes, man. Run your eyes plenty and then raise them to old Man Above. Lift them to old Wakan Tanka. Thank him. *Ha ho, woyuonihan.* By God, Morgan Bates had done it—he'd brought him his gunpowder and his red-wheeled goddam!

If Watonga had a price, this was it. His band was out of meat and powder and with a big herd of fat cows running around on the mesa above Portola Springs. *Wagh!* Any man in the business who'd been Sioux-coached and couldn't make a trade out of this tangle deserved to have his hair hoisted.

On his side of the meadow, Watonga was digging in, spreading his best shots among the rocks flanking the upcañon trail head, covering Jesse's hole as closely as the muleskinners had it covered from their side. If it was going to be a siege, the wily Arapaho was ready for it. He might be low on powder and lead, but he had a mort more of men and time than the whites.

Among their rocks, the muleskinners were imitating the chief's moves, shifting their individual vantage points to improve their rifle command of the trapped mountain man's cover. It was Jesse Callahan's move. Cupping his hands, he bellowed across the meadow: "Hi, there, Andy! Can you hear me?"

Jesse had a baritone halfway between a colicky boar pig and a sore-throat bullfrog. Apparently it was more than adequate, the bearded wagon master bellowing right back that if a couple of old North Trail hands like Jesse Callahan and A.J. Hobbs couldn't make themselves heard over 200 yards of open meadow, they were in the wrong business. What did Mr. Callahan have on his bright young mind this bracing autumn afternoon? And how would he like to hear that Mr. Hobbs had managed to bring along the whole original load of Du Pont intact?

Jesse let the thrill of that spread his rare grin about four more teeth, before calling back: "All right! Fine. Now, listen. Hold her down and watch your words. Old Blackface over there, and some of his top haircutters, they catch a little white chin music." The mountain man tried using words that wouldn't likely fit into the bobtail English primer of

Watonga's prairie education, hoped he was getting the idea across to Andy Hobbs. "And they ain't exactly got their thumbs in their ears. You get me?"

"Like as not, little man. Can you hear this all right?"

"Just right. All set, now. Watch your talk."

"I said I got you, boy. What you aim to pull? Straight trade?"

"Straight trade," the mountain man echoed him. "The Pittsburgh and Du Pont for me and the kid. What you say?"

"Bad medicine, Jesse." The old man's voice was quick with worry. "What's to keep them from accepting the swindle, and then crossing us double? They got us ten to one and nobody never got fat swallowing no Injun eyewash. I'm spooked at just giving them the Du Pont, right out."

The moment Jesse had seen the powder wagon, his mind had started turning on how best to use it. When he had set out after the Arapahoes, things had been a mort different. He had, offhand, thought that if he could bring the wagon up to the red camp on a peaceful palaver basis, with a reinforced party of whites to back up the talk, he could trade them out of the kid with nobody getting hurt on either side. But that was before a lot of things. It was before he'd had to kill Tall Elk and carve up Watonga. It was before he could have known that, when Andy Hobbs got the wagons to Fort Bridger, he would find Bridger and the other mountain men usually around the place absent from the fort and scattered God knew where. And before anybody but the old white warrior himself could have known that, old Gabe had changed his whole plan about trying to stand off Brigham Young's Danites from within the fort. Had decided to cut for the timber and not be home when the Saints dropped in.

Now, hesitating, Jesse knew Andy Hobbs was plenty solid in his doubts of turning the powder over to the unstable red men. Knew, also, that he was up against a moral decision that spelled murder. The mountain man made that decision the way he had to. Without thinking about the dirty side of it. Keeping his mind on Lacey O'Mara's kid and the dozen white men with Andy Hobbs and Morgan Bates. And keeping it on Jesse Callahan's own tender, snow-white hide. Somebody was going to get hurt now.

Watonga had taken too much loss of face off of this particular bunch of *Wasicun* goddam drivers to let them go clean and free following a peaceful trade. That was the way Andy Hobbs had it figured and he likely had it figured right. On top of that general debt, you add what Jesse had handed the giant Arapaho on his own personal account and you had a sum that toted up way too heavily for a white man to look for an even-steven trade from a red one.

Across the meadow Andy Hobbs, waiting nervously on Jesse's long silence, sang out: "Hello, Jesse! What's amiss, boy? I said I was plumb set against just giving them the Du Pont, clean out. Did you hear me?"

"I heard you." The mountain man's voice came quick now, the snap and hop of it telling a decision hastily made but finally meant. "And you needn't be skittery about giving them the powder. Not the way I'm aiming to give it to them, old salt."

"What you mean? You said straight trade, didn't you?"

"I'm changing that. I ain't saying it no more. You was right. We can't chance it."

"What you saying, now?"

"Straight Injun trade."

"Where's the difference?"

"I said straight *Injun,* old hoss. You got that? We ain't trading with old Gabe or Charley Bent, you know. Those're red Injuns over there. The whole thing's gummed up, Andy. This ain't just the ideal swap I had in mind when I took out after these sons. They got us spread so far over the barrel our butts are pointing sun high. Give one chance, the way they're gingered up now, they'd snatch the Du Pont and half our hair along with it. Brush up, Andrew!"

"Leave off the sass!" The wagon master's yell was heating up with tension. "We ain't got all autumn here. How you aiming to trade?"

"We're trading red now. Red-style. Injun honor." The mountain man dropped his call back as low as he could.

"How's that, again . . . ?" Andy Hobb's voice dropped, too, now.

"Long promise . . . short fuse." Jesse used the old frontier phrase covering the white man's belly-low opinion of his red brother's given word.

"Whoa, Nellie!" The implication in the mountain man's answer hit the old man suddenly. "You can't do that, boy. It ain't civilized. . . ."

"I ain't, neither," barked Jesse. "Now, get aholt of Morgan and ask him did he bring that coil of touch-off medicine along. And get a move on, old hoss."

Jesse could see the oldster duck away from his rock, slide quickly back and around the far side of the Pittsburgh, go to palavering with the tall Missourian. Shortly the boss muleskinner slid back along the far side of the wagon, went to rummaging in the seat box. He was back with Andy Hobbs in a moment and the two went into another discussion. Apparently something was amiss. Either that, or Jesse was getting a mite jumpy.

To the cotton-mouthed mountain man the silent seconds of the wait seemed to drag their feet louder than bonedry brakes on a sun-blistered wagon wheel. Then, just as he was about to consign Morgan Bates and his misfire memory to hell's hottest stove hole, the palaver broke up and old Andy doubled over for the quick scuttle back to his outpost. Once more safely behind his forward rock, the wagon master took up his interrupted conversation with the quietly cursing Jesse.

"Feast your peepers on her, boy! Fifty feet of the best even-burning fuse ever twisted. Morgan says you can clip it anywheres from twenty seconds to ten minutes!" With his tight-voiced call, the old man's arm waved the stiff coil of shining black loops.

Jesse let his breath go. Man! Sometimes a Minniconjou like him played in pure outhouse luck. Old Morgan hadn't let him down. Now! With the breaking off of the thought, his long arm was returning Andy Hobbs's wave. "God bless that Missouri redneck for me, Andy. Happen his touch-off medicine works for us. I'll buy him four hundred yards of the damn' stuff, for free. Set tight, boys. Here goes for the dicker with old lump jaw."

"Take your time," the old man hollered acidly. "It's your red wagon!"

Jesse went down back of the rocks, muttering and shaking his head.

"What's the matter, Jesse?" Johnny O'Mara's thin voice piped up worriedly. "Ain't we going to get away, after all? Gosh, I thought we was saved!"

"Shut up, boy. We're all right. I just got to have me a minute to think. You keep quiet and lay low."

With fifteen seconds of his minute unused, the mountain man stood up, jaw set, eyes narrowed nearly shut. While the crouching boy stared, fascinated, he picked up his Hawken, straightened his shoulders, stepped slowly and deliberately into the open meadow on Watonga's side of the rock pile.

Ten long, measured strides, rifle held butt and barrel high over his head. Ten strides counted off by the growling wave of deep, approving *hunhunhes* that rose up among the watching Arapahoes. Then he stopped, held the rifle toward the hostiles, bent forward to place it on the ground. When he straightened, his hands were held shoulder high, empty palms out, toward the Indians.

It was the peace sign—*Wolkota wa yaka cola*—by prairie protocol it could not be ignored.

Watonga walked his pony three lengths out in front of his hidden braves. His deep voice came rolling across to Jesse, but it came without the outward palm. It came with the war sign, with the chief's lowered hands firmly full of loaded rifle.

"What does Tokeya Sha want of Watonga? Why does he use the holy sign?"

Jesse let him have it quickly. The afternoon shadows were already high on the cañon walls, creeping higher by the minute. Time was running out. The mountain man's voice carried to the scowling savage, the measured Sioux cadences rolling dramatically. *Hau, kola. Hau, tahunsa.* Would the great Arapaho chief accept the gift of the red-wheeled goddam with its original load of *big hmunha*, intact? Exactly as Brigham chief had promised it to him?

Would he take the twenty-four cases of *Wasicun* gunpowder in exchange for the courtesy giving of Tokeya Sha and little Ya Slo to the goddam drivers from Big Throat's fort? Would Watonga do that?

The chief hesitated. Wheeled his pony suddenly. Rode back into the cedars without a word in answer to Jesse's wheedling offer.

Five minutes passed, every last one of them sweat damp enough to wilt the starch out of six Sunday shirts. Jesse, standing alone in the meadow, knew he was holding the biggest breath he had ever taken.

Watonga came back as abruptly and black-browed as he had left. *He-hau*, would Black Coyote accept the white goddam guide's crawling surrender? Would he accept the *Wasicun's* craven powder offer? *Hau*, he might do just that. Providing. Providing that he, Watonga, could inspect the goddam before accepting. That was flat. *Nohetto*.

The mountain man let his breath out so loudly he thought maybe the chief could have heard it, 200 yards across the meadow. *Wagh*, of course Watonga could inspect the gift. Did Black Coyote think Tokeya Sha would play him false? Lie to him? Give him short measure?

It seemed that Watonga did. *Iho*, no matter. He would come in, anyway. If he liked the looks of the powder, a deal might be made. After all, Tall Elk was gone. There was no one to care for Ya Slo. And did not the red-haired goddam guide admit that by losing the powder to Watonga he was letting Black Coyote count the biggest coup of all? Did the Fox admit that? That the Coyote was his master?

Aii-eee! Indeed he did. He did just that. He was

proud to admit it. It was a great honor to be beaten by a real chief like Black Coyote. *Woyuonihan. Hunhunhe.* Watonga was all man. Much more man than Tokeya the Minniconjou. Would he, then, now come in and inspect the Fox's surrender gift?

Hau, he would. He'd do that. And he'd bring his chiefs along, too. He would bring Elk Runner and Gray Bear.

H'g'un, that was fine. But why bring his friends? Tokeya had no friends. Tokeya was alone out there. Did Watonga fear to come alone to meet him? Was that the way it was?

Wagh! Damn! Never! Watonga's heart was big, like a bear's. He was coming. By Man Above he was coming now. All by himself!

Waste, good. Tokeya would have the old one, Big Throat's wagon chief, drive the red-wheeled goddam to mid-meadow. He would have the wagon chief make all his men come out and stand in the open so that Watonga could see none of them was hiding in the goddam. Now, would Watonga have all his warriors ride into the grass a way? Not far. Just a little way. Just so the *Wasicun* could see that none of them was going around the meadow while the talk was made?

He-hau, of course. *Woyuonihan.* Black Coyote would do that. It was only common courtesy.

Waste, all was agreed, then?

Jesse yelled the deal over to Andy Hobbs while Watonga was arranging his warriors. The old man signaled his understanding, began unhooking half of the sixteen mules which had dragged the 5,000-pound freighter up a cañon God had built to give a two-horse surrey a headache. When he was ready, he made his final yell.

"How about the *Injun* part of it, boy?"

"Five foot long. And stuff it down your crotch cloth," Jesse echoed back. "And don't forget your tinderbox!"

Chapter 13

The packed ranks of Watonga's followers sat in slit-eyed silence as their chief rode out to meet the red-wheeled goddam. In mid-meadow Jesse and Andy Hobbs stood waiting, the Pittsburgh parked and rein-wrapped, the mules standing quietly.

Black Coyote rode past them without a word or look, tied his pony to the rear wheel, clambered into the sheeted Pittsburgh. He was back out in three breaths—three breaths in which one tinderbox and five feet of black powder fuse got from one *Wasicun*'s crotch cloth to another's.

"How'd you find it, chief? You savvy, powder all there? *Waste*, good?" Andy Hobbs's scraggly beard bobbed with the rapid questions.

"*Waste*. Powder all there. *Wiksemna nunpa dopa*. Two times ten and four. Watonga says it."

"You betcha!" The beard bobbed again. "Nary a danged drachma short. Twenty-four kegs, twenty-five pounds to the keg. Six hundred pounds to the damn' ounce of the best by-god powder Du Pont ever built!"

The towering Arapaho nodded. "Good. Watonga trades. You leave powder, take boy. Get out now. Watonga come fast, bring warriors, take powder. You leave powder on ground, take goddam. *Nohetto.*"

Jesse stood, dumb as a lightning-struck ox. God Almighty, now what? Leave the powder on the ground? *Aii-eee!* There was one to twist a man's thoughts around. A real cute one. He'd sure as hell never foresighted that idea.

Watonga sensed the mountain man's hesitation, the burr of his suspicion showing its quick bristle in his demand. "How goes it, Tokeya?" He fell back into Jesse's Sioux tongue. "I smell something. And there's no wind."

"Of course!" It was a wild shot, and the only one open to the floundering mountain man. "Tokeya is a fool. You smell his bad judgment. It doesn't take a wind to smell a *heyoka*. I had not seen this softness in Watonga's nature, that's all."

"*Softness?*" The chief's scowl clouded up black as a summer cloud. "Tokeya speaks of softness. How is that?"

"Oh, nothing. Nothing at all." Jesse kept the shrug as insultingly careless as he could. "It was not in my mind to think Watonga would weaken thus toward an enemy. Aye, to think of it! Letting Tokeya make away with a thing that has been such a curse to you. Naturally I thought it would be taken and burned. To be made to count as a real coup. Especially since the chief must remember that I heard him say to Tall Elk that it was the curse of his life, and that he would rather count a coup on it than to eat fat cow all winter. Ah, well. Tokeya is grateful. Watonga is as graceful as a woman. *Ha ho!*"

"Do not thank me." The chief's huge jaw chopped

the ugly words short. "It is nothing. Thank your big
mouth for what you hear now. Watonga did *not* remember that you heard that curse. Leave it there.
Right where it is. With all the powder in it!"

With the angry demand, the Arapaho swung his
four-foot skull club and with a great shout of *"On-
hey!"*—the word shouted when the first coup is
struck on an enemy, literally: "I kill him, first!"—
smote the sideboards of the Pittsburgh a thunderous
clout.

"Now, wait! Watonga said I could take the goddam." Jesse made the objection hesitantly, hoping
he wasn't over-putting it.

He wasn't.

"Leave the goddam! That's the way it will be
now," snapped Watonga. *"Nohetto!"*

"Nohetto," sighed Jesse, bowing regretfully to the
superior power of the hulking raider. "Perhaps in
time Tokeya will learn that Watonga is all the man
he looks."

"I am going," was all the Arapaho said, turning
his roan pony with the words.

"Wait!" Jesse's hand gestured quickly. "You have
counted the powder. I have not. Would Tokeya Sha
give a gift not knowing it was all there, as his word
was given on it?"

"Woyuonihan," grunted Watonga, waving his
hand haughtily. "Be quick about it. I honor you."

Jesse was inside the wagon before the chief's
words were well out. Once there, he found the
sheeted dimness too uncertain for an honest count.
Surely there could be no objection to striking a little
light with Andy Hobbs's tinderbox, nor to getting
that damned stiff fuse out of his crotch cloth, so it
wouldn't chafe him out of being absolutely sure

Black Coyote got everything that had been promised him. A man had to have things just so, in a close deal like this one.

When the mountain man crawled back out of the Pittsburgh, a sharp eye might have wondered that he was in such a mortal hurry about it. And about the way he talked when he did get out.

But Watonga's beady orbs were busy with pleasanter prospects. *Ha! Iho!* How blind were these white antelopes? Oh, sure. Let them give him the goddam full of powder. Let them leave it there and go running for their rocks. *Hau,* let them go. It was a long way to Big Throat's fort. And did they know about the hidden way to climb out of Little Chief's Valley, back there where the grass grew wide among the cedars? The way that would let a fast pony get back to the Medicine Road well ahead of any band of *Wasicun* goddam drivers traveling down the main cañon trail? Did they know that? About that secret way Watonga would have sent some warriors to cut off Tokeya and Ya Slo had he not known he could catch them so easily without doing so? *Iho,* indeed. Here was a trade that wasn't done yet.

"All right." Jesse's hurrying words cut the chief's *wickmunke* dreaming short. "It's all there. We have traded."

"*Ni'inaei,* good hunting." Watonga grinned, making rare use of an Arapaho phrase in place of the generally spoken Sioux: "*H'g'un.*"

With the courage shout, the fleeting grin died, stillborn, leaving Black Coyote's face as blank as a basalt rock. The obsidian glitter of his tiny eyes held Jesse while a slow man might have counted five. Then he was gone, his blue-roan gelding digging on a dead gallop toward the waiting warriors.

"Leg it, Andy!" The mountain man's shout was wasted back of the dust puffs already being sent up by the wagon master's thudding boots. As the old man looked back, Jesse waved him on. "Go on, leg it! I'll get the boy."

Johnny, hearing the yell, scudded from the rocks, heading for Jesse. The mountain man scooped him up on the run, legged it for the cheering teamsters as fast as his long shanks would churn. Johnny O'Mara wasn't the only one to respond to Jesse's shout. As the mountain man grabbed the boy and ran for the muleskinners, a forlorn, dusk-gray ghost tottered out of the rocks to follow along in a stumbling trot. Heyoka, the knock-kneed clown, wasn't aiming to be left behind, not while she could still see and had the breath left in her to go after that red-haired *Wasicun*.

By the time Jesse and Johnny reached the down cañon rocks, the Arapahoes had swarmed across the meadow, surrounding the Pittsburgh and boosting Watonga up onto the wagon box. And there, mounted triumphantly on the driver's seat of Tokeya Sha's red-wheeled goddam, all six feet three of him standing, black and stark, against the white Osnaburg back-drop, Watonga, war chief of the Wind River Arapahoes, made his departing oration of acceptance.

Then, his faithful crowding the wagon hubs as close as their scrawny ponies could jam, he seized the unfamiliar wrap of the multiple reins, started the *Wasicun's* fear gift uncertainly across the meadow. His final, jeering shout at Jesse reminded the cowardly mountain man that in the end it was Watonga who had proved the better man, he, Black Coyote, who was finally going to get what was rightly coming to him. Which he did. Six seconds and one inch of fuse later.

The twenty-four kegs of powder made a nice salute to the chief's phenomenal gift of prophecy. Choice cuts of Choteau & Company mule, Indian pony, and male Arapaho, mingled with a fine selection of oak spokes, hickory whiffletrees, and drawn-iron wheel rims. The clapping thunder of the explosion rocketed back and forth between the narrow cañon walls fit to split a man's ear skins clean across.

Jesse shook his head to get the ringing out of it, peered intently under the rolling cloud of powder smoke. At first glance, he counted eight sprawling braves who were already pounding their stiffening rears up the misty trail to Wanagi Yata, another limping three dozen who would carry pieces of Pittsburgh and pepperings of Jesse Callahan's Du Pont powder buried under their smoking hides for all their days short of the place where the souls gather. One membrous figure, tottering waveringly toward the far edge of the meadow, brought a strange leap to the watching mountain man's heart. As will sometimes unaccountably happen with those who are the very closest to the source of an explosion, Black Coyote had miraculously survived. Blown sky high, dumped bare skin naked into the spiny clutch of an early berry bush, the old warrior had come out of it alive. His panicky braves, unfamiliar with gunpowder in larger quantities than buffalo horns full were hustling him aboard a squealing, wild-eyed pony, were cutting out of the meadow for all they were worth, jamming and packing the entrance of the up cañon trail head.

Watching the rout, Jesse yelled along the line of

head-drawing muleskinners. "Hold your fire, boys! They've had it. No use kicking them when they're done and down. Leave the buzzards go."

The last of the braves were crowding through the far trail head, the still reeling Watonga supported among them. The mountain man's rare grin cracked the dirty granite of his jaw.

Sure, leave the red sons go. He had set out long days ago to skin that arrogant scut of a Watonga, true. But what with his Arapaho hide still smoking from its twenty-four-keg gunpowder cure, and his hog-size Indian ego blistered worse than a lapful of hot grease, the haughty chief's peltry was hardly worth the sweat it would take a man to peel it off of him. Not to Jesse Callahan it wasn't, anyhow. Jesse was a man who never messed with any skin that wasn't plumb prime. Leastways, never killed for one that wasn't.

Chapter 14

It was a loud-talking band of Choteau & Company muleskinners that rode the shadowed reaches of Carson's Cañon downtrail of Rockpile Meadow that early fall evening. Heading them, pert as a peafowl, astride a captured calico pony, rode young Johnny O'Mara, proudly flanked by Morgan Bates and Joplin Smith. The two muleskinners had their horses trapped with feathered Arapaho headstalls, their persons dripping buckskins and beadwork, while behind them scarcely a man in the outfit failed to sport some spoils of Jesse's hard-driven Indian trade. A horsehair-tasseled buffalo lance here. A heron-plumed coup stick there. And, here and there, a sprinkling of squat Arapaho war bows, beautifully worked elk-hide quivers, tooled parfleches, quilled moccasins, bear-claw necklaces, buffalo-horn and half-kull headdresses, stone pipes, handmade skinning knives, and scarlet three-point Northwest blankets: together, the whole gaudy rag tassel of peeled-off Plains Indian war dress that told the story of ten naked braves silent amid a lonely pile of meadow rocks.

Behind Johnny and his jubilant escort, Jesse and Andy Hobbs rode in wordless quiet. Glancing at his companion, the old man marked the brooding, narrow-eyed stare, the wide clamp of the Sioux mouth, knew the gaunt mountain man was mind-riding the back trail.

"You couldn't help it, Jesse." The words came as soft as the touch of the weathered paw on his companion's knee. "You had to think of the kid, first."

"Sure," the answer came after a short silence, "I reckon. But it shames me all the same, Andy. I feel mortal bad about it, somehow."

"Ain't no call for you to feel thataway, young 'un. They was hostile Injuns and trail raiders, to boot. And any red bunch that works the Oregon Trail knows what to expect when they wipe out a settler band and carry off a young 'un."

Jesse nodded. "Yeah, Andy, I allow you're right. Watonga sure knowed what he was asking for when he hit them emigrants and hoisted Lacey's kid. Not to mention what the squaw did to the baby."

The wagon master lifted his hand from the mountain man's knee, placed it gently on his shoulder.

"Matter of fact, Jesse, I allow you done the whole Medicine Road traffic a powerful turn. Jim Bridger has had hisself twenty years' hard work building a peaceful trade with Washakie and them friendly Snakes of his'n. Him and the other traders sure can't afford to have these here wild northern cousins filtering down and getting the friendlies riled up again. And you done put a sharp, hard stop to any such notions they might've had, with that powder trade just now."

"By damn, I hope you're right, Andy. That was strong medicine I dosed old Black Coyote with. I'd feel a heap better to figure he had it coming to him for more'n just what he done to us."

"Well, you just figure he had, son. He had, and you can tie on it. And I'll tell you how it's going to be now. Old Black Coyote, he's the big chief up north. So when a dozen Missouri muleskinners and one medium-size red-head mountain man can knock the hides offen a hundred of his top warriors three times, hand running, its going to shrink the size of his teepee considerable. Time he gets home with what's left of his tail tucked atween his legs, every Arapaho north of the Platte is going to know there's easier ways of making a living than working the old Medicine Road. I allow it'll be a long, hot winter in Montany before another Arapaho chief comes down to raid the Californy traffic."

"Let's hope," said Jesse despondently. "This lying and killing, red or white, don't add up to nothing but more of the same."

"And another thing," Andy Hobbs worked ahead, patiently ignoring the mountain man. "You're square with Bridger on the powder. His Snake wife there at the fort told me Gabe's done changed his whole idee about battling Brigham for the post. Says Gabe is aiming to winter in the hills, hide out, and just leave Brigham and his Danites set in the place till spring. Figures they'll come out poorer by wintering through than by fighting. Naturally that's how come us to have all the Du Pont for your swap."

"Well, that works out slicker'n green boar grease,

for me." Jesse got his grin back, gradually. "Happen Gabe chooses to get generous, I can stand it. Though I reckon what with losing the powder I won't get no pay for my peltries."

"I allow you will," countered the old man quietly. "Bridger's Snake woman said she could guarantee that. She figures old Gabe'll be so plumb tickled to hear about how you kept Brigham from getting his saintly paws on all them supplies and turning that powder over to the hostiles, he'll give you full price for your skins and glad of the chance. You'll get your thousand dollars, Jesse."

"Andy"—the mention of the money brought other pictures than Jim Bridger and Brigham Young to the mountain man's mind, the sudden eagerness of his voice telling the nature of them—"how'd Lacey come around about the little gal? And me, and all? I had to smack her back there at Wild Hoss Bend. She was clean outen her mind about losing the baby, and I . . ."

"She's all right, son," the oldster interrupted earnestly. "I talked her around to the idee the baby was done for, anyways. I figure she really was, too. Don't you?"

"Sure, Andy. She had the lung fever, fatal bad."

"Well, you got yourself a real woman. She'll do to ride any river with."

"Yep!" The dark-faced trapper brightened. "She's prime beaver. I can scarce wait to get to Gabe's to see her. You know, Andy, we ain't rightly had a chance to talk proper yet. I broached some purty big plans about Californy, first off I met her. I sure hope she ain't been scared offen them by all this crazy-head shagging around after Injuns."

"She ain't, mister!" The old man wagged his

head, satisfied now that he had the mountain man
eased out of his dour Sioux mood. "She's hotter'n a
four-*peso* Spanish pistol for anything that's spelled
Jesse Callahan. Including his addle-pate idees. And
more, too"—the wagon master played his hole card
craftily—"you ain't going to have to wait to get to
Gabe's to find it out, neither!"

As he spoke and before Jesse could reply, the
cañon ahead flared out for its confluence with the
Medicine Road. The sloping decline of the cañon
floor spread, wide and clear, in the late twilight, letting Jesse see the bright beacons of the cook fires in
the main trail ahead.

"That's our base camp, Jesse. Some of Gabe's
Snakes, with our spare stock and supplies. We
brung everything we might need to run you and the
boy clean to Californy. I allow you can see what else
we brung you!"

Jesse had dug his heels in before the wagon master finished talking. His mount shot up through
the loose-riding muleskinners, swung in between
Morgan Bates and Joplin, swerved up alongside
Johnny's spotted pony. He made a one-arm snatch
of the surprised boy, scooping him off the pony
and onto the pounding withers of his own mount,
all to the startling tune of a long-drawn Minniconjou yell.

Following his careening ride toward the base
camp, the laughing teamsters saw the tiny figure
waiting against the flare of the distant cook fires. It
was a long, dim way, but a man couldn't miss those
lines. Especially when what made them was running and waving right at him. There was something
about the way some women moved that would hit a
man's mind and jump his heart as long as his blood

was pumping and as far as his eyes could reach. And this was *some* woman!

"It's Mom! It's my mom!"

Johnny was laughing and crying and waving all at the same time. The mountain man's response to the boy's excitement was a sound precious few humans had ever heard—Jesse Callahan laughing out loud.

"*Hii-yeee-hahh!* Shout it out, boy! It ain't your Aunt Harriet!"

Seconds later, one indignant, borrowed Arapaho horse was getting his haunch hide burned off on the dry granite of the Medicine Road, and little Johnny O'Mara was that wrapped up in a flying smother of mother hugs and kisses he couldn't get his wind to whistle. Jesse legged it slowly down off his eared-back mount, stepped toward Lacey and the boy.

"Don't be a hawg, son." The words were for Johnny but the blue-dark eyes behind them went into the upswinging, wide gaze of Lacey O'Mara. "Leave some for your old man. . . ."

He stood with the tear wet of her thick lashes locked into the hollow of his shoulder, his lean face, flushed and fever-dark, buried in the warmth of her hair.

"It's all right, Lacey honey. Everything's all right, now. We got our young 'un back and the three of us are going to make it to Californy before snow flies. And if they want, we'll take your Kansas folks along, too. Listen to me, honey. We got the world in a jug. And Lacey, gal"—his deep growl dropped softer than new snow—"there ain't nobody but God Almighty ever going to pull the stopper on us again."

The night dark came down heavily as the trail-weary muleskinners kneed their ambling mounts along the path of Jesse's campward gallop. The wiry little horses picked up to a shuffle trot, moving eagerly toward the cheery fire blooms. Through the settling dust of their passing, the last member of the returning caravan plodded unsteadily.

There was enough light to make out her pop-eyed, outsized head, her wobbling cow hocks and stiff-splinted knees, even the ugly, smoke-dirty color of her lather-stained hide. And then there was just enough light left over to mark the memorable snow flash of Watonga's eight-foot eagle-feather war bonnet, where it swung and jolted in tired and final triumph across the bony withers of Heyoka—The Clown—all that was left to signal and dignify the final skinning of Black Coyote.

After that, there was only black sky and quiet starlight over Carson's Cañon and the old Medicine Road.

About the Author

Henry Wilson Allen wrote under both the Clay Fisher and Will Henry bylines and was a five-time winner of the Spur Award from the Western Writers of America. He was born in Kansas City, Missouri. His early work was in short subject departments with various Hollywood studios, and he was working at M-G-M when his first Western novel, *No Survivors* (1950), was published. While numerous Western authors before Allen provided sympathetic and intelligent portraits of Indian characters, Allen from the start set out to characterize Indians in such a way as to make their viewpoints an integral part of his stories. Some of Allen's images of Indians are of the romantic variety, to be sure, but his theme often is the failure of the American frontier experience and the romance is used to treat his tragic themes with sympathy and humanity. On the whole, the Will Henry novels tend to be based more deeply in actual historical events, whereas in those titles he wrote as Clay Fisher he was more intent on a story filled with action that moves rapidly. However, this dichotomy can be misleading, since *MacKenna's Gold* (1963), a Will Henry Western about gold-seekers, reads much like one of the finest Clay Fisher titles, *The Tall Men* (1954). His novels, *Journey to Shiloh* (1960), *From Where the Sun Now Stands* (1960), *One More River To Cross* (1967), *Chiricahua* (1972), and *I, Tom Horn* (1975) in particular, remain imperishable classics of Western historical fiction. Over a dozen films have been made based on his work.

"I am but a solitary horseman of the plains, born a century too late and far away," Allen once wrote about himself. He felt out of joint with his time, and what alone may ultimately unify his work is the vividness of his imagination, the tremendous emotion with which he invested his characters and fashioned his Western stories. At his best, he wove an almost incomparable spell that involves a reader deeply in his narratives, informed always by his profound empathy for so many of the casualties of the historical process.

Made in the USA
Las Vegas, NV
5 September 202

Made in the USA
Las Vegas, NV
25 September 2023

78120809R00167